CODEWORD JANUS

CODEWORD JANUS

Evelyn Anthony

This title first published in Great Britain 2003 by
SEVERN HOUSE PUBLISHERS LTD of
9–15 High Street, Sutton, Surrey SM1 1DF.
First published in 1979 in Great Britain by Hutchinson & Co
under the title *The Grave of Truth*.
This title first published in the USA 2003 by
SEVERN HOUSE PUBLISHERS INC of
595 Madison Avenue, New York, N.Y. 10022.

British Library Cataloguing in Publication Data

Anthony, Evelyn, 1928-
    Codeword Janus
    1.   Nazis - Fiction
    2.   Suspense fiction
    I.   Title   II. Anthony, Evelyn, 1928- . The grave of truth
    823.9'14 [F]

    ISBN 0-7278-5990-0

Printed and bound in Great Britain by
MPG Books Ltd., Bodmin, Cornwall.

*To Paul
with my love*

Acknowledgement

*My grateful thanks to Paul Mulley
for his invaluable research.*

Foreword

One of our sons had a young German friend to lunch. As she was leaving she turned to me and said "Thank you for being so welcoming. It isn't my fault that terrible things happened in the war. I wasn't even born". That made me think quite hard.

A lot of young Germans carried the guilt of crimes committed by their grandparents.

This is the story of guilt borne by the innocent. It's also the result of chance. I spent some time researching the last days in Hitler's Bunker. There was plenty of lurid evidence – drunken parties, sex, a kind of suicidal gaiety among the SS staff and the SS girls waiting for the end. For Hitler to die so that they could try to escape. There was one very strange incident; the day before Hitler and Eva Braun committed suicide. One of his staff was shot by a firing squad after a brutal beating. His name was Fegelein. I looked further. The man murdered on the Fuehrer's personal order was Eva Braun's brother-in-law.

What had he done, this member of the Fuehrer's circle – what did he know that was so deadly that Eva Braun herself couldn't save him?

I couldn't stop thinking what this might mean. The world was never meant to know of it – but an SS soldier was captured by the Russians. Years after the war was over they released his testimony.

This book is based on that one sinister unexplained act of murder among so many millions. And while this is fiction, the Russians spent a long time following-up a persistent rumour – the reason why Fegelein had to die.

Evelyn Anthony © 2003

I

'You've had that nightmare again, haven't you?'

He was shaving and he could see her reflection in the bathroom mirror. She wore pink pyjamas with a pattern on them; without make-up she was as pretty as a doll, with big brown eyes and marvellous American teeth. Pink was a colour he loathed, yet she insisted on wearing it, and the look of concern on her face irritated him so much that he nicked himself shaving. She had been trying for years to convert him to an electric razor. A little nodule of dark blood appeared on his lower lip. 'Oh, darling,' his wife said, 'you've cut yourself.'

'Ellie' – with a great effort he kept his tone gentle – 'please don't fuss.' The reflection in the mirror shook its head at him; the curly brown hair fluffed round her shoulders.

'I'm not fussing, Max. I know you've had that dream again and it's upset you. Why won't you talk about it?'

He put down the razor, splashed his face and dried it. There was a blood spot on the white towel. Then reluctantly he turned round to look at his wife.

'All right, I did dream the same thing last night. It happens now and again; I don't know why you have to make such a drama out of it.'

'Because of what it does to you,' she said. 'I remember the first time, when we'd just got married. You were soaking with sweat and shaking all over. We talked about it and you felt

7

better. It was a long time before it happened again. We used to communicate in those days; now when anything goes wrong you just shut me out.'

'I've got an early interview this morning,' he said. 'I must get dressed.' They went into the bedroom and his wife sat on the bed; he didn't have to look at her to know that her eyes were full of tears.

'It used to be very rare,' she said. 'Now I know it's happening regularly. You can't fool me, darling. You get moody, withdrawn, you snap at me and the children – you're not yourself for days!' He was dressed, fastening his watchstrap. The watch was a gold Piaget; she had given it to him for Christmas, with a note that overwhelmed him with guilt: 'Just to prove to you I love you.'

'I'm sorry,' he said. 'I don't mean to be difficult. It's just a phase – I probably won't dream about it again for months.'

'Max, darling, you've been saying this for years,' she said. 'Why won't you see a doctor, get him to analyse what it is that's worrying you? Dreaming about the war is just symbolic of some inner anxiety....'

'For Christ's sake,' he said, 'don't start that psychiatric stuff again. There's nothing symbolic about what happened to me in Berlin. I don't need any half-baked therapist telling me it's because my grandmother took away my teddy bear. I dream about being bombed and blown up because I bloody well was! Now I've got to go – I'm going to be late.'

'Don't forget to kiss the children good morning,' she said. She got up and went into the bathroom, locking the door. He knew she was going to cry. He paused outside the kitchen door; they had coffee in their room in the mornings – Max never ate breakfast since it meant starting the day with a meal with his children. Kiss the children good morning. Otherwise they'll feel you don't love them and they'll grow up insecure. The headache which was there when he woke, intensified suddenly as he went into the kitchen and forced himself to smile at his children and the English student who was giving them breakfast. She was a nice girl, shy and ill at ease. He was

8

ashamed of the way his son and daughter bullied her. 'Good morning, Pat ... Peter ... Francine. ...'

Fifteen and twelve were said to be difficult ages, pre-teens and teens; Ellie was always saying how traumatic it was for their children to be growing up and how understanding they both had to be and how careful not to pressurize them.

His son Peter was dark and good-looking like his mother; Francine was small and fair-haired. 'Hello,' she said. Peter didn't speak at all. He was eating cereal and scowling. Max kissed his daugher and, seeing the boy's expression, decided to damage his psyche by ignoring him that morning. Both children were at the local *lycée*, at his insistence, where, in spite of their mother's disapproval, they had to work extremely hard. His son was exceptionally clever, specializing in science and mathematics. His scholastic abilities did not compensate Max for his lack of good manners and consideration for anyone but himself. His father's attempts to impose discipline early on had been successfully frustrated by his mother; by the time he was seven Peter was adept at playing off one parent against the other. His relationship with his father was hostile and competitive; he bullied Francine because he suspected that his father found her more congenial.

'Good-bye, Daddy,' Francine said.

'Peter,' the English girl pushed back her chair, 'you'll be late for school.'

Max had turned towards the door when he heard his son answer.

'So I'm late – so what's it got to do with you?'

Max didn't pause to think, he didn't take a decision, he just lost his temper as he had been losing it inwardly for years. Perhaps the dream was responsible; perhaps he suddenly saw his son through eyes which hadn't been conditioned by modern child psychology and an American wife who had been reared on a deadly combination of Freud and Spock. He turned back, reached the table in three long strides, and smacked his son across the left ear. The boy overbalanced and fell off his stool. There was a few seconds' pause of shocked silence, and then his daughter burst into tears, and his son,

9

crouching in shock and amazement on the ground, suddenly began to roar with rage.

Max looked down at him.

'Don't you ever dare to speak to anyone like that again!'

He wasn't aware till he had left the apartment and was getting into his car that he had shouted at his son in German.

It was a glorious spring day in 1970, and Paris was awake early, the shops open, the traffic clotting at junctions and traffic lights. The city had a smell which was exclusive to itself; had he been blinded Max would have known Paris from any capital in the world by that original blending of food smells and street smells, and a thousand varieties of human and artificial scents.

He had lived there for fifteen years and he loved Paris. Ellie loved it too; she hadn't liked London where they had lived when they were first married in 1954. It had been a grey, sad place after the war, pinched by austerity, its people weary and seeking change, as if the conflict which had destroyed Nazi Germany had somehow defeated them too. It hadn't been easy for Max, working in London during the fifties. Anti-German feeling was stronger in Britain than in some countries which had suffered Nazi occupation. The articles he had written on the changes taking place in post-war Britain attracted a lot of attention in European political journalism, and the by-line 'Max Steiner' appeared in leading West German newspapers and prestige political publications on the Continent. When he was offered the post of chief foreign affairs correspondent for *Newsworld*, based in Paris, he was married to Ellie and she was pregnant with their son.

Driving along the rue Constantine, the sunshine roof of his smart new Peugeot open to admit the morning sun, he ignored his headache, concentrated on the traffic, and told himself, as he had done so many times in the past year, that he was an ungrateful bastard who didn't appreciate his family and his job, and it was time he realized how lucky he was. He had no right to criticize his wife: most men were sexually bored after sixteen years of marriage, and, naturally, when sex had ceased to be an urge and become a habit, the critical faculties sharpened and trifles previously unnoticed began to grate. He had been unfaithful to her once or twice, during trips to the States, and formed a brief liaison with an Italian girl who lived in Rome. As a result his sex life at home became guilty as well as tedious, the guilt partially eased by the certainty that had Ellie known, instead of being jealous, she would have sat down with him to analyse his reasons for going to bed with someone else.

It was unfair of him to resent her intellectual limitations. What had happened to the attractive girl whose naïvete had enchanted him when they first met? Why should the plus have become such a minus that her opinions irritated him until he tried to avoid any serious discussion? ... Motherhood. He could blame that. Women changed when they had children. There at least he had reason for complaint. She had become obsessed with the children. He had definitely shifted down two places in her scale of priorities. But how much time had he spent travelling, leaving her alone with the children he resented ...?

A right turn at the end of the street and along the river. A very pretty girl in a short skirt crossed in front him, threading her way through the stationary traffic. He watched her without interest. His marriage was falling to pieces. He had hit his son. As hard as he had once been hit, so that he fell to the ground ... the dream again. They didn't speak German at home; he and Ellie spoke English and the children brought up in France were bilingual. Peter wouldn't have understood what he was shouting at him. Why, suddenly, had he lapsed into his own language, except that his wife was right and the nightmare persisted in his mind long after he had woken?

Of course, he *had* been dreaming about it regularly; it had begun after Christmas. He woke with his heart and pulse rate galloping with fear, his mind full of fire and thunder and the distortion of the dream world, but a world still real and horribly recognizable. He hadn't dared to go to sleep again. The first time he had made the excuse that he was tired, that he'd drunk several whiskies after dinner – he'd rationalized it, and remembered everything quite deliberately to disarm the subconscious that Ellie was always talking about. He wasn't hiding anything from himself. He had even written an article about his own experience in Berlin at the end.

Not everything, though. Was that the thorn embedded in his mind? He drove his car into the car park under the *Newsworld* building in the Champs Elysées, got out, closed it up and locked it.

From January onwards he dreamed about it, sometimes on consecutive nights, sometimes with a merciful gap of nearly a week. He formed a routine: he got up, went into the kitchen, made coffee, had a cigarette, woke himself up thoroughly and then went back to bed. His wife only surprised him twice, and he had lied to her. He couldn't have endured her attempts to comfort him and explain it all away. Because of course she couldn't, because she didn't know the truth. He had told her no more than anyone else when he described the last days in Berlin. And yet although he called her stupid in his private thoughts, bilious and disloyal as they'd become, she'd sensed what was happening and faced him with it that morning.

'You've had that nightmare again.'

It came nearly every night now, sometimes in episodes, at others in rich detail. He walked through the entrance to the lift, pressed the third-floor button, ascended and got out. He had an interview that morning, although it was not for another hour; lying to Ellie was becoming a need rather than a habit. He wanted to look through his notes and fix the line of his questions in his mind. He never wrote anything down when he was talking to people, nor did he produce a tape-recorder. He carried that in his pocket. People said more when they imagined themselves to be talking off the record.

He had a bright modern office, and an efficient French secretary who was too intelligent to try to be sexy. He liked her but he had never even bought her a drink.

'Martine – good morning. Could you get me some coffee and some aspirin? Don't put anyone through to me: I'm going to read over the notes on Sigmund Walther.'

Sigmund Walther was a West German politician who had graduated to politics through industry. His background was well documented: father a naval officer killed during the war, mother a member of the minor Bohemian aristocracy; a bright young man, too young to have fought for Nazism, brought up through the harsh post-war years by his mother and grandparents, his time at university followed by a spectacular career in the industrial rebirth of West Germany. Married to a member of the old *Junker* military caste; five children, all born close together – unusual for an ambitious man. Joined the Social Democratic Party and began a determined and ruthless campaign to reach ministerial level. Was known to have made a large personal fortune since the war.

Max began writing, underlining points to fix them in his memory. There were stories circulating about Sigmund Walther and his affiliations in East Germany, and rumours of his ambition to form a splinter group inside the Party. He was staying at the Crillon with his wife and two eldest children on a private visit to Paris. If it really was private it had been extraordinarily well advertised in advance, and *Newsworld*'s request for an exclusive interview had been promptly granted.

The aspirin had taken effect, and Max was totally absorbed in his work. Walther was a challenge: his personality had eluded previous interviewers; even the television cameras had failed to expose more than he intended to reveal about himself. Journalists covered themselves by describing him as an enigma.

Max prepared himself as he did his notes. No personal prejudice, no slanted questions; a man as clever as Sigmund Walther would detect immediately if his attitude were hostile and defend himself. Max wanted him off guard if possible. His telephone buzzed; he frowned and picked it up. Martine's voice reminded him that he was due at the Crillon in twenty minutes. He put his notes in his desk, slipped the little transistorized tape-recorder into his outside pocket, and went out. The secretary looked up at him as he passed.

'Is your headache better?'

'Yes, it's fine.'

'Your wife rang, but I didn't put her through. I said you were out. I hope that was all right.'

He could imagine Ellie, brimming with outrage because he had given a Peter a box on the ear, and suddenly the idea made him smile. At a safe distance he could imagine the scene he had left behind as hilariously funny. It wouldn't be so funny when he went home.

'Did my wife leave any message?'

'Well, yes.' He sensed Martine's hesitation. 'She asked if you would come home; she said Peter was too upset to go to school. I told her you were out all morning at this Walther interview but I'd give you the message as soon as you came in.'

'Thanks,' he said.

The doorman at the Crillon took his car and parked it for him. The reception desk was surrounded with people checking in and out. The service was courteous and efficient and within a few minutes a pageboy was escorting him in a lift to the Walthers' suite on the second floor. It was one of the best suites in the hotel, with a magnificent view over the Place de la Concorde; the door was opened by a tall slim woman wearing a scent he recognized because he had given it to Ellie for her birthday. It was probably the most expensive in the world, and it was his first, misleading impression of Minna Walther.

'M. Steiner – come in, please. My husband won't be a moment.'

She had an amazing figure for a woman with five children; a long straight back, narrow hips and elegant legs. She was wearing a casual coat and skirt; he noticed the lack of jewellery, the plain wedding ring on her finger.

'Do sit down,' she said. 'I'll go and call Sigmund.'

'Thank you, Frau Walther,' he answered in German. She was too Slavic in type to be beautiful: the cheekbones were too high and the grey eyes a little too far apart. She had a lovely wide smile that changed her face completely.

'I'm afraid my French is terrible,' she said. 'I'm told I have a very strong accent.'

'No worse than mine,' Max said. 'It's not an easy language for us.'

She hesitated by an inner door, touching the handle. 'How long have you been away from home?'

14

Home. It was years since he had thought of Germany as home. Or heard anyone speak about it in that way.

'Nearly eighteen years,' he said. 'I moved to England soon after I left university. Then I got married and we lived in England till we moved here.'

'I'll call my husband,' she said.

He got up and went to the window; sitting down would have placed him at a disadvantage when Walther came in. He stared down at the traffic coiling round the Place below. The breadth and splendour of Napoleon III's concept for his capital had made the site of the guillotine and the Terror into the epitome of civic elegance. Germany had revived the guillotine; those found guilty of high treason during the war were executed face upwards by Himmler's special order. He turned round as Sigmund Walther came through from the inner room. He reached Max and held out his hand.

'Sorry I kept you waiting; I had to take a call. Would you like coffee or a drink?'

'A whisky and soda would be fine.'

'I'll join you.' Walther went to a walnut cabinet and started pouring drinks.

He was shorter than Max had expected, very fit and quick moving; his skin was lightly tanned, as if he made use of a sun lamp. Blue-eyed, hair slightly thinning, impeccably dressed in a dark suit, white shirt and plain tie, he wore his forty-two years lightly. Max tasted the drink and set it down. They faced each other, Walther leaning back on the sofa, legs crossed, very relaxed, Max sitting slightly forward in the armchair. He had slipped his hand into his pocket and activated the tape while Walther's back was turned.

They began with a general conversation, designed to put the interviewee at ease; Max didn't continue for long because he sensed that Sigmund Walther knew the technique and was impatient with it. His questions became more specific. How would Walther deal with the problem of urban terrorists? Did he think de Gaulle's withdrawal from NATO or his resignation would have a significant impact on German policy towards France? Was he in favour of Britain's joining the

15

EEC? Walther's answers showed a mind at once incisive and decisive. 'Tell me,' Max went on, 'what role would you like to see West Germany play in the Community in the next five years?'

'Five years from now? I wouldn't look that far ahead – in a year I'd like to see some sort of *rapprochement* with the East German government, while keeping our links with the Community and NATO as strong as possible.'

'You don't think these aims are incompatible?'

'No. There is one thing about our people which distinguishes us from other Europeans. Our nationhood is comparatively recent. Partition, division, all the punishments inflicted upon us by the Allies and Russia after the war, have not only affected us but are responsible for the atmosphere of confrontation which bedevils the world at the moment: I believe that the principal duty of our government is to try and establish good relations with our people in the East. We must aim at polycentrism, not bipolarity.' He leaned forward to emphasize what he was saying. 'That is the policy I am advocating in Bonn.'

'And this is what you will try to bring about if you are offered a post by Brandt?'

'Yes,' Sigmund Walther said. 'I have considerable support in the Bundestag.'

'Are you really proposing the ultimate reunification of Germany?'

'If Europe is to have any hope of peace in the future our country must become a sovereign state with all our people within our own borders.'

Max gave a slight smile. 'Some might think of the word *Lebensraum*, Herr Walther, when you talk about all Germans being incorporated into Germany.' He was watching Walther's hands for any sign of tension; they were a truer barometer of inner reaction than the eyes. They didn't move from his side, and yet he hesitated before answering that gentle provocation. When he did, it was Max who was taken by surprise.

'I'm not a Nazi, Herr Steiner. I believe the desire of every

German is to belong to his country, not to Communism or Western democracy or any other ideological faction. I believe that whatever Ulbricht's dictatorship behind the Wall imposed upon our people can and will be eroded by that longing to be one nation again. But we in West Germany have to take the political initiative.'

'What makes you think that either Russia or the West would allow this *rapprochement* to take place?'

'As far as the West is concerned, I also believe that Europe has grown up politically in the last twenty years. I believe from personal contacts among senior NATO officers that the reunification of our country would be welcomed by the West.'

'You still have Russia to convince,' Max said. 'Even if France, for instance, could be persuaded to accept a strong and united Germany, is it really conceivable that the Soviet Union would stand by and allow the Eastern territories to escape her? Of course,' he added thoughtfully, 'reunification would be a marvellous platform in the elections.'

Sigmund Walther didn't answer. He picked up his whisky and drank most of it. 'You're not taking any notes,' he remarked. 'But no doubt you have a tape-recorder?'

'Yes,' Max said. 'But I find it puts people off when they can see it. Have you any objection to this being taped?'

'None at all. I just wanted to establish that you weren't relying on memory.' The easy smile came and lingered; Max could see why Walther had been so successful in industry; his reputation had begun as a negotiator. He had a magnetic charm that in no way concealed his considerable authority.

'Let me put my last question to you another way. If at any time in the future East Germany tried to form some kind of federation with Bonn, Russia would act as she did in Hungary – and in Czechoslovakia less than two years ago – to prevent it. Wouldn't what you're proposing lead to a military confrontation with the West?'

'Are you asking that question for *Newsworld*, or do you have any interest in the future of Germany as a German?'

'I'm asking the question,' Max said, 'so that *Newsworld* readers can get an answer; I'm not personally concerned.'

'That's a pity,' Walther said quietly. 'But I'll give you the answer just the same. West Berlin is the parent of the Wall; the division of the capital of Germany into two halves was dictated by vengeance and the Allies' fear of offending Stalin. An island of Western-style democracy in a Marxist sea. The concept is crazy and was very nearly fatal. The world has been closer to war over Berlin than over any other issue since 1945. If it means confronting Russia then I believe the West is strong enough to do it, exactly as America did over Cuba. Russia is not going to embark on a nuclear war with China at her back.

'I believe it will be possible to reunite Germany and not only preserve peace but restore proper balance to Europe and the free world.' He finished his drink. 'That will make a nice quote for the article you're going to write,' he said. 'Now perhaps you would switch your little machine off? Wherever it is —'

Max took the recorder out of his pocket and laid it on the coffee table. He pressed the switch to 'Off'.

'Amazing how small they can make these things,' Walther said.

'Would you like me to play it back?'

'No, thanks. In spite of being in politics, I don't enjoy hearing myself speak. I'd probably ask you to wipe it out and start all over again. And we haven't got time for that.' He got up, looked at his watch, exclaimed softly.

'I have a luncheon appointment at one — the traffic is so bad in Paris, I've hardly enough time — excuse me, I'll ring down for my car.' He turned, holding the telephone. 'Wait a moment — we can go down together.'

He opened the inner door and called to his wife. She came and stood in the doorway, smiling at him.

'I'll be back at three, my darling. We've had a very good interview. I hope I haven't given Herr Steiner too bad an impression!'

Max said good-bye to her; she kissed her husband on the cheek and shook hands with him. He had forgotten how distinctive that type of German woman was.

Walther and he went down in the lift. As they reached the foyer he turned to Max. 'How long is it since you've been back to Germany?'

'A long time,' he said. 'Your wife asked me the same thing.' They had reached the glass street doors and passed through them into the brilliant sunshine. Walther's car, the chauffeur waiting by the rear door, was drawn up outside. Walther held out his hand to Max. 'Minna feels the same as I do. Germany needs men with talent and courage. You could do a lot for your country. Why don't you come back?'

'I live here now,' Max answered. 'I'm not due to be posted anywhere as far as I know.'

'I have a lot of contacts in German journalism,' Sigmund Walther said. 'Think about coming back. I'm being quite serious about this. Just let me know.' They were still shaking hands as they talked, Walther half turned from the street facing Max, when the first shots cracked out.

There were two of them; Max saw them quite clearly seconds before he realized what was happening. Two men, with dark glasses, standing within a few feet of Sigmund Walther, with guns in their hands. It was a moment frozen in shock and disbelief; Walther's hand gripped his in a convulsion of agony; the smile of a second earlier became a hideous grimace, and still the shots cracked, as bullets thudded into his lurching body and one whined like an angry hornet past Max's head. Walther was falling now, turning a semi-circle as he collapsed, almost in slow motion; people in the street were screaming and shouting; the firing had stopped. Max scarcely saw the running figures disappear into the crowd as he held the dying man in his arms. Blood was streaming over the pavement. Walther's face had turned a deathly grey, his eyes were filming over.

His lips moved and Max crouched close to him, his hands sticky with Sigmund Walther's blood. For a moment the eyes cleared, and by a last effort of will a single word was spoken clearly: 'Janus...' Then Walther choked and his head rolled sideways as he died.

It was dark and the offices of *Newsworld* were closed up except for the nightwatchman and the office where Max Steiner sat alone. He switched his desk light on when the room grew too dark for him to see, and he sat with his elbows on his desk and the little tape-recorder in front of him. The police had played the tape back, while they took a long statement from him. Someone had asked if he wanted to see a doctor himself, if he felt shocked. He had been very calm and refused everything but coffee. He wanted a clear head unclouded by alcohol or tranquillizers. He had seen the killers: two men, one above medium height, the other slighter in build and shorter; the dark glasses had made it difficult to guess their ages but both had dark, short hair and were Caucasians. Professionals, who had escaped through the crowds and been seen leaping into a waiting car. The car had been found abandoned in a Paris suburb. Predictably it had been stolen that morning.

It was a political assassination and the newspapers and other media were blaming the Baader-Meinhof because Walther was a West German politician.

Max had gone over the details with senior men from the Sûreté and then with a couple of investigators from SDECE. He had told them everything he could remember, every fleeting impression gained in those last few moments of panic and horror. Except for the dead man's last word.

He had washed and changed his bloodstained clothes for a suit sent round from his home. He had ignored the frantic messages from Ellie, who was assured by the police that he was quite unhurt. When he was told he could go home he asked to be driven to his office. His editor-in-chief was a Frenchman who had never forgiven him for being German but was too practical to let it influence his judgement. Steiner was one of his star correspondents; he cleared everyone out of Max's office and took the story down himself. 'I'm going to write it,' Max said.

'Eye witness,' Martin Jarre said briskly. 'This is going to be your guideline. Tomorrow it mightn't be so clear. Go home and get your doctor to give you something for a night's sleep. You look clapped out.'

But Max hadn't gone home. He had switched off his telephone so Ellie couldn't get through to him, and sat on, playing the tape back once or twice.

It all looked very straightforward. Not the Baader-Meinhof but assassins from the right wing who didn't want *détente* with East Germany. Or the KGB, who didn't want it either.... The motives were there on that tape: reunification of Germany through a political understanding with the Communist regime in East Germany. A proposal that would make Walther many powerful enemies. But no more, on examination, than a political ideal to be promoted during an election, by a man who was aiming at power and popularity. Not sufficient threat to have him murdered in a Paris street, with all the attendant publicity and uproar. Walther had been killed for something else, and he had known it, and said so just before he died. 'Janus.'

It was twenty-five years since Max Steiner had heard that word, and the man who spoke it then was just about to die. In the Bunker in Berlin on 25 April 1945, when Adolf Hitler shot himself and the Third Reich came to an end.

For twenty-six days and nights the city had been under bombardment from the air and the advancing Russians, their artillery ranged around the perimeter within fifteen kilometres of the Brandenburg Gate. Within the last seven days Berlin had become completely encircled, and already the first Russian patrols had penetrated the suburbs. All who could get out had taken to the roads and were fleeing to the West and the Allied armies. A massive pall of black smoke hung over Berlin, and through it the fires from bombed and burning buildings licked and spouted jagged flame. The air was thick with rubble dust and sweet with the stench of burst drains and corpses buried in the ruins. The air-raid sirens howled continuously and the thud of explosions from Allied air attacks was competing with the crash of high-velocity shells.

Berliners had forgotten how to sleep; they dozed between

air attacks, risked a forage into the shattered streets for the meagre rations which were still being supplied, and huddled underground, waiting for the final assault upon the city. In the heart of Berlin the Führer stayed on in the Bunker below the Chancellory, directing a war which had been lost months before. Berlin, the centre of the Third Reich, its buildings designed by Albert Speer as a monument to the New Order which was to last a thousand years, burned and crumbled under the attacks of the enemies who had so nearly been defeated.

The city lived on rumours; nobody believed the lies broadcast by Goebbels' radio, or its hysterical admonitions to fight on to the last and victory could still be won. The war was lost: Himmler and Goering had left Berlin; only Hitler and his few fanatics – Bormann, Goebbels and his personal SS guards – remained to fight on and die with the people and the city. German troops, exhausted and hopeless, were entrenched in the ruins, with orders to fight the Russians street by street.

No surrender. Fight to the death. Those were Hitler's orders, and the veterans and old men of the Volksturm and schoolboys of the Hitler Jugend joined what was left of the army and prepared to defend Berlin and the Führer to the last man.

Max Steiner was sixteen; his platoon was due to take up position in the Pichelsdorf district, where savage fighting was holding the encircling Russian troops from driving through the centre. They had been issued with uniforms, ill-fitting olive green, with forage caps and belts, the insignia of the Hitler Jugend on their collars. Max, being the eldest, was the platoon commander; unlike the younger boys he carried a revolver. The others carried rifles and shoulder packs, with grenades. There were stories of children, even younger than the fourteens and fifteens in this group, who had thrown themselves and their grenades under Red Army tanks. Max's platoon had been ordered to the Bunker for the supreme honour accorded those who were about to die for the Fatherland.

Adolf Hitler himself was to review his boy soldiers; he would exhort them to hold back the invader. They had been waiting since dawn, crouching half asleep in little groups, the tumult of the bombardment muffled below ground. Max's mother was still in her house on the Albrechtstrasse; the adjoining buildings had been wrecked by a bomb but their house still stood and she and his grandmother lived in the cellars and refused to leave. There were no false heroics about Marthe Steiner or her mother-in-law who was seventy-eight years old. Only the quiet logic that countered Max's frantic pleas to join the refugees with the answer that he was all the two women had left, and they weren't leaving Berlin without him. There was no suggestion that he should run away. His father had been killed during an air raid on the Luftwaffe station at Brest, and his elder brothers shot down during the Battle of Britain.

It was his duty to fight for his country, and theirs to stay and give what help they could. His mother helped with the street kitchens and his grandmother sewed bandages for the Red Cross. None of them expected to survive the fall of their city. Max had kissed them good-bye when the order came to report for active duty; his mother was not a demonstrative woman but she had held out her arms and he had run into them, and they were both in tears.

He thought of her, and looked round anxiously in the dull light to make certain no one was awake and watching him cry. The others were silent, some sleeping, some with their eyes closed but awake. He was the platoon commander; he wiped his eyes with his sleeve and tried not to think of his family. Not of his father, or his two brothers who had seemed so splendid in their blue uniforms and were lost over the English Channel within a week of each other. It was his turn now, to prove himself as brave as they were, a German ready to die for the Führer and the Fatherland. He wished his mother and his grandmother had gone, when their friends the Schultzes packed up and left. He wasn't just afraid for himself, because he had been taught that fear was childish and unworthy in a Hitler Youth; he could contain the niggle in his stomach that was becoming a nervous pain at the idea of being shot or blown up. He couldn't bear the thought of his mother staying in that dank old cellar with his grandmother, their personal possessions heaped around them, and perhaps the house being hit by a shell or a bomb and the walls crashing down on top of them. . . .

He shifted, and eased his legs to stretch the muscles that were cramped from sitting. Albert Kramer was on the left of him, his back balanced against another boy who was crouching forward, his head on his knees. He and Albert had been at the same school and joined the Hitler Youth at the same time. A few months separated them in age, and Albert had expected to get the senior post in the platoon. They had spent a large part of their lives together, but they were never friends. Albert's father was in the Waffen SS; he had lost an eye and part of his left leg in an ambush in Poland during the retreat. Albert told them how every civilian in the area had been arrested and shot as a reprisal.

Obersturmbannführer Kramer was in an Eastern hospital; nobody knew what had happened to him when the Russians occupied the area, but Albert told everyone his father must have died fighting. The Waffen SS were the best soldiers in the Reich; Albert's eyes glowed when he talked about his father. He didn't seem to mind that he was dead. He only lost his temper when it was suggested that his father might be a prisoner. No SS officer surrendered to those Russian swine. Max could remember him shouting, and how he cried with rage. He had thought, secretly, that he would have been happy if *his* father were somehow alive. . . . But then Albert was a fanatical type. He believed in the Führer and the Third Reich the way some people believed in God.

Albert had never had a doubt about the war or about victory. He should have been made platoon leader but Max was picked instead. He knew how Albert hated him because of it. He looked at his watch: it was nearly six o'clock. He was hungry; the boys had been given a bowl of potato soup when they had mustered earlier. They were all as thin as stray dogs; food was rationed just above starvation level; anyone found hoarding or using forged food cards was shot immediately, without a trial. Max yawned, and was ashamed to see his hand shake as he covered his mouth. He was afraid; he wondered how the other boys were feeling. Otto Stülpner was barely fourteen and small for his age. He was asleep on the ground, his face pinched and sallow in the emergency lighting. There were marks on his cheeks where he had been crying. The rifle lying beside him looked ridiculously big.

Children, Max thought suddenly, and couldn't stop the rush of indignation that followed it. Children sent out to fight against the Russian army, the crack troops specially chosen to reduce Berlin ... Mongols from the East, if rumours were correct, savages with a licence to rape and slaughter without mercy. The stories from refugees fleeing their advance had filled the Berliners with terror and caused a mass flight of women and children from the city as the threat came closer. Little boys like Paul and Erwin Rapp and Fritz Kluge, who should have been sent to safety not told to go into battle with rifles as big as themselves and the children's oath of loyalty to the Führer as their reason for committing suicide. All right for boys like Albert and himself. Sixteen was old enough when men of seventy were fighting. It had to be; he accepted that, but for most of that little band of boys it was equivalent to murder. He found himself trembling with rage and near to tears. If Adolf Hitler saw them, surely he wouldn't expect them to go to fight in an area which was a hell of shelling and street fighting.... Surely if he loved his people, as he was supposed to, he wouldn't want a snivelling child like Otto Stülpner to get ripped to pieces by Russian bullets....

'I wonder how long it'll be before we see him?' Albert Kramer might almost have read his thoughts.

'I don't know,' Max muttered. 'Keep your voice down – don't wake the others.'

'I can't wait,' Albert whispered. 'I can't wait to see him face to face. Aren't you excited, Max? This'll be the biggest moment of our lives! I keep thinking what I'll say if he speaks to me. You don't even seem to care – what's the matter with you?' The boy's eyes had narrowed in suspicion; his jaw jutted aggressively. 'Don't you want to die for the Führer?'

Max Steiner looked at him and said the unthinkable. 'No,' he said. 'If I get killed, it'll be for Germany.'

'You dirty swine!' Kramer sprang up, shouting. 'You traitor! I'll report you –'

'Shut up! Come to attention, all of you! Quick!'

Max had seen the two SS officers come into the room; he stood up and saluted. Kramer froze into attention: his response to an order was instantaneous. The boys struggled up and formed themselves into a line. There were twenty of them. The senior SS officer, wearing the flashes of a Standarten-führer on his lapels, walked towards Max and raised his right arm stiffly.

'*Heil Hitler.*'

The children responded in unison; Albert's voice was louder than the rest.

'*Heil Hitler.*'

The Standartenführer cleared his throat. He was a big man who had grown thin; the black uniform hung loose on him and there were heavy pouches of fatigue and strain under his eyes.

'I am the Standartenführer Otto Helms. The Führer sends you his greetings,' he said. 'He regrets that he cannot speak to you in person today, but he reminds you of your oath of allegiance and your duty to him and to the Fatherland.' He paused and his eyes lingered for a moment on Max.

'The Führer has chosen to stay with his people and to lay down his life with us,' he said, and emotion made the harsh voice quiver. 'If we have lost the war it is because of the traitors inside Germany. One of those traitors has been dis-covered, here, at the Führer's side. It will be your privilege, as members of the Hitler Jugend, as German soldiers, to execute that traitor in the name of Adolf Hitler and the Reich!'

He spoke directly to Max. 'You come with me.'

It was a long narrow passage deep underground; their steps echoed on the concrete floor. The SS officer came to a door, shot back a bolt and opened it. He stood aside so that Max could see in. It was some kind of storeroom because there were boxes stacked to ceiling height in one corner and a fluorescent bar blazed overhead.

A man lay on the bare floor, curled up in the foetal position, knees drawn up, his arms cradling his head. There were splotches of blood on the ground and a sour, sick smell. For a moment Max felt he was going to be sick.

'That swine there,' the SS officer said, 'was the Führer's trusted friend. He betrayed him. The Führer sentenced him to death himself. You're going to form a firing squad.'

Max tried to speak; his throat was constricted with terror and disgust. The man on the ground moved a little and gave a whimpering groan.

'What did he do?' Max whispered.

'Only the Führer knows,' the Standartenführer said. 'We carried out his orders. I would have killed him myself but I have the Führer's own command. He wants him executed and he wants you to carry out the sentence. "The future of Germany depends on the children." Those were his words. "Let the Hitler Jügend shoot him. Let them see what happens to traitors."'

'He's injured,' Max whispered.

He saw the SS officer smile. 'Yes,' he said, 'but if he can't stand up we'll shoot him in a chair. You get back to your squad now; Oberst Frink will take you above ground and show you the place. He'll be brought up in a few minutes.'

He turned back into the room and closed the door. Without thinking Max began to run down the corridor. He found the SS Obersturmführer barring his way; the squad of boys was ranged up behind him.

'Line up!' he shouted. As Max hesitated he pushed him. They moved off behind the SS Leutnant, clattering up the two flights of stairs that brought them to ground level.

The discipline of his training in the Hitler Jügend kept Max Steiner on his feet, made him give orders to the rest of the squad and stopped him giving way to the impulse to turn and run from the whole nightmare. And it was a nightmare, a sequence so horrible that it was almost unreal. He saw a plain chair standing in the enclosed garden where they were waiting; the air was thick with smoke and the cinders of fires floated down on them in a light breeze. The noise of explosions was joined by the rattle of shots from street-fighting in the distance. He glanced over his head and saw a flight of birds high above, winging away. They were not just being sent out to die for their country, the frightened children of Berlin, the Pauls and Erwins and little Fritz Kluge who was clinging on to his rifle and staring ahead like a terrified rabbit. They were being ordered to kill a man in cold blood. The Führer's personal order. The Führer hadn't come to see them, to give lunatics like Albert Kramer something to die happy remembering. He had chosen them to kill a man who hadn't been tried, and whose treason was just a word to be accepted.

He closed his eyes, fighting himself and his panic and revulsion. His family were all National Socialists; his elder brother had won the Iron Cross 1st class for bombing raids on England. As a child he had grown up with the idea of Adolf Hitler as the saviour of Germany, the leader with mystical powers who had brought his people out of the chaos and humiliation of the years after the Great War and set them on their path of destiny. A strong Germany, a pure Aryan super-race whose mission was to rule the world. His father and his mother and his brothers had accepted that, and so had he. The marches, the rallies, the torchlight processions, the marvellous victories, the films glorifying war and sacrifice – nobody questioned that everything their Führer did was right, certainly not Max.

When adversity came, and the war closed in upon them bringing the dreadful air raids which destroyed cities like Cologne or engulfed Hamburg in a holocaust of fire, the people of Germany responded with courage and determination, just as his own family had done when their three menfolk were killed. Max wore the black armband that showed that Steiners had given their lives for the Fatherland, and was proud while he grieved. There had been nobility as well as suffering, and through it all the belief that the Führer would not fail, that the army's reverses were the failure of the generals to carry out his orders. With the shells falling on Berlin itself, part of the myth survived. But the reality was sending children out to die and, now, commanding that they become his personal executioners. They had brought the victim out; he used the word unconsciously.

The Standartenführer and an SS trooper were dragging him between them; he stumbled and staggered till they pushed him into the chair.

'You – cadre leader – come over here!'

Max didn't want to move; he stood as if he were paralysed, and then unwillingly his legs obeyed, and he found himself standing close to the man who was to be shot, with the two SS men confronting him.

'You know what to do?'

He looked up into the Standartenführer's face: it was gaunt and grim, but all he could remember was that brief, hateful smile ... The condemned man was conscious; his eyes were open. They had wiped his face clean but a rim of blood showed between his lips. Now he had been tied to the chair. He wore civilian trousers and a shirt which was torn and bloodstained.

Max kept on staring at him; he felt his eyes filling with tears.

'You know what to do – answer me, you stupid little clod!'

'No,' Max said, and his voice sounded very loud.

'You give the order: "Take aim, fire." If he's still alive you shoot him through the head.'

Max heard him dimly, as if he were shouting from a long way away. The man in the chair was looking at him. Not a young man, because his hair was turning grey. The eyes were agonized. They reminded Max of the expression in the eyes of a crucified Christ he had seen during a visit to the Kaiser Friedrich Museum. It had haunted him for nights afterwards. Then slowly the bleeding lips opened; the words were spoken directly to him.

'Janus ... Find Janus ...'

Max wasn't sure which of the SS men hit the man; he saw the blow, and the fresh blood, and suddenly he was shouting at them.

'No ... no ... no!'

The world rocked under his feet, tears blinded him, and a punch to the head sent him sprawling. He saw what happened afterwards as if it were a series of scenes from a film that kept breaking down. He saw Albert Kramer come out of the ranks; he was dragged to one side and somebody kicked him. Then he heard the shots which seemed to go on for ever. The man in the chair fell over. Then Max became unconscious.

He heard the voices from a distance; they came and went at first while he struggled back to consciousness. 'Poor devil – no, he's alive –' 'Christ, that one was close – here, help me . . .'

Someone was dragging him by the arms, he opened his eyes and saw the sky, rent by scudding clouds, and his ears buzzed from the shell which had just exploded nearby. Then the sky disappeared and there was grey concrete over his head and he was being helped to stand. An SS Scharführer supported him; a uniformed police guard was beside him.

'You all right, son?' The Scharführer asked him.

Max nodded; his head and the side of his face were throbbing. He remembered that savage punch that had knocked him to the ground. He had been kicked too; breathing sent shafts of pain over his ribs.

'We saw you out there,' the police guard said, 'and we thought you'd caught a shell splinter. One of the HJs going to Pichelsdorf, weren't you?'

'Yes,' Max mumbled. 'They shot the man. . .' He put his hands over his face and began to cry. The SS Scharführer glanced at the police guard.

'Come on, son,' he said. 'You've just got a bit of concussion, that's all. Think yourself lucky you got knocked out and didn't get to bloody Pichelsdorf – suicide squad, that was – come on, we'll take you downstairs.'

'I'm on duty in the watchtower,' the police guard said. 'All I see is the Red bastards getting closer every minute. Take the kid below; he looks green. . . .'

Max had recognized his surroundings as they talked; he wiped his eyes on his sleeve and choked back more tears. They were in the porch under the exit from the Bunker. Outside was the garden where the man had been executed.

'Mind the steps,' the Scharführer said. 'You're not going to puke, are you?'

30

'No,' Max mumbled. 'No, I'm all right.' The stairs seemed to go down and down; they had been comparatively few when he had hurried up them with his squad in the early-morning. At the foot of the stairs they were met by three SS officers, headed by a man wearing the insignia of a Sturmbannführer.

'What are you doing?' he shouted to the Scharführer who was ahead of Max, and the man snapped to attention.

'Carrying out orders, sir.'

'All exits into the garden are closed?'

'Yes, sir.'

'What's that boy doing?'

'We found him lying outside – he's all right, just got a knock on the head.'

Max watched the Sturmbannführer's face; it was haggard and the lips quivered; there was a look of frenzy in the eyes.

'Get him away from here – at once! This corridor is to be kept clear!'

The SS Scharführer saluted and grabbed Max by the arm, hurrying him forward. He saw two doors on the right of them as they hastened through a long wide room with chairs and a long table and wall maps. The second door was partly open, and he glimpsed the black uniforms of the SS inside. He had an impression of a blanket-shrouded figure being held by two men, but even as they passed the door was slammed shut, and by now the Scharführer was forcing him into a run.

They came out of the long room which looked as if it were used for conferences and into another room of the same size: it was full of people, men in uniform, women wearing the military-style garb of the female SS staff. Nobody looked at Max or seemed to notice him; faces were dazed and no one spoke. Two women, one of them young and pretty, wept without making any sound or attempt to check the tears which streamed down their faces. Max was hustled through them and to another flight of stairs; his head was quite clear now and he recognized the route he and the squad had taken earlier; through the dining area of the upper Bunker, past the passage and the storeroom where he had seen the executed man for the first time. They reached the bulkhead before a shorter flight of steps, and at the top of these they came into a room which was also full of people.

'Stay here,' the Scharführer said. 'Ilse, come and look after this one; get some of that liquor they've been hiding in the kitchen.'

'You hurt?' The girl was in civilian dress, a brown skirt and a white blouse; she had fair hair severely pinned back in a bun and her face was very pale, with puffy skin under the eyes. Max shook his head.

'No. What's happening? Why is everyone in here – that other room below was full of people ... I saw some of them crying. ...' He caught hold of her arm. 'Is the war over? Have we surrendered?'

She had a glass in her hand and was pouring wine into it. She drank some herself before giving the glass to him, and wiped her pale lips with the back of her hand. 'Don't say that word,' she said. 'Not till we know for sure he's dead. You must have come up through the Führer Bunker. Did you see anything?' She was watching him closely, speaking very low.

'They were clearing the corridor and closing all the doors outside,' he said. 'I thought I saw somebody dead, wrapped up in one room, but they slammed the door –'

She gave a deep sigh, and suddenly her eyes were filled with tears. 'He said good-bye to us all last night,' she said. 'He came and shook hands with us. We knew what it meant. Somebody started a gramophone in the canteen and we began to dance. It was about three in the morning – I work in the kitchens here, doing the catering. Do you know, one of the senior officers in his bodyguard – a Standartenführer – he danced with me? I knew it was the end then. Everything was breaking up. ...' She caught hold of Max by the shoulders. 'You don't understand me, do you? You don't know what I'm talking about?' Her hands dropped away from him. 'The Führer's dead,' she said. 'If they're closing everything up like that, and you saw a body – those rooms are his private suite. Him and Eva Braun. She came here to die with him.' She took the glass away from Max and poured more wine into it. Again she drank half herself.

'It's all over,' she said. 'Now we can make peace, while there's anyone left alive – my husband's fighting with General Wenck's army. We kept hoping they'd come to Berlin and drive back the Ivans, but they didn't . . . I expect my man's dead anyway. I haven't had a letter for weeks –" She paused; it was as if she had been talking to herself rather than him. Now she looked at him as a person, and hesitantly touched the bruised and swollen side of his face.

'That's nasty,' she said. 'What are you doing down here – we haven't any HJs on our staff –'

'Our cadre were sent for last night,' Max answered. 'We thought we were going to see the Führer, before we went to fight at Pichelsdorf – he didn't come. There was a man shot this morning –'

'That's what we heard,' Ilse said. 'Someone said he was caught with E.B.'s diamonds, getting ready to run. Listen, where's your home?'

'My mother lives on Albrechtstrasse; I want to get back and see she's all right. How can I get out of here?'

'Stick close to me,' the girl said. 'Now that the Führer's dead there's nothing to stay for – not to get caught by the Ivans. The Scharführer's a friend of mine' – she looked briefly sly – 'the one who brought you up here. Josef Franke, that's his name. They're shooting all the SS, as they capture them. Josef's not going to get himself caught by them. . . . Some of us are going to try and run for it. I'll ask him if you can come along.'

'I want to get home,' Max insisted.

Someone had come up behind him. He was a tall, thin young man in the uniform of a Luftwaffe staff officer. 'And where's home, cadre leader?'

'Albrechtstrasse, sir. My mother and grandmother are there.'

The thin man shook his head. 'No good trying to get there,' he said. 'The Russians have got control of the whole section. They broke through to Schöneberg this morning. If you're found on the streets in that uniform you'll be shot dead.' He moved away. 'Albrechtstrasse' – Max heard someone else say

33

it – 'there's not a house left standing. We got a message from the Volksturm commander before they surrendered. Poor old devils, there were just a handful of them left.'

He felt Ilse's thin arm go round him. 'Never mind,' she murmured. 'Never mind – it's the same for all of us. You come with Josef and me. . . .' Max leaned his head against her narrow bosom and wept for the loss of his family and his home. By five o'clock that evening, his olive-green Hitler Jugend uniform exchanged for an ill-fitting assortment of civilian clothes, Max Steiner crept out through the vast ruined Chancellory building, with Ilse and Franke, now wearing army uniform, and some of the clerks and domestic staff from the Bunker and the Foreign Office who had taken shelter there. As they left the shattered building, its marble and malachite walls cracked and crumbling from Allied bombs and Russian shellfire, the group of fugitives noticed, without realizing the significance, two thick black columns of smoke rising from the Chancellory gardens. They came from the petrol fire that provided Germany's Führer and his lover Eva Braun with their Viking funeral.

He had fallen asleep at his desk, his head resting on his folded arms, and the tape-recorder shone its red eye unheeded, waiting to be switched off. The window grew lighter, showing the outline of roofs on the opposite buildings, and the sky changed subtly from grey to pink and then to a sulphurous yellow as the sun rose. He woke stiff-necked and aching, with the nightbeard bristling on his chin, and a staleness in his mouth. It was too early for the office staff to have arrived; he heard the distant hum of a vacuum cleaner in the corridors. He needed a bath and a shave and first, some coffee. There was a machine outside his secretary's office, and he got a plastic cupful, so hot and black that it burned his tongue.

He went back to his office and lit a cigarette. The thought of Ellie nagged him; he needed to go home and use his own bathroom, change out of the suit he had slept in. But going back to the apartment meant facing his wife, submitting to the

34

questions and the fussing and the reasoned reproaches. He stretched, loosening the muscles in his back and shoulders. He was behaving badly, like a coward. He was sure she hadn't slept all night; his children must be worried, shocked by his involvement with a violent murder. He switched on his portable radio and caught the eight o'clock news. There were no new developments; the police were conducting a nationwide hunt for the two killers; he listened to the clichés that concealed a lack of fresh news, and then switched the set off.

'Janus.' The nightmare had not come; he had slept deeply and without disturbance. But his memory was running as clear as if he were watching a film of his own past; incidents long forgotten came crowding and jostling for recognition, linked by the dying word of Sigmund Walther, and the whisper of the condemned man in the Berlin Chancellory yard. He had got out of the centre of the city, with Ilse, the girl from the kitchens, and her SS lover, Franke. How clearly he remembered their names. Then an American patrol had picked them up; the Red Cross had arranged his repatriation to his father's sister in Bremen. With her family, he had begun to reshape his life and go to school and then to university. He had kept the secret of his last days in Berlin to himself. There had been no point in returning to Albrechtstrasse to look for his house; it had been destroyed. His mother and grandmother were never heard of again.

As a young journalist he had written of his flight from the doomed city, of the shelling and fighting he had lived through and his arrest by the Americans. But he had never mentioned his presence in the Bunker to a human soul. But whatever the condemned man had known and tried to communicate to him, Sigmund Walther had known about too. He knew exactly what he had to do, and the decision brought with it a sense of extraordinary relief. He picked up the telephone and dialled the Crillon; no calls were being put through to the Walthers' suite. He persuaded them to send up a message, and he waited, holding onto the telephone.

When he heard her voice it shocked him; it sounded thick with tears.

35

'This is Minna Walther. You wanted to speak to me.'

'Yes,' Max said. 'I'm sorry I had to intrude on you, Frau Walther. Please believe me, this has nothing to do with my paper. Your husband said something before he died. I didn't mention it to the police. But I'd like to talk to you about it. Will you see me?'

There was a slight pause; he heard her clear her throat.

'Yes,' she spoke slowly, carefully. 'Yes, of course I will. My elder children are here – there are arrangments to be made this morning. I'd rather not see ordinary journalists.'

'That's very natural,' he said. 'What can we do, then –'

'I shall arrange to be alone at lunchtime,' Minna Walther said. 'Come and see me just after one o'clock.'

'Thank you, Frau Walther,' he said. She hung up without saying good-bye.

2

'Why doesn't she cry? Why won't she let go for once?' Helmut Walther stopped pacing the sitting room and turned round to his sister. He was pale and red-eyed from a night spent weeping for his father; he looked very much like him. He was eighteen, and going to be reading law and economics at Heidelberg University. He faced his younger sister and asked the same angry question. 'She loved him – for Christ's sake, why can't she show what she's feeling?'

Freda Walther shook her head. She too resembled her father, except that she had inherited her mother's tall, slight build. At seventeen she was a pretty girl with the promise of beauty when she matured.

'She doesn't want to upset us,' Freda said. 'You don't understand Mother, you never have. This isn't the time to start criticizing. She's just thinking of us!'

'Oh no, she isn't,' Helmut said. 'It's the shit Prussian attitude – no human feelings, no tears – only the lower orders cry! I remember Grandpa saying that to us, and so do you! I tell you, Freda, I don't know how Papa lived with it –'

He sat down and covered his face; his shoulders moved as he sobbed. His sister got up quietly and went to comfort him. He was a brilliant student, but the most impulsive of the family; he laughed and cried easily, loved and hated on intuition. He would be a great man, Sigmund used to say

37

gently, when he learned to control himself and think first before he spoke. Freda loved him; she stroked his hair and murmured to him. He had worshipped his father; although she was not as clever as he was, she understood that venting his anger upon their mother was only part of his grief.

'Come on,' she repeated, 'come on, Helmut – Papa would not want you to go on like this. He'd want you to be brave and help Mother now. We've all got to stick together and look after Hedda, Willi and poor little Magda – we'll be going home tonight and we've got to think about them.' She hugged her brother close to her for a moment. 'You're wrong about Mother. I was awake last night and I heard her crying her eyes out. Papa absolutely worshipped her, you know he did.'

Her brother slipped an arm round her waist.

'All right,' he said. 'I suppose she can't help it – none of that generation could. Oh God, how we're going to miss Papa! I still can't believe it –'

'Nor can I,' Freda said. 'I keep thinking he'll walk in from the bedroom . . . why – why did anyone want to kill him?'

'Because he was a liberal German,' Helmut said fiercely. 'He wanted to bring us all together. I know who murdered him – the bloody right wing!'

They heard the bedroom door open and together they looked up and saw their mother. She was very pale and though it was a trick of the sunlight through the window, her blonde hair seemed almost white. She stood and looked at them for a moment; Freda moved first. She went and put her arms round her mother.

'How do you feel, Mama? Did you sleep?'

Minna clung to her daughter for a few brief seconds, and then released her.

'I'm all right darling. Helmut –' She approached her son with hesitation.

There had always been antipathy between them; she had married Sigmund Walther at eighteen and been a mother by her nineteenth birthday. The strong-willed, volatile boy had grown up into an adversary, as close to his father as he was distant with her.

38

'I spoke to the Ambassador this morning. Arrangements have been made to fly your father home. They've booked us on a Lufthansa flight this afternoon; they're very worried about security, so the Ambassador suggested you and Freda should go round to the embassy at lunchtime, I'll join you later and we'll be driven to the airport together.'

'Why aren't you coming with us?' Helmut asked. 'If there's any danger, you should go to the embassy too. You've no reason to wait on here, Mother.'

'Someone is coming to see me,' Minna said quietly. 'He's coming to the hotel.'

'Who is it?' Her son spoke sharply. 'It's not a reporter is it? I said last night we wouldn't give any interviews or talk to anyone on the media. I thought you agreed to that –' Minna looked at him. He was the head of the family now that his father was dead; there was a silent confrontation, witnessed by Freda. Then Minna Walther spoke. Her voice was cold and there was anger in it.

'The man who is coming here was with your father when he died. I have a right to see him, and it is nothing to do with you, Helmut, or anyone else. The embassy car will be here at twelve. You'll both go, and I shall join you later.'

She turned her back on her children, went into her bedroom and closed the door. She didn't come out until she knew that they had left. She checked herself in the mirror; it was habit, not vanity. Nineteen years of living in the spotlight as Sigmund's wife had conditioned her to looking right, whatever the occasion. She had not worn black, although she possessed a black suit; but her husband had detested mourning and the ritual of death. He had been a man to whom life was all-important; a man with a personality that radiated energy, optimism and hope. She would never wear black for him.

She went into the empty sitting room; it was full of sunshine. She poured a glass of whisky and water, lit a cigarette; went to the windows and looked out over the Place de la Concorde. The evening they arrived from Bonn, she and Sigmund had stood in front of the window, he with his arm around her, enjoying the spectacular view of the Place at night, jewelled with lights, the traffic flashing diamond head-lights in a glittering moving pattern. He had said suddenly that he felt everything they had worked for was coming closer; he told her how much he owed to her support, and asked her, as he often did, if she still loved him. They had made love that night. She remembered it, not seeing the panorama beyond the window. The cigarette was finished. She stubbed it out and went to the sofa, sipping the whisky. She sat down to wait for Max Steiner.

Max Steiner was right when he supposed his wife hadn't slept; she had spent a long time calming Francine and reasoning with Peter, who was still sullen and hostile towards his father. The more she emphasized the danger he had been in when the West German M P had been assassinated, the more hysterical Francine became and the less her son responded. In the end Ellie took the girl into bed with her, and left Peter dourly watching late-night television with the English girl. Love for her children masked Ellie's own anxiety and hurt feelings until Francine was asleep and she was awake in the darkness. She loved Max, and she was in love with him; she admired his intelligence, his grasp of events, his brilliant journalism. Her role was supportive; to mother his children and care for him, to be lover and companion, and to apply her own brand of simple wisdom in dealing with his difficult temperament. She had never consciously put the children first; they were child-ren and automatically claimed priority over either of their parents. It pained and troubled Ellie that Max had grown so apart from them, and from her in the last year or more. She had accepted the change in him, rationalized her own disappointment and continued to do her best. In the dark-ness her daughter stirred uneasily beside her. He should have come home; he should have thought first of his family's anxiety and at least telephoned. By the morning, Ellie had recovered her composure; she was pale and her head ached from weariness and tension, but she saw her children off to school, kept up a bright chatter with the English girl, and refrained from telephoning the *Newsworld* office until ten o'clock. There Max's secretary told her that he had been called out, and gave her his message. He would be back after lunch, and she was not to worry. Everything was fine.

She was reading the *Figaro* and drinking coffee in the kitchen when the doorbell rang. 'I'll answer it, Madame Steiner,' Pat said. Ellie nodded, deep in the editorial which was devoted to the significance of Sigmund Walther's murder. A moment later Pat was back.

'It's someone called Durand from the Sûreté,' she said. 'He wants to see you.'

Ellie frowned. 'Okay, Pat, thanks. Bring us some coffee, will you please?'

He was a small, square man, holding his hat rather stiffly at his side. He wore thick-rimmed spectacles. Ellie took him into the sitting room and sat opposite to him.

'I'm afraid my husband isn't here,' she said. 'I got a message he'll be back this afternoon.'

'Have you any idea where I could find him, Madame?' The eyes behind the lenses were small and blue; he had an intent look that made Ellie feel uncomfortable.

'I haven't. I'm sorry. His secretary said he was called out, that's all I know.'

'Your husband was very lucky not to have been killed yesterday,' the Sûreté detective said. 'It's surprising they didn't shoot him too.'

Ellie shivered. 'Don't even talk about it,' she said. 'You'll have some coffee, won't you?' Pat put down the tray, glanced briefly at the policeman and went out.

'I was hoping to talk to your husband,' Durand said, 'but perhaps you can help me. What exactly did he tell you about the killing – anything, even the smallest detail, could help us find the murderers.'

Ellie shook her head. 'He didn't tell me anything – I haven't seen or spoken to him since it happened. He was down at the Sûreté yesterday making a statement. I guessed he was back there this morning –' she paused, and then spoke her thoughts aloud. 'I wonder where he is?'

'Maybe with SDECE,' Durand said. 'They're a law unto themselves; they don't believe in co-operating with us or anybody else. I'm sorry I've bothered you for nothing. It's just that sometimes the memory plays tricks after a shock; your husband might have remembered something talking to you which he'd forgotten when he made his statement to us.'

'Can I get him to call you when he comes back?' The detective stood up. His coffee cup was full; he hadn't touched it. 'No, thank you, Madame Steiner. We'll contact him.' They were on the way to the front door when he stopped.

'Has anyone else tried to see him this morning – have you had any telephone calls?'

'No,' Ellie said. 'Only from friends wanting to know he was all right – nothing official. Why?'

The pale eyes focused on her face. 'Your husband was a witness, Madame. He saw the assassins. I'm a family man myself. I would persuade him to get out of Paris and take a trip somewhere. It might be a good idea if you and your children went with him.' He set the soft hat on his head, tweaked the brim till it came down on his forehead, made her a little gesture like a bow, and let himself out.

Ellie stood in the narrow hallway; slowly her hands came together and locked.

'Oh, my God,' she said.

Minna Walther held out her hand; Max took it. It was cool and quite steady. He thought she looked ill; the skin around her eyes was taut, emphasizing the Slav cheekbones; there were black shadows under her eyes.

'Help yourself to a drink,' she said.

'No, thanks,' Max said. He noticed the half empty glass beside her chair. Tension crackled in the air like electricity after a storm.

He had gone to a barber's for a shave, and spent an hour walking along the Seine near Les Invalides, thinking thoughts that had taken him a long way from Paris. As he faced Sigmund Walther's widow, it could have been a lifetime since he had taped that interview in the same room, instead of twenty-four hours. He had a sense of sharp anticipation, a flutter in the stomach, as he waited for her to speak.

'You have something to tell me about my husband,' she said.

'Yes,' Max answered. He found a cigarette, offered one to her, and lit them both.

'Please,' he caught the tension in her voice, 'please tell me.'

'I held your husband as he died,' he said quietly. 'He said one word, and it didn't come out by accident. He meant me to hear it. "Janus."' He watched her as he said it. No shade of expression passed over her face. The large grey eyes returned his look. 'Was that all? He said nothing else?'

'No. He died immediately afterwards,' Max leaned a little forward in his chair. 'What did he mean, Fräu Walther?'

'I don't know. Janus was a Roman god – it doesn't make sense.'

'You've never heard him mention it?'

'No, never.'

Max felt suddenly depressed. 'Could I change my mind and have a drink now?'

'Of course; I'll get it for you – what would you like?'

'Don't move, please, I'll get my own. One for you?' He was surprised when she emptied the glass and held it out to him; she didn't seem the type of woman who drank except to be polite.

He poured whisky for them both and his depression deepened. He hadn't expected her to lie. 'Janus.' She hadn't been surprised; he had the feeling that she had been expecting him to say it. He sat down opposite her.

'Your husband was murdered,' he said, not looking at her. 'Janus was the reason, that's what he was trying to tell me. If you want to get the people who killed him, you've got to tell me what Janus means. Before you answer, Frau Walther, I'd like to tell you something. It's not the first time I've heard it said by a dying man.'

The rigidity went out of her so quickly that she sank back in the chair and closed her eyes. 'Who are you working for?'

'Why should I be working for anyone?' he countered. 'Stop lying to me, Frau Walther. Who is Janus?'

'A Roman god with two faces,' she said. 'That's all I know. It's a code of some kind. Sigmund was trying to find out what it meant.' She raised her head and looked at him. 'When did you hear it first?'

'In 1945. It didn't mean anything to me then; it was just part of a nightmare. Since then it's become a real nightmare; I dream about it – something in me won't let it rest. Then your husband gets shot down, and it's right back in the present day. You asked me who I was working for – I'm not working for anybody but myself. I want to know who or what Janus is, that it can kill a man like Sigmund Walther.'

'And the other man,' she asked him, 'the one you mentioned who said it before?'

'That's a long story,' Max Steiner said. 'Let me ask you something – do you want to find your husband's murderers?'

There was a spot of colour blazing on each cheek when she answered him. 'I'll do anything, pay anything – how could you even ask –'

'Because I want to be sure,' he interrupted. 'You may prefer to let the police handle it. Their record for finding high-grade political assassins like the two who shot your husband isn't all that impressive. You may be frightened for yourself – or for your children. . . . I'm just on the fringe of the thing; you may know far more than you're prepared to tell me. But I'm going to find out what this means, and I came here to ask you to help me.'

She didn't answer. She got up from the chair, wearily, as if she were exhausted, found a cigarette and lit it. The lighter closed with a snap that could be heard, the room was so quiet.

'Sigmund was an old-fashioned man,' she said suddenly. 'He loved his country. It's been fashionable for a long time among certain Germans to reject their race and their history, as if denying them could wipe out what happened in the war. It can't, and Sigmund knew that. We have to forget about the past and concentrate on the future. I'll help you to find out what Janus means. Not just to find the men who killed him, and the people who sent them to do it. But to carry on his work for Germany.'

'And Janus is connected with that work?' Max asked her.

'Yes,' Minna Walther said. She stood leaning against the fireplace, looking down at him. 'You'll have to come to Germany.'

'I was planning to,' he said. 'One thing: we've got to trust each other. You've got to tell me everything your husband knew.'

'I will,' she said quietly. 'I'm flying home this afternoon. I'll go through my husband's files and have everything ready for you to look at. When will you come?'

'When is your husband's funeral?' Max asked her.

'The day after tomorrow. In Hamburg. Our home is there.'

'His family came from Silesia,' he said.

'So did mine,' Minna Walther answered. 'Where were you born, Herr Steiner?'

'Berlin,' he said. He stood and for a moment they faced each other.

'I'm very sorry about about what happened,' he said.

'He had a good life,' she said softly. 'A lot of people loved him. Telephone me and I'll meet you at the airport.'

He took her hand once more and held it. He hadn't kissed a woman's hand since the war, but he did so then. Outside in the corridor, walking down the thick-piled carpet to the lift, he thought suddenly, Christ, Steiner – what's got into you? Then the lift came and he stepped inside, as he had done the day before with Sigmund Walther by his side. He went back to his office and wrote a special article on the murder and the short political career of the dead man, for the end of the week issue. It was easy to do; he avoided sensationalism, and at the back of his mind was the fact that Minna Walther and her family might read what he had written. He gave it in to the editor-in-chief, and waited while he finished it. Martin Jarre put the script down.

'Good. It'll be the lead story and we'll run a cover with

Walther's head in a mock-up. You're looking better this morning – get a good night's sleep?'

'No,' said Max. 'I didn't go home. I stayed in the office. I'm glad you like the piece, but it's just the tip of an iceberg. I want to do an in-depth investigation job on this. Walther murder.'

'Why?' Jarre frowned. 'What have you held back?'

Max picked up the script. 'Something that could bring his killers after me,' he said. 'But they don't know I know anything. I'm asking you for a *carte blanche* on this one: expenses, time, the lot. If I succeed in finding out what I'm after, you'll have a big story. Very big. If I don't, you can kick my arse. Or pay the funeral expenses.'

Jarre's frown became a scowl, and then cleared suddenly. 'All right, Max. Write your own ticket. Be careful.'

'Thanks, I will. I'm going to Germany on Thursday. I'll report back when I've got something. I'd like a credit account opened in the Deutsche Bank in Bonn, with facilities in West Berlin and Hamburg. Twenty-five thousand marks as a start.'

'I'll make the arrangements,' Jarre said. 'It would help if I knew what you were looking for.'

'It'd help if I knew myself,' Max Steiner said, as he went out.

The men who had killed Sigmund Walther boarded the Swissair flight to Geneva less than two hours after the murder. They carried Swiss passports, made out in the names of Kesler and Franconi; the elder of the two was grey-haired, wore glasses and carried a briefcase, the younger was blond, soberly dressed, and carried a small handcase and an armful of the financial papers. They were described respectively as a civil engineer and an accountant. The dark wigs they had worn for the killing had been pushed into a rubbish bin en route for the airport. The two handguns, all serial numbers erased and never used before, had been dropped in a paper bag into the Seine. They abandoned the stolen car, picked up the self-drive which had been left parked in the car park

46

behind Les Invalides, and driven to Orly airport to catch their flight.

They didn't sit together on the journey. Kesler took papers out of his briefcase and studied them, making notes, and Franconi read the London *Financial Times*. Kesler ordered a vodka and tonic: Franconi asked for coffee. The flight was uneventful; after a time Kesler put his papers away and stared out of the window at the piercing blue sky. He had been killing professionally since the late fifties; five years in the Foreign Legion had provided him with a hiding place. It was full of people like him, with false names and war crimes behind them, men too unimportant to merit the help of the SS escape organization, Odessa; Poles and Ukrainians and Germans, members of the terrible Einsatzkommandos who had exterminated Jews in the East, concentration camp guards, rankers in the Waffen SS who had thrown away their uniforms and papers and crossed the Italian frontier with the refugees and the army of displaced persons that roamed Europe.

Kesler was a Pole by birth; the Legion accepted him and thousands like him, and sent them to fight for France in Indochina. He had survived the siege of Dien Bien Phu, and returned to civilian life with skills in every kind of modern weapon, and a reputation for ruthlessness that filtered through to people interested in recruiting such men. He went to Marseilles, because he had contacts there through the Legion, and worked for a narcotics ring. That was where he met Maurice Franconi and fell in love. Franconi was an Italian Swiss who had been in petty crime since he was a boy, graduating from male prostitution to theft and extortion from his victims.

Kesler set up an apartment with him, and began to teach him to better himself. He had proved quick and skilful; after a few months he was as good as Kesler with a knife or a handgun. Employment was found for him too, and between them they murdered seventeen people, five of them women, in the next two years. This had been their biggest assignment; the payment was in proportion to the importance of the victim and to the risk involved. After this, Kesler thought peacefully, he and Maurice could retire, buy a little place in Tangier, where they had friends. . . . The sexual aspect of their lives was less important than when they had first met; their relationship was tender, at times almost as of father and son. They liked music and the theatre; Maurice had become a keen reader of the classics, under Kesler's tutelage. Kesler's own background had been middle-class in his native Poland; he was a cultivated man and he enjoyed improving his lover's mind and introducing him to the arts. They had a perfectly balanced relationship and, unlike some of their homosexual friends, there were no stormy quarrels, no jealousy. At the end of their first two years together, they had gone through a ceremony of homosexual marriage, and both men wore wedding rings on their right hands.

The plane landed on schedule at Geneva airport; they met in the car park, where the car hired the previous evening was waiting for them. Kesler paused with his hand on the door. 'To be on the safe side,' he said, 'let's just check it, shall we?' Franconi crouched down and opened his handcase. He took out a small pencil torch with a surprisingly strong beam and, getting his knees dusty, inspected the underside of the chassis by both front and rear doors. Kesler said, 'We may as well make sure of the rest of it. No harm in being careful. I'll do the top half if you'll get underneath.'

Franconi nodded and smiled at him. He had fine white teeth, and when he smiled he was handsome. He stripped off his jacket and crawled under the chassis. Kesler checked on everything above; the boot swung open when he was sure the lock was clean; it was empty. The wipers satisfied him, so did the bonnet. He opened the passenger door and checked that the mechanism for opening the bonnet was free of even a hair-trigger wire, and then opened it, so that the engine could be inspected. He was looking inside when Franconi came up from underneath. He had dirtied the back of his shirt and trousers, and there was a smudge on his face. 'Nothing,' he said. 'Did you find anything –'

'No,' Kesler said. 'Turn round and I'll brush you down. The car's all right.'

'You don't trust anybody do you?' Maurice said.

'That's why I'm still alive.' Kesler helped him put on his jacket. 'I've checked cars ever since we started working for them. I don't say for a moment they'd get rid of us – we're much too useful – but you never know. There was a man used to work for Gabriel – the drug boys got a lead on him and he made a deal. Somebody passed Gabriel the word, and they fixed his car for him. He'd been told to check but he forgot one thing. The cigarette lighter.'

Maurice got in and started the car. 'I'm hungry, aren't you, Stanis? I could do with a good lunch. I suppose the restaurant will be closed by the time we get in.'

Kesler looked at his watch. 'Nearly four – yes, I'd think so. But we'll get something sent up. We can nibble away while we count the money.' He put back his head and laughed. Then he placed his hand lightly on Franconi's knee.

'You were great today,' he said. 'It was a beautiful job. One of our best.'

Maurice frowned. 'They didn't tell us there'd be another man with him,' he said.

'Don't worry about that,' Kesler said. 'He saw the same as everyone else. Two men in dark glasses. We'll listen to the radio and it's sure to be on the T V now. We're out and clear, like we always are, eh? And this time, we've got enough to give up working.'

Franconi glanced at him and flashed the gleaming smile. 'You'd get bored, Stanis. You love working.'

'I love you,' Kesler said. 'I don't want the luck to run out. I want to go and live in the sun with you; you'd love Tangier. We'd be very happy there. And we could always take a trip if you wanted a change.'

'I'd be happy wherever we went,' Franconi said, 'so long as we're together. That's all that matters to me.'

The hotel had a two-star rating; it was comfortable and catered for businessmen and families. Kesler and Franconi had stayed the previous night there and found the food excellent. Franconi parked the car at the rear of the hotel, while Kesler went to the reception desk.

'Good afternoon,' he said to the clerk. 'I'm expecting a package – has anything arrived for me?'

The clerk checked in the pigeonholes and glanced under the desk. He shook his head. 'No, M. Kesler. But there's a gentleman waiting in the lounge for you. He's been here some time.'

'Ah,' Kesler said. 'Thank you.'

There were a number of people in the lounge; tea was being served. Kesler recognized the man sitting alone at a table, and went up to him. His eyes noted that the man was carrying a briefcase similar to his own. He went over and shook hands.

'What's this?' he said under his breath. 'We weren't expecting you – where's the money –' He gave a wide smile and said loudly, 'How nice of you to wait for me – come on upstairs –'

They went up the two floors in the lift without speaking. Kesler unlocked the door of his room; Franconi had the room adjoining. Then he shut the door and turned to the man who had seated himself on the bed. There was no smile on Kesler's face. 'What the hell is this? I was supposed to get a package – nobody told me you were coming!'

'I've brought the money,' the other man said. He had been their contact for the last five assignments. He was known only as Paul; he spoke French with an accent that suggested he came from east of the Oder, but when Kesler tried him out in German and Polish he refused to talk at all. He was a thin, dour, nondescript human being, with deep-set eyes. Franconi nicknamed him 'the undertaker'.

Kesler held out his hand. 'Give it to me.' The briefcase was passed to him and the man Paul tossed him a key. Kesler put the case on the chest of drawers and opened it. The money was neatly packed inside: Swiss francs, in used notes. Kesler didn't trouble to count the packets. He knew his employers had never cheated on a payment. He shut the case again and turned to Paul. Franconi came into the room; he stared at the other man and looked sharply at Kesler. 'What's he doing here?'

'He brought the money,' Kesler said.

The man seated himself on the bed again and drew an envelope out of his pocket. 'I've got a proposition for you,' he said in his ugly French. 'You've got two hundred thousand francs in there –' he jutted his mean chin towards the case. 'You could earn three times that.'

'Oh?' Franconi sneered. 'Who's the target – the American president, for instance? How do you fancy ending like Lee Harvey Oswald, Stanis – nice bullet in the belly –' He said something obscene in Italian. Paul ignored him; there was a natural antipathy between them. He addressed himself to Kesler.

'I've got a list in here –' the envelope was raised like a torch, and then lowered. 'There are four names on it. No presidents – not even the Pope.' His teeth showed in a grimace trying to be a smile. Kesler matched him.

'Maurice and I are Catholics,' he said. 'I'm glad it isn't the Pope. Four people – six hundred thousand francs. That's a lot of money. And a lot of risk.' He shook his head. 'We're not interested.'

'Wait a minute,' Maurice said. 'Who are the four targets?'

'I can't give you the envelope till you've agreed to the job,' the man said. He put the envelope back into his pocket. 'All I know is there's no one that imporant.'

'Then why so much money?' Kesler asked. 'Six hundred thousand francs. Nobody pays like that unless it's in proportion to the risk. We've done the Walther job and we want to enjoy the money.'

'Show us the names,' Franconi said. 'If they don't trust us, then get someone else. I'm not going into anything blind and neither is Stanis.'

The thin man hesitated. They were the best in the business. Reliable, efficient: a perfect killing mechanism. He took out the envelope, opened it and handed the sheet of paper to Kesler. There was silence in the room for a minute while Kesler read the list and then read it again. He looked up and frowned at Paul.

'Who are these people?'

'I don't know,' the thin man said. 'What do you care – just find them and get rid of them. You've got a month to do it. But no fuss, no publicity.'

51

'Don't try teaching us our job,' Franconi snapped. He came over to Kesler and studied the list. He shrugged. 'It's a fortune,' he said softly. 'Just one month, Stanis. Think what we could buy for ourselves with money like that –'

'I am thinking,' Kesler said. He looked at his lover. 'You want to do it?'

'Why not? One month and we've got enough money to have everything we want. There's nothing in this –' he tapped the paper with his index finger. His nails were manicured and lightly polished. He had sensitive, well-kept hands. 'It's a package deal, that's all. No problem.'

Kesler turned back to Paul. 'Some have no address,' he said. 'Just relatives. This makes it complicated.'

'That's why you're being paid so well,' the man said. 'You find them, get rid of them nice and quietly, every one an accident – that's important.' He waited, looking at Kesler for confirmation.

'We'll do it,' Kesler said. The thin man nodded, gave the grimace which was meant to be a smile, and left them.

Franconi waited for a moment, and then, crossing to the door, opened it suddenly. There was no one in the corridor. He turned back to Kesler.

'I don't trust that little bastard – and I don't trust that list.'

'Then why did you make me agree?' Kesler seldom got angry with Maurice but his face had reddened. 'I didn't want to touch it – we've got two hundred thousand besides the money we've saved! Why did you have to be so greedy?'

'Because it's the biggest chance we'll ever have to be really rich!' Franconi's voice rose. He hated quarrelling with Kesler: rarely as it happened, it unnerved him and he felt sulky for days afterwards. 'You talk about living in Tangier – yes, all right we can go there and hole up and watch the pennies for the rest of our lives, not being really *in* – if we do this last job we can be *rich* – we can buy a lovely villa, do it up nicely, entertain.... Oh, Stanis, don't you see it's worth it?'

'I suppose so,' Kesler said slowly. 'But something about it stinks. Come on, let's not row about it. We've said we'll do it and we will. Let's put that case in the hotel safe till we can bank it, and get something to eat. Then I want to watch the TV news. I have a gut feeling that we'll learn something more about that list.'

For the first time in years, Ellie Steiner surprised her husband. He had rehearsed the scene, every line of dialogue already spoken in his mind, his own attitudes and hers plotted out. He was ready for tears, appeals to his responsibility to her and the children, followed by the patient arguments which so infuriated him because they were full of surface logic. When he came into the apartment, the children were at school, and his wife was alone, watching an educational programme on TV.

She got up slowly and stared at him for a second or two, before coming across very quickly and putting her arms round him.

'Oh darling,' she said. 'Thank God you're back.'

She made them both tea and they drank it together in the kitchen. The kitchen was Ellie's kingdom, gleaming with copper and pine, equipped like a spaceship with every gadget that came on the market. She was a marvellous cook. He watched her while she got the cups and a plate of biscuits. He noticed that she looked very pale and tense. He told her about Walther's assassination; without intention, he hardly mentioned the murdered man's wife. She reached out and placed her hand over his. It was a touching gesture, and he squeezed it hard, nerving himself for what had to be said next. That was when she surprised him.

'Max darling, a man from the Sûreté came here this morning. He wanted to talk to you. He said we could be in danger; you and me and the children. He told me to take them and go away for a while. He said you should come too.'

'Why would the Sûreté send someone round here? And, for God's sake, why would you and the children be in danger –'

'Because you saw the killers,' she said. 'He terrified me; he said the people who murdered Walther could be after you. We've got to get away – you've got to go to Jarre and tell him you want leave!'

53

'Wait a minute,' Max said. 'Wait a minute – this doesn't make sense. I spent hours down at the Sûreté yesterday, making a statement – nobody said anything to me about any risk – as for seeing the killers, so did half a dozen other people.... Who was this man, do you remember his name?'

'Yes, Durand,' she said. 'Durand.'

'Christ,' he said, 'that's like Smith. I'm going to call Regnier and find out what the hell they're playing at.'

Ellie stayed in the kitchen, setting the cups in the dishwasher; she heard Max's voice and the 'ting' of the telephone. She stood by the kitchen door and listened. He hated anyone by his elbow when he was talking on the telephone; he had his back turned towards her. On the other end of the line, Inspector Pierre Regnier told Max to hold on, while he made inquiries. Certainly, he had not sent anyone to the Steiners' apartment. Max turned round while he waited and saw Ellie in the doorway.

'He's finding out about it,' he said. 'He didn't send a man round himself.... Yes, hello –'

Regnier's voice was sharp. 'We have no one called Durand on the Walther case,' he said. 'Whoever saw your wife this morning, he wasn't one of our men. Could be some crank – but she says he showed a card?'

'He could have shown her a credit card for all the difference my wife would know,' Max said. 'Someone says they're a policeman, you believe them. I'll call you back when I've talked to her again.'

He saw Ellie's pale frightened face and his heart thumped when he thought of the man she had let into the flat that morning. He listened while she told him what the man had said, and fear began to prick along his skin. Whoever he was, and he didn't accept Regnier's suggestion of a crank, he had tried to prise information out of Ellie which she didn't have, and then tried to panic her so that she in turn would panic him.

'I've booked for all of us on the first flight to London tomorrow morning,' she said. 'I'm not risking keeping the children here. If that man wasn't from the Sûreté, then, for God's sake, who was he? Oh, Max, I'm really scared!'

'You did the right thing,' he said slowly. 'He could have been some nut, trying to frighten you. But it's better you and the children get out of Paris for a while.'

'You're coming with us – you're not going to stay here. If there's any danger, we've got to be together!'

'I shan't be in Paris,' he told her. It was slotting into place, like pieces in a puzzle that was making a picture. 'I'm going away on an assignment for Jarre. It'll take three weeks, maybe a month. Where are you going to stay in London – with Angela?'

'Yes,' She seemed thrown off balance by the question. Angela was married to a solicitor; she and Ellie had been close friends. They had stayed with the Steiners in Paris the previous autumn.

'Max,' she said. 'Max, where is this assignment?'

He didn't lie to her, although he was tempted. 'Germany,' he answered. She kept on looking at him, the brown eyes seemed to widen until they overpowered her face.

'Sigmund Walther's murder – is that what you're going to Germany for?'

'Yes,' he said. 'I'm determined to do it. I want to know who and why, and a whole lot of other things. And it'll help to know you and the children are safe in London with Angela and Tim.'

'And if anything happens to you, are Angela and Tim supposed to take care of us?'

Oh, he said to himself, Christ, here it comes. 'Nothing will happen to me,' he tried to sound reassuring, instead of angry. He didn't succeed because he added, 'Anyway, I'm heavily insured.' She gave him an odd look, and he thought she drew her body back and upright, as if something unpleasant had passed close to her. He felt suddenly alarmed, as if he had taken a step too far in a direction he hadn't intended. 'Ellie, I'm sorry. Try to understand, will you? This is terribly important to me. I have to find out why Walther was killed, not for bloody *Newsworld* but for myself! For my own peace of mind –

I know you're scared and upset, and you want me to come with you, but I can't. I can't give up the chance to find out something –'

He stopped, and in the seconds that followed, he tried to retrace that step towards the brink, by telling her the truth. He didn't get the chance. She brushed her skirt with both hands, as if she were dusting off an apron, and her face was small and pale and set tight like a fist.

'I understand one thing,' she said. 'Me and the children come second. I've accepted it for a long while, and I've tried to explain it to them so they wouldn't be hurt. But now we're threatened with God knows what, because of you and your goddamned job, and you have the gall to tell me you're not coming over to protect your family! You're going to Germany instead, while we sit in someone else's house and let them take on your responsibility. Okay, Max, you go and play detective, and I'll think up a good reason for Peter and Francine why their father's gone off and left them.' She swung round and walked away; at the door she half turned. 'They'll be really glad to know you're insured.'

He drove them to Le Bourget at eight o'clock the next morning; his daughter was excited about going to London; his son had been morose and ill at ease the night before. He had muttered provocatively about being happy to miss school, but Max had ignored him. Ellie had been bright and artificial in front of the children, who quickly recognized that there was trouble between their parents, but when they were alone she refused to speak to him. At the airport he said good-bye, and it was forced and awkward. He kissed Francine, who started to cry from nerves and excitement, embraced his son, who went stiff, and kissed Ellie on the cheek.

'Safe journey, darling. I'll call you tonight.'

'That would be nice,' his wife said. 'Come on, Peter dear, Francy, take hold of my hand –' Then they were gone. He ignored the funny pang of loneliness that nagged at him all the way back from the airport to his office. He spent the day in the cutting room, and the reference library, and at the end of the day he had completed a set of notes. He did not give them to his secretary to type out. He took them back to the apartment, where the English girl Pat cooked him dinner, and then he settled down to read them and the books he had brought with him. The subject matter was the closing days of April 1945 and the fall of the·Bunker in Berlin.

There was a six-hour time difference between Washington and Bonn; the telex from the Director of C I A West Germany reached the Director in Washington a little before two o'clock. It was decoded and passed straight through to his personal tray, because of the double prefix T P, which it carried. The Director lunched in his office; he arrived there at eight o'clock prompt and set no limit on the hours he worked. He read the telex through carefully:

INTERPOL REPORT PROGRESS NEGATIVE. OUR
INFORMATION RULES OUT TERRORIST
RESPONSIBILITY FOR ASSASSINATION. ANALYSIS OF
MOTIVE AND METHOD TALLIES WITH CONTACTS
HERE; UNCLE VANYA OPERATION PROBABLE TO
CERTAIN. REQUEST WASHINGTON LIAISON WITH
APPROPRIATE AUTHORITY AS SOON AS POSSIBLE.

The Director pressed a button on his telephone and spoke into it. 'File on Sigmund Walther, right away.' He lit a pipe and puffed gently while he waited. They had been keeping a careful watch on the West German politician from the moment he had first declared his belief in *détente* with East Germany. His private telephone had been tapped and his office in Bonn infiltrated by an agent. There had been no evidence of complicity with the Russians, or of any motive but the one he proclaimed publicly: the reunification of Germany.

The Director was a man of boundless cynicism in respect of human beings ’and their motives. He believed nothing unless it showed evidence of venality, and Sigmund Walther was too good to be true. He was bidding for power, and he had chosen a policy which had the appeal of patriotism and peace, and *détente* which was fashionable, and stood no chance at all of

57

becoming a reality. So the Director believed he was a fake. That belief didn't satisfy him because it left the true motivation of the man in doubt. Power alone was not sufficient explanation. To become leader of his party, to aim at the Chancellory itself – these were the obvious explanations why Walther projected himself as he did, but to the Director's subtle intelligence they were too obvious. There was a muted trumpet in the dulcet tones of Sigmund Walther's political pronouncements, a faint Wagnerian murmur that caught the Director's ear. West Germany was stable, prosperous and firmly tied to NATO and the Western alliance. She didn't need a saviour. There were no scandals about Walther. His business and private life was investigated over a long period without turning up a single dubious incident that could be used against him. Again it was too good to be true; the Director rejected it and told his people in Bonn to dig deeper and go back further. There had to be something discreditable. They hadn't found anything more heinous than a succession of love affairs with girls in his student days, and there were no pregnancies, abortions, drugs or suicides to make them worthwhile. Since his marriage to Minna Ahrenberg, he had never been involved with another woman. An upright businessman, succeeding through sheer ability and personal effort, a model husband, a devoted father, an incorruptible politician with high ideals. It was all a gigantic lie; the Director was convinced of it and let his counterpart in the West German Intelligence Service know exactly what he thought. And there, strangely, he had met resistance.

The head of German Intelligence had credentials which the West considered impeccable. He had led active resistance to the Nazis and to the SS Intelligence Service, when serving as a young officer under Admiral Canaris. He had been arrested after the Generals' Plot of 20 July, and sent to Mauthausen concentration camp, where he had withstood torture and protected his associates. He had been released by the Americans, held for a long interrogation, during which he helped to track down senior members of the SD, including two of Reichsführer Himmler's aides, and by 1947 he was working for the

Gehlen organization against the Russians. He had proved himself an anti-Soviet as well as an anti-Nazi; his name was officially Heinrich Holler, but he had several other names, including the one which he had been given at birth. He had astonished the Director in Washington by defending Sigmund Walther, and insisting that he was exactly the paragon he appeared to be.

The Director was adept at reading files, skipping the irrelevant details, mentally processing the facts. Walther had a lot of powerful friends among the old military establishment; that was a consequence of his marriage to a member of it, but they made odd bedfellows with the new rich industrialists, the lawyers and journalists and Social Democratic politicians who were part of his circle. Now he was dead; murdered with the maximum publicity in the heart of Paris, accompanied by a well-known political journalist. Uncle Vanya, the top man in Bonn had said. He certainly needed a specialist to help unravel this one. The Director closed the file; thought for a moment and then pressed a button on his second desk phone. 'Send a message to Curt Andrews in Houston. Tell him to fly up here and be in my office by nine tomorrow. I have an assignment for him.'

3

Sigmund Walther was buried in the family grave at Ohlsdorf cemetery in Hamburg. His father and mother were buried in the small plot, and he followed them on a beautiful sunny day, with a light breeze stirring his widow's black veil. His eldest son watched the veil covering his mother's face and tried to see if it concealed tears. He was angry with her for now adopting the conventional trappings of a ritual she had earlier said his father had always despised. His own concession was a black armband, though Freda had followed her mother's example and dressed in black, as had their cousins and the few close friends invited to the private burial. A public memorial service would be held later. They reminded Helmut of a flock of black crows gathered round the grave, his mother a little apart, seeming even taller because she held herself so upright. He forced back his own tears as the coffin was lowered. His father had left no instruction in his will; Minna Walther had rejected cremation, which Helmut thought was cleaner than the archaic committal to the ground. He didn't believe in a life after death; Sigmund had derided it. It didn't matter what happened to a body; life was the only important thing, and when that had gone it was a flame snuffed out that didn't rekindle anywhere else. Helmut was returning to university that afternoon; Freda and the younger children would go back to school; his mother insisted that she would be better if normal family life were resumed immediately. There was a lunch at their house for the cousins and the friends, which Helmut, the eldest, dreaded. He would be expected to be the host, support his mother, behave with gravity and self-restraint. All he wanted to do was shut himself in his room and cry his heartbreak out. When it was over, he took his mother's arm and they walked to the car. Inside she pushed back her veil. He saw how white her face was, but felt guilty because he did not undertstand her.

'The little ones were very good,' Minna said. 'Willi didn't cry – they were very brave.' Her son didn't answer. He had seen his brother's drawn face, and the way he kept biting his lip and fidgeting. Prussians, he thought. Thank Christ there's none of it in me. I'm just like my father. . . .

'I don't think the younger ones should go to the memorial service,' he said; he was trying to take an adult view. 'This has been quite bad enough for them.'

'There's no question of it,' Minna said. 'I want them to get back to normal. I just wish the lunch was over too, and I didn't have to see anyone.'

'It was your idea,' her son said. 'It didn't have to be done like this.'

'No.' Minna turned towards him. 'No, your father could have been cremated and popped into the ground; I've seen those funerals. It's the way you bury your pet dog.' Immediately she regretted the harshness of her answer, seeing it had upset him; he would never understand how much his hostility upset her.

She turned towards him, but he was staring out of the window, and he didn't look at her until they arrived back at the house. By four o'clock they had all gone. Helmut was on the train to Heidelberg, Freda and the younger children had flown back to Bonn where they were all at school. The house-keeper brought Minna a tray of coffee, and went out, shutting the door very quietly. Minna poured a cup and then left it to get cold; she smoked several cigarettes. The big room was silent; a small mantel clock ticked like a metronome. There were photographs on the tables and on an old-fashioned grand piano: they showed Sigmund and the children. There was a wedding group in a silver frame. People had sent flowers to her and the family; there were big vases displaying them, and they made the room seem artificial, as if it were a setting for a party. She stretched out her right hand, and looked at the gold wedding ring. She drew it back and forward on her finger; it slipped easily over her knuckle. Her hands had got thinner. She got up and opened the antique cabinet which had been converted to hold drinks, and poured herself a whisky.

Max Steiner was arriving at the airport at eleven twenty the next morning. She had booked him into a modest hotel, and told nobody that he was coming. Steiner knew about Janus. It was the most extraordinary coincidence; Walther would have called it Fate, that sent him to the Crillon that morning. It meant that what her husband had begun could be continued. The men who had killed him were merely instruments, she knew that. They hadn't known why he had to be murdered. Those who sent them believed that without Sigmund, it would all come to an end. She wouldn't be expected to carry on, or even to know the significance of Sigmund Walther's dying word, if she had ever heard it. Janus....

They hadn't calculated on the existence of Max Steiner. Minna carried her glass across to the piano, and picked up the wedding group. Nineteen years ago. The clothes were very dated; Sigmund looked self-conscious and her own expression was shy. She looked very young, even for eighteen. Her father was there, tall and straight-backed, her mother in a pale blue hat and dress that matched her eyes. It was a good marriage for her; in his mid-twenties Walther was already successful, and the Ahrenbergs had no money, and no possessions. Ivan had swallowed up the house and the lands in Prussia. His drunken soldiers had looted the furniture and the silver and smashed up what they couldn't load up to steal. Sigmund Walther was a good husband for a penniless general's daughter. She hadn't known what love meant; she hadn't wanted to marry him or not wanted to; it had happened and she accepted it. He had made her love him afterwards. He was an accomplished lover, and he wanted her to enjoy it. Sex meant a great deal to Minna, and he was intuitive enough to develop that aspect of their early life until she was completely in love with him. He had encouraged her to have children; he wanted a large family unit; a beautiful pregnant wife was something a man prized like a decoration on his breast. Her own intelligence earned her the place in his confidence that no one else enjoyed. She held the wedding photograph for a minute and then put it face down on the piano. She took her glass back to the cabinet, refilled it, and went out to her husband's study. It was a businesslike room, with modern furniture, filing cabinets, a tape-recorder and a portable television set. She had promised to show Max Steiner what was in that room. She addressed herself in thought to her dead husband.

He would not be defeated, even in death. The search would go on.

Max flew into West Berlin the following day; *Newsworld* had a leg man in the city who had met Max in Paris, and they were friendly. He was at Tempelhof airport to collect him with a car. His name was Hugo Priem. As they shook hands, a tall man in an American-style suit and buttoned-down white shirt bumped into Max, and excused himself. He carried a suitcase and a Leica camera strung round his neck. Max didn't know it, but he had his first encounter with Curt Andrews from the CIA in the arrivals hall at Berlin airport.

He and Priem lunched together in a restaurant on the Kurfürstendamm. It was a bright day, and the wide avenue passed under their window, the traffic moving steadily; the ruined steeple of the Kaiser Wilhelm Memorial Church pointing its blunt finger to the sky stayed as a reminder of what war had done to the city.

The restaurant was full, the food excellent; he enjoyed the wine. West Berlin was blooming with prosperity. The luxury shops along the Kurfürstendamm were as opulent as anything in Paris. The women he saw were expensively dressed, well made-up, escorted by men with money. There was a lot of laughter round them. Priem was being a good host, but he was uneasy. If there was a feature to be written about West Berlin, then he didn't see why a man from the Paris office should be sent over his head to do it.

Max leaned forward. 'Have a look at this,' he said. He pushed a folded sheet of paper towards Priem. 'I want to find out where they are.'

Priem read the few names, and then looked up. 'Why – what's the angle? Nobody wants to know about the Bunker now – certainly not in Germany. It's been hashed over till people are sick to death of it. Besides, the Russians caught most of them. These three –' he put his finger against the names – 'these were released. I remember that. In the sixties. They wouldn't talk to anyone then. The others could be dead or still in prison in Russia.'

'How can we find out?' Max asked him. 'And don't think I'm stepping on your feet. This is part of an investigation into the Sigmund Walther killing.

'What the hell would the end of Hitler and the people in the Bunker have to do with that?' Priem stared at him.

'I'm not sure,' Max said carefully. 'But there is a link. How good are your contacts in the police?'

'Very good. I make sure they are. I've got an expense account to prove it.' He laughed. 'And there's nothing but praise for the good job they do when I write anything. Which happens to be true. They're a good force, and a clean one.'

'Including the expense account?' Max lit a cigarette.

Priem shrugged. 'Lunch now and then, dinner with the wives, the odd tickets for this and that. Anyway, you want help. And the best way of getting it is to go to the headquarters on Tempelhoferdamm and see one of my friends. He'll know whether you can contact any of these people, and what records we have of them.'

The Inspector took them down to the records office. A computer operated the filing system. The names were fed in one by one. Erich Kempka, SS Standartenführer, serial no. 1877438, chauffeur and bodyguard to Adolf Hitler. Herbert Schmidt, valet to Adolf Hitler, Gunther Mühlhauser, SS

Obergruppenführer, chief liaison officer with Reichsführer Himmler, serial no. 335150. Sturmbannführer Otto Helm, serial no. 977430. SS Scharführer Josef Franke, serial no. 400896. Fraulein Gerda Christian, secretary to Adolf Hitler. Fraulein Johanna Wolf, secretary to Adolf Hitler. Albert Kramer, Hitler Jugend, last known address Hildebrandstrasse 33, Berlin.

They sat round smoking cigarettes; the Inspector was a large, pleasant man in his mid-forties. He was obviously on good terms with Priem. To Max he said, 'What's the object of this inquiry, Herr Steiner – Hugo says your paper is doing an investigation. It's not another Bormann story, is it? War criminals again?' He stubbed out his cigarette and didn't wait for an answer. He looked hard at Max. 'Personally, I think it's time we Germans stopped rubbing our own noses in the shit. It's a long time ago and we ought to forget about it.'

'It's nothing to do with war crimes,' Max said. 'Or Bormann.'

Priem shouldn't have said it, but he did. He wanted to protect his own interest with the Inspector. 'Steiner's doing a piece on the Walther assassination.'

He saw the disbelief on the policeman's face, and raised his hands in a gesture which was mockingly Semitic. 'Don't ask me what all these dead heads have got to do with it; ask him. He doesn't know either.'

'Just so long as it's not an anti-German angle,' the Inspector said.

'I am a German,' Max said, suddenly angry. 'When will we get those answers?'

'Now,' the Inspector said. The computer assistant came up to them, carrying a sheaf of papers. The policeman didn't hand them to Max; he read through them quickly first. 'Best of luck,' he said. 'Excuse me, I've got work to do. I'll sign you out.'

Max went back to his hotel; Priem offered an invitation to dinner with his wife, said he knew of a nice girl if Max was interested. He wasn't and he refused the dinner. Priem didn't quite conceal his relief, shook him hard by the hand, and drove off.

There was a bar and grill in the hotel; Max found a corner table and ordered a steak. He had brought the computer's answers with him; he wasn't sure why but he didn't want to leave the papers in his room.

Kempka, the chauffeur; Schmidt, the valet; Mühlhauser, Himmler's assistant: all three returned alive from captivity in Russia. Kempka was dead, lung cancer in a Stuttgart hospital three years ago. Schmidt was alive, living at Berchtesgaden, Max noted that: the Führer's favourite 'Eagle's Nest', perched high in the Bavarian Alps, Berchtesgaden was a Nazi shrine. He made a red pencil mark against Schmidt's name. Günther Mühlhauser. He had served fifteen years in a Russian prison, spent two years in hospital, was now employed in the personnel section of A. G. Hoechst, Hamburg. Address Goethe Allee 18, Hamburg, tel. no. 768029. Married, the second time, Hilde Ploetz, one child, female, aged six. Mühlhauser. There was a red mark against his name. Otto Helm, officer in the elite SS guarding the Bunker. Surrendered to the Americans, tried and was convicted of war crimes, sentenced to life imprisonment, released five years ago on compassionate grounds after two strokes. Living in West Berlin, Apartment 2, Regensdorfstrasse, home of daughter and son-in-law, Dr Heinz Mintzel, tel. no. 967252.

The two women, Gerda Christian and Johanna Wolf, secretaries to Hitler, were no longer traceable by the computer. Both had left Germany for Central America, in 1951 and 1952, and vanished.

But Josef Franke was, by the luckiest coincidence, working in a department store as a security man, also in Hamburg. Franke, who had pulled him out of the Chancellory yard and, together with the skinny girl who worked in the kitchen, guided him through the shattered streets of Berlin away from the encircling Russians. He had very clear memories of Josef Franke, and they were all good. He had saved Max's life. Franke had taken him and the girl out of the Bunker that same night. According to the records Max had been investigating, the main group, including the secretaries and Martin Bormann and Artur Maxmann, had waited until 1 May, when it had been virtually impossible to escape the Russian patrols or survive the bombardment. He circled Franke's name in red.

Albert Kramer was adviser on industrial relations to the Social Democratic government in Bonn. He was a director of one of the largest banks, chairman of a plastics company, on the boards of three major nationalized industries, gas, electricity and the railways. He was married, with two children, and his address was in the exclusive residential suburb of Puppelsdorf, just outside Bonn.

Albert Kramer. The steak arrived, with a bottle of red wine, and Max began to eat. He hardly noticed the food. It was a big steak, popular with tourists, too large to eat before a third of it got cold. Albert Kramer. He could remember him as if it were the day before that they last saw each other. The cropped fair hair, the blue eyes with the aggressive stare, the Hitler worship. He had jumped forward to take Max's place as officer in charge of the execution squad. Half stunned as he was, Max could see him standing over the man lying, still tied to the chair, on the ground, pointing a revolver at him and firing. . . .

Albert Kramer was a powerful businessman, and high in the council of the Social Democratic government of West Germany. That was going to be a very interesting interview. He put the paper away in his inside pocket; he had memorized one telephone number. He went to the foyer to telephone; the directory checked with the address on the list in his pocket. Heinz Mintzel, Regensdorfstrasse.

A woman answered him; he sensed the wariness of the doctor's wife against a call in the middle of his supper.

'Is that Frau Mintzel speaking?'

'Yes; what can I do for you? I'm afraid the doctor's not available at the moment.'

Max smiled, his intuition proved right. 'I'm not making a sick call,' he said. 'My name is Steiner. I wondered if I could call and see your father. I used to know him in the old days.'

There was a long pause; he heard muffled sounds and knew she had covered the telephone with her hand and was speaking to someone. 'My father's an invalid,' she said. 'He's partially paralysed. I don't think it would do any good your coming to see him, Herr Steiner. But I could tell him you called.'

'I'd like to come,' Max insisted. 'I'm trying to trace a cousin of mine. They were together in Berlin in forty-five. If your father could help me at all, I'd be very grateful. There's some family money involved. And I'd like to see him again. Could I come round for ten minutes?'

He waited, while she mumbled in the background. The doctor mightn't be available to a patient, but he was certainly there beside her.

'All right,' she said. 'But I doubt if he'll be able to help you. His memory's very bad. If you can come round in half an hour we'll have finished our supper.'

It was a modest street, tree-lined and the houses built within the last ten years. Each had a small patch of garden in the front and a garage. The house where Otto Helm lived with his daughter and son-in-law was on the corner, and it had been converted into three self-contained flats. Max pressed the bell for the second floor, and the door opened. The stair was narrow, carpeted and the walls were papered in a cheerful yellow. It was a good conversion, and he decided that it must belong to the doctor. He could imagine the type; frugal, honest, very hard-working, a man who had risen by his bootstraps after the débâcle of the war to a profession and a small property. The kind of man who wouldn't let space go to waste when it could earn him money. He had his father-in-law, the war criminal and ex-convict, to support.

He had formed a character in his imagination, and when the door opened he was so wrong that he hesitated. A young man in his thirties stood there; grinned at him, held the door open and offered him his hand. 'I'm Heinz Mintzel. Come in.' He was untidily dressed, in a sweater and a badly tied tie, which he had loosened; his hair was on end. Max realized with a start that his impressions of his countrymen were long out of date. This was not the starched *Herr Doktor* of his youth, whom his patients treated with respect and children with positive awe. This was a young German. 'Trudi! Herr

68

Steiner's here –' He turned to Max and the friendly grin was rueful. 'I've got to rush out, I'm afraid. I've got a call. My wife'll look after you. I'm afraid the old man won't be much help, but it'll cheer him up to have a visitor.' Trudi Mintzel didn't fit in with his notion of her either. She was about the same age as her husband, a little plump, wearing jeans and a bright shirt, and round spectacles with heavy frames. She shook hands with him; a little frown appeared as she looked at him. 'I thought you'd be much older,' she said. 'You couldn't have known my father, surely?'

'I did,' Max said. 'I was only a boy, but I knew him.'

'He didn't remember you,' she said, 'but then he wouldn't. Half the time he doesn't know who he is himself. Come on in; he's looking forward to seeing you.'

It was quite a large bedroom; the bed was an iron-framed hospital type; there were bright reproduction prints on the walls and a big bowl of greenhouse plants on the table. Sturmbannführer Otto Helm sat in a chair by the side of the bed, with a blue rug over his knees. His daughter raised her voice.

'Dad, here's your friend come to see you. Herr Steiner. Sit down, won't you? I'll bring you a beer, or would you rather have coffee?'

'Nothing, thanks,' Max said. He perched on the side of the bed. Otto Helm looked up at his daughter, and then at Max. He had thin hands, with veins standing out under the pallid skin. One lay palm upward, like a withered claw, in his lap. The hair on his head was white and translucent as candyfloss; it crowned a skull-like face, which was tilted in a frozen grimace on the left side. Then he spoke, the words slurring but still intelligible. 'I don't remember you,' he said. 'Trudi says you knew me in the old days. . . . I don't remember you.'

'I was in the Bunker,' Max said.

'They jailed me,' the old man said. 'It wasn't my fault. I only did my duty.'

'Yes,' Max answered. 'I know that.'

A thread of saliva slipped down one side of the old man's mouth. Max felt a sudden nausea. He wanted to get up and

69

leave the room and the pitiful wreck in the chair, telling himself that it was useless, that Otto Helm couldn't possibly help him.

'I forget things,' the sludgy voice went on. 'I had a stroke and then another but I didn't die.' The lips twisted in a terrible smile, showing the teeth and gums on one side. 'They let me out,' he said.

'The Führer died, though.'

Max waited in the silence; there was a smell of antiseptic in the room. He felt he could have heard a leaf fall from one of the plants in the bowl. 'Yes,' he said at last very slowly.

'The Führer died. He had a man shot that day. By a firing squad. Don't you remember that, Otto?'

'No.' The lids closed over the eyes like a tortoise going to sleep.

'Think,' Max said. 'Think about the day the Führer died. There was a man; you said he was a traitor. You told me about him; I was there. With the Hitler Jugend. You can remember that, can't you?'

The eyes opened again. 'He was shot,' Otto Helm murmured, as if Max wasn't there and he was thinking aloud. 'Swine. She tried to get him off, but no – the Chief wouldn't listen. Didn't listen to her. . . .'

'Who tried to get him off?' Max leaned close to him, he put a hand on his arm and gave it a little shake. 'Who was it? Tell me. . . .'

'E.B.,' Helm sniggered. 'But the Chief wouldn't listen.'

E.B. The girl who had escaped with him from the Bunker had used those initials but they hadn't registered. He'd forgotten them until he started reading the Allied reports and Trevor-Roper's definitive account of the last days in Berlin. *Eva Braun*. Eva Braun had tried to save the man from execution. Adolf Hitler hadn't yielded. He brought himself very near to Otto Helm.

'Who was he?'

'Eh? Who? I don't know – I don't remember things. Where's Trudi – I want the bottle.'

'You can pee in a minute,' Max Steiner said. 'When you

think back. The Bunker, the last day – who did E.B. try and save, Otto? Come on, you tell me and I'll get Trudi for you.'

The eyes were looking into his, and there was a clear intelligence in them. 'Fegelein. He was trying to escape – betray us. I never told them about that. They put me away for all those years.... I never said anything about that.'

'No,' Max said. He felt as if he'd been winded. Fegelein. Herman Fegelein. The man who had whispered to him to find Janus had been Eva Braun's brother-in-law.

He got up, and went to the door. 'I'll get Trudi for you,' he said.

He found her in the sitting room, watching television. She looked up and smiled. 'You haven't been long,' she said. 'Was Dad able to help?'

'No,' Max shook his head. 'I didn't worry him too much. He's pretty confused.'

She stood up and there was something awkward about her. 'He was in prison more than nineteen years,' she said. 'I was eight when he went inside. My mother kept things going till she died. I don't know what he was supposed to have done, Herr Steiner, and I don't care. He's my father and I'm not ashamed of what he was. There are people around here who'd spit on us if they knew he'd been in the S S.'

'He wants the bottle,' Max said.

'Oh, God,' she said. 'Why didn't you say so?' She hurried out. He looked round the pleasant little room. More potted plants, photographs of herself and her husband on a skiing holiday, outside the Mayor's office after their wedding; modern furniture and bright colours. All his preconceived ideas about Otto Helm's family were ludicrously wrong. The house didn't belong to them; they were tenants, not owners, a young couple, not long married, looking after the wife's invalid father. He remembered so vividly that it sickened him the last time he had seen Otto Helm, standing over the bound and bleeding victim in the Chancellory yard. He had been right not to mention that incident to his American interrogators. He might have been hanged instead of going to prison. To his daughter, and probably to her decent young husband too, he

71

was a sick and helpless old man who had been punished for serving his country.

There was nothing he could say to Trudi Mintzel that made any sense now. He let himself out of the flat and began to walk slowly down the road. He was booked on the ten-thirty flight to Hamburg the next day.

Minna Walther had promised to meet him at the airport; it was understood that there would be an exchange of information. He went on walking; there was a tightness in his stomach that followed the nightmare, only he wasn't dreaming now. He took a bus to the sector where his hotel was. A pretty girl sat next to him and smiled; the atmosphere was genial, different from his remembrance of the city where he had been born. But then he only remembered the war, and the grim years afterwards when he had paid a visit to Berlin before taking up his post in London. The people had rebuilt out of the ruins; they lived with the Wall running through the city like a scar, and behind it lay the dead heart of Nazi Germany, the site of Hitler's Chancellory, now razed to the ground by the Russians. The Bunker itself. The dead heart of Nazi Germany. It was a good phrase, and he could use it one day. But that heart was beating still; the murder of Sigmund Walther proved that. He and Fegelein had died because of Janus. Whoever or whatever Janus might be. He went to his room and put through a call to Ellie in London. Tim, the solicitor answered. Ellie and his wife and the children had gone to the cinema. They were all fine and enjoying their stay. He sounded offhand, and Max could imagine what Ellie had told them. He left affectionate messages and rang off.

Hamburg tomorrow. His wife and children, the disapproval of Tim, the good family man – he'd forgotten them as he put the phone down. The tension in his stomach kept him awake; when he dozed images chased through his uneasy sleep. The crippled old man in the chair, Minna Walther by the window in the Crillon with the sunlight on her face, the crack of shots in the Chancellory garden that became the gunfire in a Paris street. Janus. A Roman god. A God with two faces. The symbol of Deceit. . . . At twenty minutes past eleven the next morning, Max Steiner walked through the domestic arrivals gate at Hamburg airport and found Minna Walther waiting for him.

Curt Andrews arranged to meet the Inspector who had given Max Steiner his list of names and addresses in a restaurant in the Old Tempelhof district for an early lunch. Andrews no longer looked like an American tourist. He wore German casual clothes and when he took his table his accent was South German. He ordered beer and waited for the Inspector to come. There had always been a close liaison between the C I A and the West Berlin police and Intelligence services. His check with the Inspector had produced a surprising reaction. Something of interest had come up, and the Inspector wanted to talk to him urgently. They had arranged to lunch in an inconspicuous place where they could discuss their business without interruption. Or bugs, as Andrews thought cynically. Not even a police station was safe in West Berlin. It was one of the most sensitive areas in the world, penetrated and counter-penetrated by agents of East and West. The policeman was on time; Andrews had arrived early. He liked to look over a rendezvous before he used it.

He listened quietly while his informant talked. 'What's the information on Steiner – any political tie-ups?'

'Not that we know,' the Inspector said. 'When he gave me this list of names I thought, Christ, here we go again, another Nazi scare story. But when he said it was tied in with Walther – then I knew you'd be interested.'

'We are,' Andrews said. 'That's why I'm here. We want to know who killed him and why. So does Steiner, if he was telling the truth. It won't be hard to check. But this list of names – how do you figure them?'

'I don't,' the policeman said. 'But they all have one common denominator. They're all people who were in the Bunker when Hitler died. Except for Kramer, the industrialist.'

Andrews lit a pipe. 'So it looks as if the snow-white knight Walther had some Nazi connections after all? My Director never believed in him.'

'It could be anti-Nazi,' the Inspector suggested. 'We have a theory that he was murdered by the extreme right. It could be he had started to get close to something certain people mightn't like discovered. He had a lot of political enemies with his pro-East attitude.'

'And German reunification,' Andrews puffed hard. 'The Soviets wouldn't like that. If you put it all down, pretty near everyone on both sides had a reason for getting rid of him. The right and the left.'

How about the CIA, the policeman thought but didn't say. You've put a few people away. . . . He watched the American. He knew the type. Thorough, cold-blooded, ruthless bastards. But a deal was a deal and allies were allies.

'Is there anything we can do to help?'

Andrews paused; a waitress was passing their table. 'One of those was a Berlin address,' he said. 'You could find out if Steiner's made contact, and what sort of questions he asked. I'm going over to Bonn. You'll be able to contact me at the Königshof Hotel.'

'I'll send someone round,' the Inspector promised. He left before Curt Andrews, and made no attempt to pay the bill.

The two Swiss businessmen had asked for adjoining rooms. They had flown from Geneva to Munich via Frankfurt, hired a car at the airport and driven to a *pension*. The proprietress looked at the booking, and briefly at them. She was used to homosexuals, although neither of them gave that impression. They signed the register: Stanislaus Kesler, Maurice Franconi. They had booked in for a week. They were shown to their rooms, and when they were alone in Kesler's bedroom Franconi brought out his road map. They studied it together.

'Berchtesgaden – we take the Ell, branch off here' – Franconi's finger traced the red line of the autobahn – 'the last exit in Germany at Bad Reichenhall, and we should reach it in about two hours.'

Kesler frowned. 'We could start at the convent,' he said. 'Settle the one at Berchtesgaden and then go on to Berlin.'

'I don't fancy the convent,' Franconi said. 'I was brought up by nuns.'

'She's not a nun,' Kesler pointed out. Franconi shrugged and went back to the map. It had taken exactly twenty-four hours to locate the people they had undertaken to murder. Their contact was a detective agency in Cologne with informants in Interpol and the major European police headquarters. A sum of money substantial enough to satisfy the agency's principal contact in the Federal German police had produced the addresses to fit the names.

'I think we should start at Berchtesgaden,' Franconi persisted. 'It's a nice drive. I'd rather get to hell out after we've dealt with *her*.' The tip of his finger touched a name.

'All right,' Kesler agreed. 'We'll set off as soon as we've unpacked. We can have lunch on the way.'

'I like Bavarian food,' Maurice said. 'But it's terribly fattening.'

'You don't have to worry,' Kesler protested. 'I'm the one with the belly.'

Within the hour they were driving their rented Opel through the centre of Munich and on to the autobahn Ell, heading towards the majestic range of the Bavarian Alps. The tops of the mountains were crowned in snow, and they sparkled in the clear sunshine. The countryside was green and wooded; they left the autobahn, drove through picture-book villages and stopped in one at a roadside café to eat a large lunch. At four in the afternoon they arrived in the small hamlet five miles outside Berchtesgaden. Franconi parked the car in the little square opposite the church. They began to walk at a leisurely pace along the quaintly cobbled street with timbered houses on each side. They stopped at the fourth down on the right, glanced at each other, smiled, and knocked on the door.

An elderly woman answered. She held the door open and said, 'Yes?'

Kesler was spokesman. His German was flawless. 'We've

75

come to pay our respects to Herr Schmidt,' he said softly. 'My friend and I have travelled from Munich. Would you tell him we're here?'

'He's not expecting you,' she said. She looked uncertain. Kesler had spoken with authority. 'I wrote to him,' Kesler said. 'Hasn't he received the letter –' He took a step forward and she let him pass through into the house. Franconi followed.

'I'm his cousin,' the woman said. 'I look after him. If you'll wait in the front room, I'll go and see – What's the name, sir?'

'Fritsche, Colonel Hans Fritsche. I've brought Captain Emden with me. How is Herr Schmidt – not sick, I hope?'

'No, no,' she was becoming more flustered, because Franconi had managed to get in front of her and she didn't like to push past him. 'He's quite well, considering.'

She hesitated. When Schmidt was first released from the Soviet prison camp, there had been a stream of visitors. Newspapermen, sightseers, old friends. And that was after the Allied military authorities had released him from their long interrogation. Those were the days when the controversies about how the Führer had died and whether Bormann had in fact escaped alive were breaking out all over the world. Herbert Schmidt had been the first man to see his master's body. Everybody wanted to hear his version. But that was years ago. Nobody had been near the house for a long, long time.

'Take us to him,' Kesler said. 'Please?'

She passed the young, good-looking man, trying not to brush against him in the narrow passageway. She led them to a small room at the back of the house. The man who had been the personal valet to Adolf Hitler got out of his chair as Kesler and Franconi came in. 'These gentlemen have come to see you, Herbert,' the woman said. 'They wrote you a letter – you didn't tell me about it. I'd have got the front room ready....' Kesler saw the bewildered look on the old man's face, and hurried forward. 'Colonel Hans Fritsche. My comrade Captain Emden. We did write, but obviously the letter went astray. It's good to see you, Schmidt.' He reached out and shook the man's hand. Franconi clicked his heels and gave a slight bow. Herbert Schmidt had spent eleven years in Soviet captivity. The frame was that of a big man, with broad shoulders, but the body had shrunk away, leaving the large skeleton in clothes that hung loose. The face was lined and taut, the eyes had a glaze of suffering in them which was a permanent memory. Franconi and Kesler observed this, and Kesler thought quickly that he was very feeble and wouldn't be difficult to kill.

The woman went out, and Herbert Schmidt asked them to sit down. He was embarrassed because of the letter. Kesler offered him a cigarette, but he shook his head. 'Gentlemen,' he said, and the voice was husky and trembled, 'what can I do for you?'

'My friend, Captain Emden, would like to know about your time in the Russian labour camp,' Kesler said. 'And I want you to accept this; your services to our Leader have not been forgotten.' The gold pencil gleamed in Kesler's fingers as he held it out. Herbert Schmidt reached towards it, and Kesler brought it up level with his face and thrust it so close that it almost touched his mouth. The tiny deadly puff of cyanide caught his breath.

Franconi held him as he collapsed and lowered him into his chair. Kesler counted three minutes on his watch, and kept up a loud monologue in case the woman should be listening. He nodded at Franconi, who felt for a pulse in Schmidt's neck. There was no sign of life. Together they flung open the door and shouted for Schmidt's cousin. She was running down the street to the post office to telephone for a doctor as Kesler and Franconi quietly left the house. She told the doctor, when she got through to him, the same as Kesler had told her. Herbert Schmidt had suffered a heart attack, and she couldn't be sure but she thought he was dead....

Kesler and Franconi drove back to Munich, stopping for dinner on the way. The next morning they searched the local newspapers, and Franconi found a tiny item at the bottom of the home news page in the *Münchener Merkur*. It reported the death of Adolf Hitler's former valet from a heart attack. There was no other mention. 'Well,' Franconi said, 'that's one we can cross out. A beautiful job.'

He glanced at Kesler. 'I suppose we'd better get on with the next one.'

'No hurry,' the older man said. 'We've got time in hand. This job can't be rushed; it won't be so easy, getting to her. I want to keep the place under observation for a day or two – see if we can make a contact with anyone who works inside. Find out when she comes out and where she goes.' He folded up the papers and pushed them aside. They were having breakfast in the restaurant. 'You're bothered about this, aren't you?'

'Yes,' Franconi admitted. 'I am. It's just the idea of a nun – I know she's not an actual nun, but it just turns me up a bit.' Under the shelter of the table, Kesler pressed his knee.

'Superstition,' he said gently. 'But I've got an idea. If you don't want to do this one, why not leave it to me? You could go ahead and settle one of the others. How about the one in West Berlin? Old invalid, living with his daughter. It won't be difficult; you know I won't let you take on a heavy job without me, but the one in Berlin is easy.... Why don't we do it like this? We'll have a few days here, keep an eye on the place and find out what we can, and then you go off to Berlin and I'll see to the business here?'

Franconi covered Kesler's hand with his own.

'I'd like to do that,' he said. 'You're very good to me, Stanis. You're sure you don't mind? You won't need any help?'

'One woman? Don't be silly.'

Minna Walther drove back from the airport. Max had expected a car and driver; the Porsche was a surprise, and so was the speed and dexterity with which she cut through the traffic. He had seen her immediately among the crowd by the arrivals gate, because of her height and the green suit she was wearing. They shook hands and she led him to the little sports car. 'What are you doing in Berlin? I thought you were coming from Paris,' she said.

78

'I was,' Max answered. 'Then something struck me as worth looking at, before I came here. So I went to Berlin first.'

She didn't turn to look at him; she cut through an intersection in a way that made him clutch his seat. 'Was it to do with Sigmund?'

'Yes,' he said. 'Indirectly. I went to see someone; watch out for that car, it's coming across –'

He saw her smile. 'Don't worry, I can see it. I'm a very safe driver.'

'I'm sure you are, Frau Walther; you're just a bit positive, if you don't mind me saying so.'

'My husband couldn't bear me driving,' she said. 'Men are nervous passengers, I've noticed that. I suppose it's because they don't think women know what they're doing. Here we are!'

He looked up at the house as she got out her keys and opened the front door. It was not very big, red brick and rather ugly. There were some fine trees surrounding it. He went upstairs to wash, and his journalist's eye noticed the comfort without ostentation. *Newsworld* had done an article on the 'Millionaires of the German Miracle.' The wealth and, in some cases, the almost nineteenth-century vulgarity of the lifestyle of some of the big industrialists had made marvellous copy. But Sigmund Walther had refused to be interviewed. That, as Max remembered, was before he went into politics. As he crossed the landing, he saw a door had been left open. There were draped net curtains and a big bed; Minna Walther's green jacket was lying across it. He hesitated, staring into the room, at the bed, and then hurried on downstairs. Her bed had nothing to do with him.

She was waiting for him in the sitting room, smoking, looking very elegant in a silk shirt that matched the green of her suit. He looked tired, she thought suddenly. Such a different type of man from Sigmund, who always looked glowing with health. Very dark for a Berliner – there must be Bavarian blood in him somewhere. A restless man, keyed up with nervous energy. He lit a cigarette, and she noticed his hands. They were strong, but sensitive, without hairs. She hated a man's hands to be hairy. He wore a wedding ring. She noticed the silence and didn't know how to break it. They were mentally circling each other, seeing the sex of the other as they hadn't done before. Like animals deciding whether they were scenting friend or foe. . . .

She knew that Max was seeing her as a man taking stock of a woman, just as she had noted his hands, the dark colour of his eyes, the way he sat opposite to her, leaning a little forward. . . . The moment of mutual recognition lengthened; she felt the colour in her face, and a sensation that was almost panic. Ten days. She'd been a widow for ten days and already she was reacting to a man. . . .

'Frau Walther,' Max Steiner said. 'You have something to show me. And I've got things to tell you. Where do we start?'

Like a stone flung into water, the question dispersed the reflection of themselves which each had permitted to emerge, and each had looked at. The moment was gone and the danger with it. Minna Walther said, 'We have to trust each other. I trust you, Herr Steiner. But I don't know why you want to find out about Janus, if it isn't to make use of it. As a political journalist. I've brought my husband's file here from Bonn, but before I show it to you, I have a right to know what your motives are.'

'Finding your husband's killers isn't enough?' Max asked.

She shook her head. 'No. A lot of other people have that motive. The police, for instance, his friends – I want to find them more than anyone. But it's not just that with you. It's Janus. Why?'

He paused for a moment, and then made up his mind. They were going to be allies, working together. They had to trust each other; she was right. He remembered saying the same thing to her when she lied to him the day after Walther's murder. No secrets, no holding back.

'I was in a Hitler Jugend cadre in April 1945,' he said. 'We went to the Bunker; Hitler was going to shake hands with us and send us off to the Pichelsdorf bridge to get blown to bits by the Russians. We never saw Hitler; we were detailed to act as a firing squad, I was the platoon leader. The man had been beaten up, probably tortured. He spoke to me. He said, "Find Janus."'

'And you shot him?' Her voice was low, shocked.

'No,' Max said. 'I didn't. Something just snapped in me; the whole Nazi mess blew up in my face. My father and my two brothers were killed, my mother and grandmother were under shellfire, we were all going out to die for Hitler. That was enough without being told to kill a man they'd half murdered already; the Führer's order – that's what the SS told us. He couldn't even stand; they'd had to tie him into a chair so we could shoot him.'

'Don't,' she said, and her hand covered her face for a moment.

'I said no,' Max went on. 'So the Standartenführer knocked me flying and laid a few kicks into me, and my squad carried out the execution. Then I passed out. I used to wonder why they didn't shoot me. Still,' he shrugged, 'maybe a few shells started falling near and they took cover. One of the guards picked me up later and brought me down into the Bunker. I didn't know what was happening at the time, but apparently Hitler and Eva Braun had committed suicide and they were going to burn the bodies, so everyone was cleared away from the Chancellory garden and the exits.'

'How did you escape?' she asked. 'Nobody got away from there – the Russians killed or captured all of them –'

'The guard who found me in the garden and his girlfriend slipped out that night, and took me with them. They disap-- peared together when we got near the American patrols, but I was picked up and sent to a camp. Eventually I got back to my aunt in Bremen through the Red Cross.' Minna got up, and he stood with her.

She didn't say anything, she walked across to the mahogany cupboard and opened it. He saw the ranks of bottles shining inside. She came back with two glasses of whisky. He took one of them. 'I never told anyone about it,' he said. 'But I had nightmares occasionally. I'd dream the whole thing, and wake up shaking like a leaf. It doesn't sound very manly, does it, but I was never the Nazi Superman type –'

81

'How old were you?' she asked.

'Sixteen. It's an impressionable age. I made my life, got married, got myself a very good job, and I still dreamed about the man who said I had to find Janus. In the last year I've been having the dream nearly every night. I began to think I was breaking up. Then I met your husband. And now you know why I have to find out what Janus means.'

'Yes,' Minna said. 'I see. Thank you for telling me. Bring your glass and we'll go into my husband's study.'

He sat in Sigmund Walther's chair, and she put the thick brown hessian file on the desk in front of him. Then she sat and sipped her drink.

'It was a million to one chance that Sigmund heard about the defector,' she said. 'He'd just got elected to the Bundestag, and he was very friendly with someone in the Ministry for Internal Security. He told Sigmund about the Soviet trade delegate who had asked for political asylum.'

'When was this?' Max had the file open.

'Last year. You'll find it there. He brought a lot of information with him; apparently he was a senior KGB officer who felt he was falling out of favour at home, and took the chance to come over to us.'

'Trade delegations usually have a couple of them, to watch the delegates,' Max said. 'Vladimir Yusevsky; I remember him –' he was glancing quickly at the first sheets in the folder. 'There was a fight between the British and the Americans as to who got hold of him. The Americans won. But not before our own people had got their hooks into him by the looks of this.'

'I'll leave you for a while,' she said. 'Call, if you want anything.' She closed the door so quietly that Max didn't hear her go. He turned the first page in Sigmund Walther's file and began to read.

There was no complete transcript of the Soviet defector's information; that would have been classified as top security. What Walther had assembled were copies of available Russian documents which had been released long after the events they described, with notes appended to clarify or implement the information. These notes were marked with 'V. Y. deposition' and a date. The first document was written by Sigmund Walther in longhand. No secretary had been trusted with this material. Vladimir Yusevsky had asked for political asylum in the autumn of '69, during a trade delegation visit to Bonn. The Federal government had granted him temporary asylum while negotiations were in progress with the Soviet government for his return. During the negotiations, he had been discreetly interrogated by the West German Intelligence Service, under the personal direction of Heinrich Holler; his co-operation was a condition of the Federal government stalling Russian attempts to get him back. It had been arranged for him to escape to the Embassy in due course, and from there he was flown to the United States.

He had talked very freely to Holler and his team. There were references in Walther's report of a Soviet network being exposed within the Federal government itself, and a link through to Brussels and NATO which caused a spate of resignations, three arrests and a suicide. Yusevsky had blown a hole in his native Intelligence operations, which had been satisfactory for the West. But he had brought something else, as a bonus for his German hosts. A copy of the original Russian autopsy reports on the bodies of Hitler and Eva Braun. The findings had been released by the Soviet authorities in June, three months after the discovery of the dead Führer and his wife in a shellhole grave in the Chancellory garden. Max had already read brief extracts in his initial research in Paris. The reports were accompanied by photographs of the badly burnt corpses, and long, ghoulish descriptions of their teeth and internal organs. The identity of Adolf Hitler had been established beyond doubt by the capture of his personal dentist, complete with his and Eva Braun's dental records. The Soviet doctor in charge had been a woman, A. Kretchinova. She and her assistants had carried out thorough post-mortem examinations on all the bodies discovered in the Bunker itself and in the graves in the garden. Goebbels and his wife had taken cyanide, after poisoning their six daughters. The evidence set out identified the bodies of Hitler and

Eva Braun beyond any dispute; the Russians found that the Führer had taken poison, rather than shooting himself. It tarnished the martyr image, and ignored the skull shattered by a bullet wound. It detailed primly that the leader of the Third Reich had only one testicle.

Max Steiner was reading, slowly, concentrating on every word. The autopsy on Eva Braun: her age, her height, her teeth, fillings, crowns, bridgework, the evidence of cyanide in her mouth, tiny glass crystals from the bitten ampoule, the smell of bitter almonds when the body was opened. And the findings of the meticulous Soviet woman doctor which had been omitted from the autopsy report released to the rest of the world. Eva Braun had had a child.

4

'You've found it,' Minna Walther said. She had come into the study, and Max got up slowly, holding the file in both hands.

'Yes,' he said. 'I've been trying to think what this means.'

'It means that Adolf Hitler left an heir,' she said quietly. 'Have you read everything?'

He nodded. 'I want to go through it again. I want to make notes and put together what I've got. My God, I can't believe it –'

'Neither could Sigmund,' she said. 'But it's there, and it's true. The Russians found out, and they must have tried to find the child. That's why they wouldn't let the British or the Americans talk to any of the people they captured from the Bunker. The ones they released didn't know anything. When Yusevsky defected, the secret came with him. American Intelligence knows about Janus.'

'Why that name?' Max said. 'Why did Hitler choose that as a code?'

'Sigmund thought it represented himself and Eva,' Minna Walther said. 'The god at the gate of the city, facing attack, defending his people at one and the same time.'

'The child was never found,' Max said slowly. 'That's why your husband was killed. He was searching for it, wasn't he?'

'Yes,' she said. 'Sigmund knew that if Hitler had a son, he represented the greatest danger to world peace and to the future of Germany. He may not even know who he is, but there are others who do, and they're waiting for the right moment to produce him. Sigmund was convinced that he hadn't been found; Yusevsky was very close to the investigation after the fall of Berlin. He said they'd been unable to trace it.'

'How do you know that? It doesn't say so in here –'

'Heinrich Holler told us,' she said quietly. 'He was trying to help Sigmund.'

'Why should the head of our Intelligence need someone like your husband to do the work for him?' Max asked. 'Surely finding the child was his job?'

'You've been away from home a long time,' Minna answered. 'There are men in positions of power in Germany who wouldn't want Holler to find that child. Men in his own service that he couldn't trust. He was helping Sigmund do what he couldn't do himself.'

'It's twenty-five years,' Max Steiner said. 'You're not telling me there are Nazi sympathizers running Germany today?'

'Not running it,' she corrected. 'But they're there. And memories begin to blur; people forget the horrors and remember the propaganda, the successes. Now we're divided, split down the middle with our capital cut in half by that disgusting Wall. . . . There are people who could look back to Adolf Hitler and think he wasn't all that bad. I know, Herr Steiner. I've heard those views expressed by sensible, decent people, who wouldn't hurt anyone. That's why my husband believed so passionately in Germany being one country again, whatever the compromise. If once we come together, we'll make ourselves independent and free!'

Max listened to her, and noted the colour in her cheeks and the intensity in her voice. Not so cool and composed now, the Prussian aristocrat had changed into a woman of passionate convictions. There was a lot of fire behind the ice.

'Now that you know,' she said. 'What are you going to do?'

He was sitting hunched forward, elbows on his knees,

looking up at her. 'I'm going to find Janus,' he said, 'if you'll help me.' He hadn't expected her to do what she did. She moved quickly and came and sat beside him. She put her hand on his arm. Once again he could smell the scent she used, the one he had given Ellie for her birthday.

'We'll work together,' she said. 'I've got friends who can help. We'll find this child.'

'It'll be a grown man,' Max reminded her. 'And if we do find him, what happens then?' She turned away from him. 'I don't know,' she said.

'Supposing it was a girl?'

'Sigmund was sure it was a boy,' Minna said. 'It makes more sense. It *was* a boy. The Führer's son.'

'It makes me shudder,' Max said, 'just to imagine what could be done with a trump card like that to play.' He lit a cigarette and gave it to her. He noted that she took it and that she let their fingers touch. Sexual excitement rose in him; he fought it down. The time would come for that; he knew it would, just by sitting close to her. 'I made a list of people,' he said. 'I saw one of them in Berlin last night. SS Standartenführer Otto Helm. He was the officer who ordered the shooting in the garden. He told me who the man was. Herman Fegelein, Eva's brother-in-law. He knew about Janus, and that's why they killed him, because he was trying to escape. They couldn't risk the secret getting out. So if he knew about the child's existence, then his wife must have known a hell of a lot more. Her name is down in your husband's notes. But there's no record he ever went to see her.'

'He tried, several times,' Minna said. 'But she wouldn't agree. She wouldn't see or talk to anyone; she lives in a Catholic convent in Munich. She's a lay sister, and the Reverend Mother refused flatly to see Sigmund or discuss Gretl Fegelein.'

'We'll have to try again,' Max said. 'I've another call to make, at Berchtesgaden. Hitler's valet lives there; it's a bit of a long shot if the Russians let him out, but there might be some clue he could give us.... We can try and get to Gretl Fegelein on the same trip.'

'We?' Minna Walther questioned. Max looked at her and nodded.

'A woman has a much better chance of getting into a convent than a man,' he said.

They had dinner in the house; his suitcase was still in the boot of the Porsche. Max had gone back to the study and spent the afternoon reading through every item that Sigmund Walther had collected. . . . Then he processed the information, discarding the irrelevancies and the dead ends, set out the facts in Walther's file and the facts which he knew himself. The outline was finished by the evening; he gave it to Minna to read. Walther had been painstaking and imaginative in his investigation, helped by the guidance of Heinrich Holler, whose memory of the old Abwehr records was invaluable. Admiral Canaris had kept detailed files on the Führer and all his associates; so had the Intelligence Service of Reinhard Heydrich and Himmler. Both services, outwardly in truce, but in mortal rivalry for control of the internal and external security of the Reich, put their spies into every department and every private house.

Until the failure of the generals' bomb plot in July 1944, Canaris and his successor had compiled a report of the activities and routine of every person who stayed at Hitler's retreat in the mountains at Berchtesgaden. There Eva Braun lived in seclusion, with her two terriers for company, appearing in front of Hitler's intimates only on his command. It was a strange love affair; her role as mistress expanded with the years, until her dances and exhibitions of athletics, loyally filmed by her mentor Heinrich Hoffman, became part of the entertainment offered the favoured few who shared their leader's relaxation. There was no doubt that she loved Adolf Hitler with a mixture of naïveté and mysticism which submitted without question to a life of loneliness and restriction. She was a simple woman whose appeal lay in her natural prettiness, and homely ways, regarding herself as divinely appointed to serve the Leader. The Abwehr spies at Berchtesgaden reported that she was in poor health during the early summer of 1943, and that she had gone to stay with her sister Gretl in Munich after Christmas, returning to Berlin in late February. The agents' report suggested that she might have fallen out of Hitler's favour, and this was the reason for her illness, which seemed to be neurotic in origin, and her return to her sister. If this was the case, then her position was even stronger after she and the Führer became reconciled.

Unfortunately for both the Abwehr agents and their former chief, Canaris, the bomb planted beside Hitler during the conference in July did not achieve its aim. He escaped with cuts and bruises, and thousands of people were executed in a purge that destroyed Admiral Canaris himself and delivered his records into the hands of his enemy the Gestapo. It had seemed to Sigmund Walther, as it did to Max, that the 'illness' from which Eva Braun was suffering was pregnancy, and the stay with her sister had been to cover up the birth of the baby.

The execution of Fegelein and his knowledge of the code-word Janus reinforced this theory. With Holler's assistance, Walther had compiled a long report on Gretl Fegelein, the pre-1945 data taken from Gestapo files. In the early part of 1944 she had entertained her sister Eva; there was no record of anything unusual during their stay together. The sisters were friendly but not intimate. There were few visitors, Herman Fegelein was one of Reichsführer Himmler's most trusted assistants, and he was seldom able to leave Berlin. His wife was a retiring woman, who felt uneasy with the Führer's inner circle and refused to take part in the intrigues and power politics that surrounded him. She was a practising Catholic, and continued to attend Mass in spite of pressure from her husband, who feared Hitler's disapproval.

Walther's report on Fegelein's execution was the official one. He had been caught hiding in a flat in Berlin, having slipped away from the Bunker; Swiss money and his sister-in-law's diamonds were found on him. Hitler ordered his immediate return to the Bunker, where he was interrogated and shot. His body had been buried in a bomb crater and dug up by the Russians. Walther had tracked down the two surviving servants who had lived in the Fegelein household during Eva's stay. One was an old woman, a war widow, who lived on a pension and helped out with a Munich family's washing twice a week. She had seen very little of the famous Eva; what she did see was when she brought her breakfast in bed during the morning. She remembered being sent a message during the visit, that the ladies were going away for the weekend and she wouldn't be needed till the Monday.

The other survivor of the household was an ex-SS man, called by the unlikely name of Schubert, who acted as chauffeur and bodyguard. His story was the same as the maid's; nothing unusual occurred while Eva was staying there, except that he too had been dismissed for the same weekend.

There followed a long and fruitless series of inquiries at hospitals and doctors in the city, none of which yielded any information linking them with Eva Braun or with the delivery of a baby in suspicious circumstances. There had been a private clinic ten kilometres outside the city, but it had been closed down at the end of the war, and the building demolished. There was no trace of the doctor who ran it or of any of his staff. The evidence pointed to Eva having had the child induced over that weekend, the baby itself being taken away by a foster-mother.

Bombing, chaos and disruption followed by Allied occupation had made it impossible to track down anyone who knew anything about the clinic or its medical staff. And there the trail had ended for Sigmund Walther with the refusal of Gretl Fegelein to see him, and of the convent to accept letters or messages for her. He had made a note of Holler's suggestion that the Reverend Mother's reluctance to assist them might be on direct orders from her superiors in Rome. There was nothing to be done officially, since the investigation was a private one, and Gretl Fegelein had not committed any breach of the law.

'We've got to see her,' Minna put the report down. 'She helped to arrange the birth and she *must* know who took the child! Her husband knew, too. That's what he was trying to tell you – find Janus!'

'It must have been kept secret from everyone else,' Max said. 'Somebody would have given it away, at Nuremburg, or tried to do a deal to help themselves. Read the rest of it; there are one or two people left on my list who just might be able to lead somewhere.'

He watched her reading, a slight frown drawing the fine eyebrows together.

'There are two in Hamburg,' she said. 'Mühlhauser and Josef Franke. Why don't you see them first – then we can fly to Munich. She's not going to disappear out of the convent.'

'I didn't know what Janus meant when I drew up that list,' Max said. 'But Mühlhauser was a very important man, the last liaison between Himmler and Hitler in Berlin. The Russians got him, and what bothered me at the time is how he got released. It bothers me even more now. He and Fegelein were Himmler's men. And Himmler was trying to make peace behind Hitler's back. Fegelein knew about the child, and I'm beginning to think he told Himmler. And if Himmler knew, then Mühlhauser would have known too. Maybe we should see Mühlhauser first. Josef Franke was the guard who got me out; he can't tell us anything, but I'd like to see him again anyway. I owe him a drink, at least.'

He saw that she wasn't listening; she was looking at the list again and this time the frown deepened suddenly, and then disappeared.

'Albert Kramer – why is he on this list?'

'Do you know him – of course, you would do,' he said. 'He's a powerful man in Germany today; he's got a finger in everything, including government policy.'

The coldness in her eyes surprised him. 'He is one of our closest friends,' Minna Walther said. 'What could he have to do with this?'

He felt suddenly angry; the last person he had expected to find ranked with Minna Walther and her husband was Albert Kramer. He wanted to shock her, to repay the snub with the truth about what her oldest friend had done in the Chancellory garden that day. But he didn't. Instinct stopped him, and he obeyed it.

91

Albert Kramer, and a patriotic idealist like Sigmund Walther, with a wife of Minna's integrity and devotion. Albert Kramer must have changed a lot from the boy who emptied his revolver into the dying Herman Fegelein. He would have another motive now for meeting him again.

'I'd better go to my hotel,' he said, 'it's getting late. Can I phone for a cab to take me there?'

'Where are you staying?'

'The Parkhotel.'

'It's not a very comfortable hotel, I'm afraid,' she said. The eyes were innocent; there was no subtle invitation in them. 'It *is* late; they'll be closed except for a night porter, it's that sort of hotel. Why don't you stay here tonight?'

'That's very nice of you, Frau Walther. I don't want to be a nuisance,' he said.

She smiled, and the strain which had arisen between them was gone. 'It's no trouble at all. I always have a room ready; we never knew when someone would call and need a bed. I left my car keys on the table in the hall; if you get your case, I'll take you upstairs.'

He followed her up to a room on the first floor. It was some distance from the bedroom he had seen that morning. She opened the door and switched on the lights; it was a warm and pleasant bedroom, impersonal as all guestrooms are.

'I hope you'll be comfortable,' she said. 'What would you like for breakfast?'

'Just coffee, I never eat anything,' he said.

'Nor do I,' Minna said. 'Goodnight.'

'Goodnight, Fräu Walther.'

He picked up his case, dropped it on the bed and began to unpack. The sight of his pyjamas reminded him of home and the room he shared with Ellie. She seemed so insubstantial that it shocked him; she and his children were receding like shadows into the background of his life. Time was running backwards; with every hour spent in that house, immersing himself in the world of the war, he was losing his identity as Max Steiner, French-domiciled with a wife and children and a bright career in political journalism. The past was closing in on him, seizing him and dragging him back into it. His youth, his lost family, they were taking shape and becoming more real than the living. He could see his mother as if she were in the room with him; her face was lined with tiredness and grief, the brown hair prematurely grey. His father, and the dimmer figures of his brothers, killed in the war which was to make Germany the ruler of the world.

He went to the washbasin and, instead of cleaning his teeth and making preparations for bed, he spent a long time staring at himself in the mirror. The man started dissolving into the boy, the member of the Hitler Youth since he was eight years old, the youngest son of a proud National Socialist family. Adolf Hitler, the saviour of his people. Somewhere in the world outside, a man carried within him the seeds of that supremely evil genius, and only an optimist or a fool would imagine that the heir to the Fourth Reich was not being nurtured and prepared to claim his inheritance, under some other guise. He had a clearer picture of Sigmund Walther after the hours spent reading his work and seeing into his mind. He had a vision of Germany which was based on his faith in the people themselves. He saw them united in peace, their talent for hard work, self-sacrifice and honesty overcoming the ugly dogmas of the left and the narrow hysteria of the right. He saw their vulnerability through partition, and recognized that a moment of frustration might emerge which could be seized and turned to an advantage. He knew his country's weakness. Germans needed a hero to reflect their ancient culture and the deep-seated racial myths which were a part of the Teutonic ethos. If Germany was to be safe for the future, the heir of Adolf Hitler had to be found. Walther had set himself this mission and he had died because of it. The responsibility had fallen on Max Steiner; it was no longer a selfish quest, or a journalist's coup of the decade. It was a mission.

He fell asleep quickly.

In her big lonely bedroom across the passage, Minna Walther stretched out to the empty pillow beside her, and began to cry for her husband. And for herself, because she knew she wasn't going to be faithful to his memory.

Maurice Franconi had bought himself a puppy. It was a black and white terrier, and it gave him the excuse over the last few days to walk up and down the street where Otto Helm lived with his daughter and son-in-law. Nobody commented on a man walking his dog; he lingered by the house, saw the doctor leave on his morning calls, worked out a routine for the family. Otto Helm's daughter went shopping in the morning, but she didn't leave the old man alone. Maurice had telephoned when she and the doctor were both out, and put the phone down with the excuse of a wrong number when a woman answered. Probably there was a neighbour in one of the other two flats who stayed with the invalid till his daughter came back. It wasn't going to be quite as easy as Kesler had imagined.

There was a limit to the number of times he could appear with his terrier in that street when he wasn't a resident. Otto Helm would have to be dealt with at night. Franconi had a room in a small *pension* not too far away. He bought himself a can of petrol and a plastic bag of polystyrene filling for cushions.

The littler terrier licked his hands, and Franconi patted it. He liked animals, but Kesler was allergic to dogs and cats. He wouldn't be able to take the puppy back with him, but he enjoyed her company while he laid low between visits to Regensdorfstrasse, trying to teach her tricks she was too young to pick up, though she played enthusiastically, licking his face and responding to his voice.

He had dinner at a café, paid his bill at the *pension* and said he would be leaving very early in the morning. He walked the dog past the house at just before eleven o'clock; there were lights in the first-floor windows. Otto Helm and family were at home. The doctor's car was parked outside.

Franconi went back to the *pension*; he had hired himself a little VW under the name of Hubert, with one of the forged driving licences he and Kesler kept in reserve. He packed his case, shushed the terrier, who was scampering by his feet, and packed the petrol and polystyrene in a big holdall. He had provided himself with matches and a long twist of rag. He

94

looked round the bedroom, making sure he had forgotten nothing. Kesler had taught him to pay attention to detail; even a book of matches left behind could help identify a man. Nothing. Nothing but the terrier. He opened the door, picked up the case and the holdall and called it softly. 'Hella – come on. . . .' A single light burned in the narrow hall below; he checked his watch. It was nearly twelve-thirty. Everyone had gone to bed. There was a pay telephone in a cubicle near the desk. He slipped inside, paid twenty pfennigs, and dialled the doctor's number. It rang for nearly a minute. Then a man's voice answered; it sounded sleepy. Franconi spoke rapidly, urgently. There had been a bad accident, three cars involved; one of the victims had given the doctor's name. Come, please, at once – it's too terrible down here – he gave the location about five miles away at a well-known junction near a shopping centre. Then he hung up, grabbed his cases, and ran silently through into the street and got into his VW. The terrier bounded in after him. He parked outside the house on the other side of the road. He saw the doctor come out of the front door carrying a surgical bag. He jumped into his own car and drove off, swerving at the corners. Maurice got out, carrying the holdall, and went to the entrance. He pressed the bell marked 'Mintzel.' The buzzer sounded and he went up the stairs. He saw the door open and a slant of yellow light cut across the dark landing.

'Heinz?' Trudi Mintzel called. 'What have you forgotten –'

He reached the door and threw his weight against it. He had a brief sight of a young woman in a short nylon nightdress with her mouth opening to scream. He hit her so quickly that she didn't have time to make any noise. She fell backwards, and he had a glimpse of her thighs and lower body exposed; he looked away. Women disgusted him.

He opened the doors till he found Otto Helm's bedroom. The room was in darkness but the old man's snoring rattled. Franconi switched on the light, but he didn't wake. He was propped up on the pillows like a dummy, white-haired and waxen, his paralysed face twisted into a sleeping grimace.

Franconi brought the holdall into the doorway; he piled the polystyrene into a heap by the bedside, and poured petrol over it, sprinkling the rest round the curtains and the furniture. Then he went back and picked up Trudi Mintzel. The blow had broken her neck. He laid her down by the bedside, near the heap of polystyrene. He backed out of the room, lit the twist of rag with a match. It was nylon and highly inflammable. It flared immediately and he stepped forward and threw it on to the mound of plastic fibre. There was a thump and a bright flash as the petrol exploded. Franconi shut the bedroom door and waited outside for a minute. The crackle and hiss of the fire was joined by wreaths of deadly smoke seeping under the door. Polystyrene gave off lethal fumes. Franconi thought he heard a faint, gurgling cry from inside the bedroom, then he left the flat, slipping the latch on the front door as he left. He hesitated in the entrance, but there was no one in the street.

He didn't look back until he was in the V W, with the engine switched on, and the terrier Hella was trying to lick his hand because she was pleased to see him. Flames were shooting out of the first-floor window. Franconi let in the clutch and drove away. The first flight back to Munich was not till eight in the morning. He drove to the centre of Berlin, parked the car, and went to an all-night movie showing sex films. He slept through them until six o'clock. He felt tired and dirty and his head ached. The terrier was curled up in the passenger seat, waiting for him. He climbed inside, and picked up the little dog to break its neck. She whined and struggled, licking joyously at his face.

Franconi hesitated; she had bright, button brown eyes and a short tail that wagged and thumped against him.

'Good Hella,' he said. 'Good girl, then. . . .' He opened the door and put her out. 'Someone'll find you,' he said, and drove off. In the driving mirror he could see her racing after him, until he outdistanced her. He caught the plane to Munich and had lunch with Kesler. He told him everything, and Kesler complimented him warmly. He had been working hard on his assignment at the convent, but there hadn't been an opportunity yet. Franconi looked disappointed. He had hoped to find it settled.

He let Kesler reassure him, while he sulked. He didn't mention the terrier Hella.

'There's a pattern,' Curt Andrews said. He laid a long finger on the paper in front of him, and looked at the head of West Germany's Intelligence Service. Heinrich Holler, the legend. Andrews wasn't impressed by reputations; he liked to make his own judgements. Holler was small and slight, with grey hair, and a limp, the legacy of his imprisonment by the Gestapo. He had pale, clear grey eyes in an intelligent face and the kind of mouth that is described as humorous. He made Andrews feel big and clumsy, which he wasn't. The two men didn't like each other, but it was a well concealed hostility, invisible to anyone else. Their personalities were at variance: Holler, the intuitive intellectual, with his crippled leg and European education, was the mental and physical opposite of Curt Andrews. Andrews stood over six feet two inches and weighed two hundred pounds; he was built like a fullback, which he had played in college; he was a veteran of the US Intelligence Service in Vietnam, had gravitated to the CIA after discharge, and proved himself one of its most ruthless and able operators. Vietnam had dehumanized him; it was a pitiless war, distinguished for its corruption, failure and brutal disregard for human decencies.

Andrews had no illusions about his fellow men when he returned to America. Years of negotiating the labyrinth of Washington political life had confirmed his opinion that humanity was shit, and the only important thing in life was power. He had a keen, fierce intelligence and an instinct for deception in others; he was inordinately brave, and quite without scruple. He would have been surprised to know how much he reminded Holler of certain members of Himmler's infamous Black Knights. But he was the Director's man, and Holler worked very closely with the British and American Intelligence Services. He had considerable reservations about the reliability of the French, and carefully monitored information destined for Paris.

'Two deaths,' Andrews said. 'Both connected with Hitler, both present in the Bunker.'

'One accident, one natural death,' Holler murmured. 'A fire and a heart attack. Hitler's valet, and one of Himmler's top liaison officers. Not to mention his daughter, who was in the bedroom when it caught fire!' He offered Andrews a cigarette, and accepted a light in return. 'I wouldn't see any connection if both Schmidt and Helm weren't names specifically asked for by this man Steiner from *Newsworld*. Our people gave him the information he wanted, and within a few days two of the people on that list are dead. According to the woman who looked after Schmidt, he was visited by two men, and died suddenly while they were with him. Helm's son-in-law, Dr Mintzel, said the old man had also been visited; his description of the man fits Steiner, but doesn't tally with the two who went to Berchtesgaden.'

'And Steiner was with Sigmund Walther when he died,' Andrews pointed out. 'This isn't just coincidence, Herr Holler. Walther is murdered –' He saw the pain on the older man's face, knew they had been close friends, and went on more forcefully. 'Steiner comes to Germany, digs up information about a list of people who have only one thing in common – they were all with Hitler in Berlin at the end. He goes to see one of them; right. Somebody else goes and sees another on the list. Within a week, both men are dead. In my book that makes a pattern, starting with Walther.'

Holler tapped his cigarette ash into a metal bowl; he was a heavy smoker and it was full of stubs. 'I had an autopsy done on the valet, Schmidt,' he said, and the light eyes glanced up at Curt Andrews. 'Very discreetly, of course. He died from cyanide poisoning. Probably fired from a pen or pencil. You know the kind of thing.' Andrews knew very well. He had used them and authorized their use. His department called them 'toys.'

'Then it was a professional job,' he said.

'So was the fire,' Holler said. 'The place was practically

gutted, but we found traces of polystyrene in the bedroom, and there was no furniture with that filling in the room. And one other thing – I have a feeling they're connected, but it's no more than that. A stray dog has been running round that street since the night of the fire. People the police contacted said it belonged to a man who walked it round the street, but he hasn't been found and nobody recognized him.'

'Where is it?' Andrews asked.

'I have it at home,' Holler said. 'My wife likes it – it's a nice terrier puppy. I think that the man who walked it near Otto Helm's house, and then abandoned it, had something to do with killing him. And his daughter. Polystyrene is just like a poison when it's lit.' He was speaking reflectively and so low, that he might have been talking to himself. 'But examination showed she had a broken neck. There were traces of urine on the sitting-room carpet; she was killed there and put in with her father afterwards. Very professional again.'

'Why haven't you pulled in Steiner?' Andrews demanded. 'He's the one link we've got – the killing of Walther and these other people are all connected. It looks to me like Uncle Vanya.'

'If it is the Russians,' Holler said, 'we have to know why. They had political reasons for killing Sigmund. His re-unification policy was gaining support. But why the tie-in with Hitler and the Bunker?'

'Maybe Walther was a neo-Nazi.' Curt Andrews tipped up in his chair and beamed his hard stare at the German. 'Certain people at home suspected it.'

'They also suspected that he was working for the Russians,' Holler said. 'They were just as wrong. I knew Walther well. He wasn't a Nazi and he certainly wasn't a Red. He was a man who loved his country.'

'If you say so.' Andrews set the chair back on its four legs. 'But whatever he was, he got killed for it. And this reporter is nosing around among the corpses. 'I'd like to talk to him. I'd like to ask him why he went to see Helm, why he wanted to interview these other people.' He waited, silently exerting pressure on Heinrich Holler. A man who loved his country.

99

He had never heard such crap said seriously before. A smart-ass politician, loaded with money and ambition, aiming for the top....

'You'll have the opportunity,' Holler said. 'When I decide to ask him myself. But he wasn't in Berlin the night Helm was murdered, and he didn't see Schmidt. He is certainly a link but he's not the killer.'

'And where is he now?'

'In Hamburg. Where two more names on his list are living. Both are being watched by our people. He's staying with Walther's widow. His investigation seems to have her blessing.'

'What's the run-down on her?'

'Old Prussian military family, married at eighteen, five children, very happily married. I know her quite well, though not as intimately as her husband. She was always a great help to him. There's no scandal or political ties there.' He seemed to say it to irritate Andrews. 'Just a woman in love with a fine man.' He didn't allow himself to smile, but the shift in Andrews's expression showed that he had scored. It was odd, Holler thought, that a man as young as Andrews should dislike human nature so much that he couldn't bear hearing virtue ascribed to man or woman. Perhaps it was the only way he could do his job. Holler had known a number of men with the same attitude. They had big offices in Gestapo Headquarters in Prinz Albrechtstrasse, and in a later generation they had surrounded a president of the United States.

He had to co-operate with Curt Andrews and what he represented, but he wasn't going to let him touch Max Steiner, or cast his shadow close to Minna Walther. He smiled, and got up from his desk. 'Let me take you to lunch, Herr Andrews. Then you might like to fly down to Hamburg with me. I think it would be useful to see these two men on Steiner's list. Just to find out what questions he asked them.'

'Thanks,' Andrews got up, aware that he towered over Holler, and it didn't give him a feeling of power. Just size. 'Let's hope we find them alive to give an answer.'

Max had gone to call at the address where Josef Franke and his wife Ilse lived. He had spent the day studying Walther's notes again; Minna had met him with an excuse the next morning, asking if he could entertain himself as she had made an appointment for lunch that couldn't be broken. She looked pale and her eyes were strained. He guessed that she had been crying before she went to sleep. The housekeeper brought his lunch into the study. He was hungry and the food was excellent; there was a superb chocolate dessert topped with whipped cream and walnuts. He had forgotten the richness of German cooking; when he was a little boy just before the war, there had been no shortages. In the early years of war, too, the fruits of victory were shared liberally among the German civilians. They had the guns and the butter too; French cognac, scent, silk stockings and underclothes, furs, all the luxuries looted from the countries under occupation flowed into Germany, and everyone lived better than ever before.

He could remember the family dinners when his brothers were on leave. They had a Polish girl to help his mother; Max hadn't understood why she was always red-eyed and sullen. He hadn't heard of forced labour, whether it was digging trenches or washing the floors for a German family. He was reminded of those meals, of the beer and wine that he was allowed to share, while his brothers sat on either side of his mother, looking like young gods in their Luftwaffe blue.

Ellie had weaned him away from what she called unhealthy eating. She made him lose weight, which was a good idea, and introduced him to the delights of low-cholesterol cooking and American salads. He had never equated her distrust of rich Continental cooking with the fact that his children were allowed to stuff themselves with biscuits and rot their teeth with Coke and sweets.

He sat in Walther's study and wondered how Ellie was and how his children were, and ended up thinking of Minna Walther instead. She had not wanted to spend the morning with him; he sensed that the lunch was an excuse. She had seemed tense and uneasy, and he didn't know what to do to reassure her. Except to keep out of her way. He had decided to go and see Josef Franke that evening, when the store where he worked was closed. He had telephoned, but there was no reply. Probably the wife worked too. If they'd had children they were probably grown up by now. Minna came in during the afternoon. She looked better; there was a faint colour in her face, and he thought suddenly: She hasn't been to lunch, she's been walking. . . .

'I hope you've been all right,' she said. 'Did Paula look after you?'

'She certainly did,' he said. 'I nearly fell asleep after lunch. Did you have a good day? Enjoy your lunch?'

'Yes, yes, very much.'

He tried not to look at her; he hated it when she lied, even though it was so innocent a lie. There was a quality about her which made him associate her with honesty and truth, even in unimportant things like an excuse.

'I'm going round to see the Frankes tonight,' he said. 'They won't have anything to tell me, it's just for old times' sake.'

'For saving your life,' Minna reminded him. 'Of course I needn't come with you. Getting into the convent is different.'

He looked at her, and let the moment lengthen.

'I want you to come with me to see Franke,' he said. 'I want you to go every step of the way with me.'

'Why?' She said it quietly, and the question floated between them, full of meaning. Because I love you. He could have said it then, because it came straight into his mind and almost escaped into words. And you want me. I know you do; I feel it every time you're near me. But 'I need you' was what he said.

'Sigmund wouldn't let me get involved,' she said suddenly. 'I wanted to so much, but he said no. It wasn't a woman's business to get mixed up in something so – so dangerous. I'm glad you want me to help. I'll be glad of the chance. Glad to have something to do. Thank you, Herr Steiner.'

'Max,' he corrected. He reached out his hand to her and she took it. He saw the shame in her eyes and the flash of desire it extinguished. He kissed her hand as he had done that day in the Crillon, the morning after she was widowed.

'We'll do it together,' he said quietly. 'We'll find Janus.'

He got up quickly and went out of the room before he ruined everything by taking hold of her and kissing her on the mouth. She sat very still and watched him go; she covered the back of her hand with the other and gripped it tight until the fingers lost all colour. The telephone rang; it shrilled until she went to answer it. The voice was deep and familiar. She held the receiver close as she heard it, as if it could bring her comfort.

'Minna? My dear, how are you?'

'I'm all right,' she said slowly. 'Thank you for your letter; it was wonderful. I shall always keep it.'

'I want to come and see you,' Albert Kramer said. 'If you feel ready to see anyone.'

'Yes,' she said. 'Oh yes, Albert, I'd love to see you.'

'This evening,' he asked her, 'just for half an hour?'

'Please do; I'd be so happy to talk about Sigmund – you were such a friend –'

'I'll be with you at seven,' he said.

The Frankes lived in a big post-war block of flats just outside the centre of Hamburg; Max took the lift up to the twelfth floor, and rang the bell of apartment 27. It was opened very quickly, and a woman stood framed in it, looking up at him, her expression changing from expectation to surprise. He had last seen her in 1945, her body hidden in a mannish white shirt and brown skirt.... His memory of her was so vivid that it seemed to Max he was looking at two images, blurring and separating the girl Ilse in the Bunker from the older Frau. She was still thin, but her hair was short and curly and she wore a bright coloured dress with flowers.

She stared at him. 'Yes?'

'You're Ilse Franke, aren't you?' he inquired.

She nodded, and her eyes were wary. 'That's right. Who are you – what can I do for you?' She had closed the door so that she could slam it instantly.

'I came to see you and your husband, Josef,' he said. 'You won't remember me, it has been such a long time. Is he in?'

'Not yet,' she said. 'I thought it was him at the door. He forgets his keys sometimes. . . .'

'Can I come in and wait, please?'

'What's your name?' she demanded.

'Max Steiner,' he said. It meant nothing to her. She had never known the name of the boy in the Bunker. 'All right, come in then. Josef won't be long.'

He glanced round the sitting room; it was comfortably furnished, the colours too bright, and a garish reproduction of Tretchikov's Chinese woman glared at him from the main wall. There was a TV set and a trolley laid out with bottles and glasses.

He sat down, and she asked him if he would like a beer. 'Or gin, maybe? We've got some Bols, if you'd like that.'

'No, thank you,' Max said.

She seated herself on the chair opposite, her hands clasped primly on her lap. 'Where did you meet Josef – I don't place you at all, Herr Steiner. How long ago did we meet you?'

'We were in Berlin,' he said. 'The last day of April, 1945. I was the Hitler Jugend troop leader you helped escape from the Bunker.'

She was a sallow-skinned woman, and when the colour drained she looked a pasty gréy; her eyes opened wide in horror, and she brought both hands up to her mouth.

'Oh my God! My God – it's you? It can't be – Oh, Jesus Christ!'

'Why be so upset?' Max said quietly. 'You saved my life; your husband certainly did. I've come back to see you both and thank you. There's nothing for you to worry about.'

'Oh no? Where the hell have you been all these years then – nothing to worry about! After we've got ourselves settled and Josef's in a good job. . . . Listen.' She got up and glared at him. 'You get out,' she said. 'We don't know anything about the Bunker and we don't know you.'

'What's the matter, love?' Josef Franke was in the doorway; he wore a dark brown uniform, with the insignia of a well-known security force on his shoulder. He was still a big man, though smaller than Max remembered, with broad shoulders and a powerful neck. His hair was cropped very short and completely grey. He stared hard at Max. He would have been a match for most men, in spite of his age. 'Who are you?'

His wife answered. 'It's the kid we brought out of Berlin.' She hurried over and caught his arm. 'You remember – tell him to get out, Seff; we don't want anyone like him coming round, making trouble!'

'I'm sorry,' Max said. 'I didn't mean to upset your wife. I've just come back to Germany and I wanted to look you up. Just to say thank you.'

'Well, you've said it,' the woman snapped at him. 'Now go away and leave us alone.'

'Ilse,' her husband said. 'Ilse, shut up!' He went over to Max and held out his hand. 'Don't mind her,' he said. 'We had a rough time after the war. I'm always glad to see an old comrade. Sit down and have a beer; I often wondered what happened to you.'

'The Americans picked me up,' Max said. 'I was sent to my aunt in Bremen. I live in Paris now. I'm just here on a visit. What happened to you?'

'The Americans arrested both of us,' Franke said. 'They found the serial number I'd had tattooed under my armpit. I had to admit to being SS, but I said I was a deserter from the Eastern zone. I went into the bag for a couple of years; they didn't hold Ilse and she waited for me.' He glanced at her and his expression softened. 'Kept me going with food, got herself a job cooking for an American colonel. Robbed the bastards right and left and they never caught on – when I came out we got married. And it was rough. No jobs for people like me, after the war. Nobody wanted to touch us with a ten-foot pole. And I wasn't a bigwig so Odessa didn't bother with the likes of me. We scraped by; Ilse had a baby but it died.' He shrugged and reached for the glass of beer Ilse had given him. 'Never mind, we're all right now. I got this job with the security force and we live very well. Nice little place, this, isn't it?'

'Yes,' said Max. 'Very cosy.'

105

'What's your job?' Josef asked. 'Why do you live in Paris? I never liked the French – crawl up your arse one minute and stab you in the back the next!'

'I work for a news magazine,' Max said. 'I'm on a story at the moment, as a matter of fact. I'm doing a story on the last days in the Bunker.'

'Oh?' For a moment the older man's face darkened with suspicion. Max saw it and recognized the same sensitivity to anti-Nazi propaganda that he had found in the police inspector in West Berlin. He decided to make good use of it.

'It's about time,' he said, 'that people knew the truth about us; all the world's been fed is horror stories, concentration camps, six million Jews killed, all the old anti-German stuff that keeps on turning up. I'm going to write about it as it *really* was. About my mother and my grandmother being killed, about the old men of the Volksturm and the children in the Hitler Jugend going out to face Russian tanks to defend their city and their homeland. That's what I'm going to write!'

Josef Franke's face had reddened. He leaned forward and slapped Max on the knee. Beer breathed over him.

'About time! It's about time someone put over our side of it. The Yids have been yelling their dirty heads off ever since the end of the war! I'd like to see an article like yours – telling the world we weren't all swine and sadists, just patriotic Germans fighting for our country against the bloody Reds! Isn't that so, Ilse?' She had come behind him, her hand resting on his shoulder. Her pale eyes burned.

'My God, I'll say it is! They've got their Russians now, haven't they? Breathing down their necks! Serves the bloody Western world right – they destroyed us when we were fighting Communism! Now they can get on with it. I hope you say the lot!' She came and sat beside her husband. 'I'm sorry I was rude,' she said to Max. 'But if you knew what we went through because Josef had served in SS. . . . Another glass of beer?'

Max shook his head. 'No, thanks. I'm going to do quite a piece on the Bunker itself. The way people stayed with the

Führer right to the end. I won't mention ourselves, just generalities. I want to convey the atmosphere at the end. It was a real "Twilight of the Gods".'

He had won them completely; he felt a qualm of guilt about deceiving them when he owed them so much, but it jarred him to find that neither had changed their old attitudes, or faced the reality of what they had brought upon their country and themselves. The *Heil Hitlers* were vibrating in the air.

He turned to Ilse. 'You remember they shot Fegelein that morning,' he said. 'You said something about it to me. Didn't he have Eva Braun's diamonds and a lot of money stacked away?'

'Those were the rumours,' she said. 'But Josef would know more about that.'

'I was in on the interrogation for a bit,' Franke said. 'Standartenführer Helm was in charge. I thought he'd kill Fegelein the way he was going at him.' He grinned, and the last twinge of guilt at his deception left Max as he saw it. 'He had her jewels all right, and money. But what Helm was really giving it to him for was something he'd told Obergruppenführer Mühlhauser. He punched Fegelein in the charlies, and yelled at him that he'd betrayed the future of Germany. I didn't know what it was all about.'

Max finished the last of the beer. Fegelein had betrayed the future of Germany. That meant he had told Gunther Mühlhauser about the existence of Janus. Or where he was hidden. Josef looked at him, and shook his head. 'You're not going to mention that, are you?'

'Why should I?' Max said. 'I'm interested in the heroes of Berlin and the Bunker, not the rats like Fegelein.' He stood up and shook hands with them. They came to the door with him, and as he turned to say good-bye again, Josef Franke straightened and brought his heels together. '*Heil Hitler*, comrade. I know you'll do us justice.' He raised his right arm to shoulder level, in the old salute.

Max didn't answer. He nodded at both of them and hurried out into the passage and the lift. He breathed in the cool air, and began to walk at a fast pace as if he were trying to leave something behind. Franke had given him a clue, when he had chanced a question without expecting an answer. Herman Fegelein had passed the secret of Janus on to Himmler's aide and confidant; that was why Hitler had ordered his death and Eva Braun had at last accepted it. He had told Mühlhauser about Janus, as part of the package Himmler was assembling to make peace with the Allies and divide the West from Soviet Russia. Only no one had considered making peace with Himmler, and he had fled, only to be arrested by a British patrol and commit suicide like the leader he had at last betrayed. But Günther Mühlhauser had been captured in Berlin. By the Russians. He went on walking, making his way back to Minna Walther's house; he had lost the sense of time. A clock chimed midnight, and he stopped suddenly, checking his watch. He had been walking through the city for almost two hours.

He found a cruising taxi-cab and gave the address. He felt tired and jaded, and his spirits were low. Mühlhauser knew about the child. He could well have been told where to find it. And it was beyond reason to hope that he hadn't passed that information to the Russians, in exchange for his life and ultimate release.

Albert Kramer had kissed her hand and then her cheek. She disliked the smell of his aftershave; it was musty and rather strong. It lingered wherever he had been, advertising his presence. She had mentioned it once to her husband, who laughed and said it was supposed to attract women. Minna had wrinkled her nose and said it had the very opposite effect on her. It was the only fault she could find with Albert Kramer; he was a loyal supporter of Sigmund in politics and a charming, intelligent friend of the family, who exerted himself to win her affection. Sitting in the pleasant drawing room, sleek and blonde and handsome as ever, he looked at her and shook his head.

'You're pale,' he said gently. 'And a little too thin. You mustn't grieve, Minna; Sigmund wouldn't want that.'

'I'm all right,' she said. 'You mustn't worry about me.' He had been married and divorced in the ten years she had known him. His wife was a bright, hectic girl, with a doting father who had made a fortune out of textiles since the war. She had a child by a previous marriage, and a dubious reputation which Albert chose to ignore. He had waited six years and had a three-year-old son before he divorced her. By that time he had become one of the richest and most influential industrialists in West Germany. His enemies attributed his forebearance towards his wife with the use he made of her father, and its sudden ending with his emergence as a power figure in his own right. Minna didn't listen to gossip; she hadn't liked his wife because they had little in common, but she had accepted her because she was a part of Albert. He had been very tactful when he arrived; his mention of Sigmund was brief and gentle. He talked about the children, asking after her eldest son Helmut, and she knew this was an effort, because Helmut was opinionated and abrasive, and Albert instinctively reacted against him.

'He's a clever fellow,' he said. 'Remember, Minna, I've got interests all over the world, and if Helmut wants to start with any of my organizations, I'd be only too delighted. I mentioned this to Sigmund before.'

She smiled in gratitude and shook her head. 'It's very sweet of you, Albert, but I don't see my son settling down to capitalism for a long time. His head is full of notions and ideals, and he thinks making money is a crime.'

'I wonder how he came to terms with his father's fortune, then?' He lit a cigarette, and offered one to her. He carried a heavy gold case, long out of fashion.

'Everything Sigmund did was perfect,' she said. 'If he made money it was only to finance his political career and advance his plans for Germany. Helmut worshipped him. He wants to go into politics, and before that, he's determined to be a journalist. He was terribly upset by his father's death; it was harder for him than any of the other children. Unfortunately, I'm no substitute; we've never been close.'

'That's surprising,' Albert Kramer said. 'I hoped he'd be a

support to you. Do you want me to talk to him?' She saw the hard line of his mouth and the glint in his eyes, and imagined the furious confrontation that would take place if he tried to lecture her son.

'No, thank you, Albert. Helmut will settle down in time.'

'And you,' he asked her, 'what will you do now, my dear?'

She didn't answer immediately; she hesitated. Sigmund had often spoken of Albert as one of his closest friends. She didn't know whether that friendship extended to telling him about the secret of Janus.

'I shall go on with Sigmund's work,' she said, and she watched his face for a sign. There was none. Only a faint surprise that irritated her.

'You're not thinking of politics, surely – Minna, that kind of world isn't suited to women, at least not to ladies.'

'I don't see why not,' she said. 'Women have to live with political decisions made by men; why shouldn't they have a say in what affects them?'

He smiled, and there was a gentle condescension in it, which made her suddenly very angry. 'I never thought of you as a feminist,' he said. 'Or a militant.'

'How did you think of me?' she asked him. 'As some kind of ornament?'

'Not at all,' Albert said. He thought how desirable she looked, with the angry colour in her cheeks. 'I thought of you as a perfect wife and mother, and Sigmund as the luckiest man in Germany. How *do* you intend to carry on his work? – please, I'm being quite serious. I'd like to know, and maybe I could help.'

'I'm going to commission a biography,' she said. 'And there's a journalist who wants to do a series about him. I've got to keep his name alive, until someone comes forward to take up his work for the reunification of our country.'

'Have you someone in mind?' He was taking her seriously, as he'd said; there was no male chauvinism in his attitude now.'

'Sigmund had a lot of colleagues with the same ideas. But the man has got to be politically reliable. He's got to have authority in the world outside Germany, like Sigmund.'

'With friends in the right places,' Albert Kramer said. 'Yes, a man with a sound political record, and independent of the party machine. Rich, like Sigmund, so nobody could buy him.' He stood up, brought out his gold case and lit another cigarette. He had a good figure; he and Sigmund used to play squash together. She sat still and watched him; there was tension in the atmosphere and it was growing.

'Minna,' his voice was low, but emotion made it deeper, 'Minna, I want to ask you a question. A very important question, and very personal to me. I loved Sigmund as much as I admired him. I believe in his ideals and I want what he wanted for my country. A united, free Germany. If I offered myself as his successor, would you give me your support?'

'You mean go into politics full time? Give up your businesses?'

'I've done all I can do,' he said. 'I want to serve my country now, out in the open. I'll seek election to the Bundestag next spring, on the same platform as he did. *Détente* with the East German government and ultimate reunification. I can do it, Minna; I've been thinking about it for a long time. I can gather his supporters together and I've a lot of influence in the government itself. I'd be a force to reckon with. But I need you to give your blessing. And more than that, I'd need your help in co-ordinating Sigmund's policies through his personal papers. I'd have to think through his brain to start with.'

'Yes,' she said, 'I see. I think I'd like a drink. Will you have one with me?'

She got up and went to the trolley, and poured herself a whisky. Albert shook his head and frowned.

He didn't approve of women drinking spirits like that. And she hadn't answered his question. He came and stood close to her, so that she was looking up. It gave him an advantage. 'What do you say, Minna? Can I count on you?'

He had hot blue eyes, and there was something besides ambition and urgency in them; she knew that he was bidding for more than her dead husband's political career. He wanted her, too, and she had always sensed that, even when Sigmund was alive. She had a flash of memory, and the hand holding the glass of whisky tightened. Sigmund saying to her one night as they undressed for bed after a party, where Albert Kramer had been the host, 'Such a pity he won't join with us – we could do with his influence and his brains. But he says politics bore him. I had a good go at him this evening to try and make him change his mind, but not a hope of it. . . .' That had been less than two months ago. She put down the glass and stood up slowly; they were face to face and he was close enough to touch her.

'Let me think about it,' she said. 'Give me a few days. I'll telephone you, Albert. Now, please forgive me, but I'm rather tired.'

He held out his hand and she had to take it. His lips pressed hard against her skin and they were moist.

'I'll wait to hear from you,' he said. 'And I shall hope. Goodnight, my dear.'

She closed the door on him, and waited until she heard the sound of his car starting outside. Then she went back to the room and sat down, with the glass in both hands. His name was on Max Steiner's list. He hadn't told her why.

She was still sitting there when Max came in, and she called out to him. He looked tired and downcast. He came and sat in the chair Albert Kramer had used.

'What happened?' she asked him. 'You've been such a long time.'

'I was walking,' he said. 'I saw the Frankes; they didn't give me good news. I had to think out what it meant, that's why I went on walking.'

'What did it mean?'

'Fegelein was shot for telling a man called Gunther Mühlhauser about Janus. Josef Franke was in the room during the interrogation. He didn't know what it was all about, but I believe Fegelein told Mühlhauser that Hitler had a child. Mühlhauser was Himmler's personal aide. And he was captured by the Russians. You know, his name's on my list and he's living here in Hamburg. If the Russians released him, he must have told them what Fegelein told him.

Which means, if the boy is alive at all, he's in Russian hands.'

Minna Walther shook her head; the light behind gleamed in the blonde hair, turning it into a halo.

'They got their information from the autopsy on Eva Braun,' she said. 'They may have got confirmation from this Mühlhauser but I don't believe for a moment that they got the child.' Max raised his head and looked at her; he felt weary and pessimistic. He didn't recognize it but the pessimism stemmed from that moment in the Frankes' flat when he heard once more the words *Heil Hitler* spoken in modern Germany.

'Why?' he said. 'Why are you so sure?'

'They never found him,' she said. 'Sigmund was convinced of that. And not just Sigmund. I had a visitor tonight. Your friend Albert Kramer.'

'*Your* friend,' he corrected.

She nodded. 'I want to ask you something. Why is he on your list of people connected with the Bunker?'

'You won't like this,' Max said. 'He may have been a friend of your husband's, but he wasn't always one of the bright lights of German liberalism. He was in the Hitler Jugend with me. We grew up together, and he was one of the most fanatical bastards in the unit. His father was in the Waffen SS, and Albert Kramer was just like him. He took over the firing squad when I refused; I saw him standing over Fegelein, pumping bullets into him as he lay dying.' He saw the look in her eyes, and said, 'Maybe he changed after the war. People can change. But that's how I knew him.'

She got up and stood by the fireplace, facing him. 'He *was* a Nazi?' she said. 'He's kept that hidden very well. Sigmund trusted him and liked him. He came here and said he wanted to go into politics and carry on Sigmund's work for Germany. He asked me to help him.' She leaned against the mantelpiece, one foot balanced on the fender. The line of the thigh was provocative; Max forced himself to look at her face.

'He talked about loving my husband and wanting the same things for Germany. He was very convincing. Except that only two months ago Sigmund asked him to join him and he

113

refused. Now he wants to take his place. Which is a lot of nonsense; he wanted an excuse for going through his papers. He said that – "I'll need to co-ordinate his policies through his personal papers." That's why he came here and told a pack of lies. He wants to see the file. He knows what Sigmund was looking for, and he's trying to find it too. I realized that, suddenly, tonight. I didn't know his background. I didn't know he'd been a Nazi.' She stepped away from the fireplace and stood in front of Max. 'Don't you see – that boy has never been found by the Russians or anyone else. But people know he exists. Albert Kramer knows, and he saw a chance to follow up on Sigmund's leads. And he was ready to throw everything in the balance to get his hands on the information Sigmund had collected.'

'He hasn't changed,' Max said slowly. 'He's just gone under cover for the last twenty years.'

'If he's a neo-Nazi,' Minna said, 'that means *they* haven't got the boy. I don't think you should wait to see Mühlhauser; I think we should fly to Munich tomorrow and see Gretl Fegelein in that convent. I believe she has the secret.'

'All right,' he said. 'We'll go to Munich. Why don't we go to bed now?'

She didn't step back when he put his hands on her shoulders; she didn't move when he brought his body close and bent down to her mouth. 'Don't hold back from me,' he said. Her lips were open and her eyes were shut. He kissed her slowly at first, and then harder, his hands bending her in to him. He felt her nails digging into his neck. There was a moment when he was undressing her when she broke free and said, 'I hate myself . . . I hate you. . . .' He put his hand over her mouth.

5

It was the first time Maurice Franconi had seen Kesler despair of an assignment.

'We've tried everything,' he exploded. 'I've spent a small fortune bribing the tradesmen who deliver to the convent, I've hung about for days on end in case she came out, they hung up on me when I phoned and said I was a relative! There's no way we can get to her!'

When in difficulty Maurice favoured what he called a blanket operation. 'We could set the place on fire,' he suggested. He had a weakness for this method.

'Don't be a fool,' Kesler snapped irritably. 'With our luck, she'd be the one to get rescued. I don't know how to tackle this – I really don't.' He slumped down on the bed and swore in Polish. Maurice put an arm round him.

'Come on,' he said. 'Cheer up. We've never failed yet. And anyway we can't afford to fail on this one. Think of all that money!'

'I am thinking of it,' Kesler said. 'It was your bloody greed got us into this in the first place!'

'Oh, all right, blame me –' Franconi turned away.

'If you're going to bite my head off, I'm going out!'

Kesler threw up his hands. 'I'm sorry,' he said. 'I didn't mean to take it out on you. But this one's getting on my nerves. It's not like any ordinary woman working in a convent. They're not an enclosed order, she could come and go and see visitors. They've built a wall round her. If we do get inside, we're not going to be able to fake an accident like the other two. And the orders specified that. Make them look accidental. No police, no investigations. You realize we won't *get* the money unless we carry through the whole contract?'

'I know that.' Franconi still sulked. 'I had an idea, that's all.'

'Tell me, for Christ's sake,' Kesler said. 'What have you thought of – come on, don't be sulky. I said I was sorry.'

'They must have a priest who hears confessions,' Franconi said. Kesler looked up. 'Yes, they must. So?'

'So we find out who he is,' Maurice said, 'and we make a substitution.'

'That's very clever,' Kesler said warmly. 'Very clever thinking. Something happens to the regular priest and a strange one goes instead. He asks to see Gretl Fegelein and, because he's a priest, she'll come. Maurice, you're a genius!'

'I'm a Catholic,' he grinned. 'I know a bit about convents and the way things work. So do you, you old sinner. I'm surprised you didn't think of it.' He was delighted by Kesler's praise. 'It shouldn't be difficult to find out who the regular chaplain is. I think we should try the nearest parish church.'

Kesler got up. 'We will,' he said. 'starting today. I'm sick of this place. I want to get it over as quick as we can, and move on to the next one.'

Franconi nodded. 'Bonn,' he said. 'I've never been there.'

'I have, once,' Kesler said. 'It's a dreary hole – we won't want to hang around there for long. Now, let's get a street directory and find the nearest church.'

Twenty-five minutes later he circled the Church of St John the Apostle with a green biro pen. 'There we are. Two streets away from the Convent of the Immaculate Conception. We'll try there first. Then this one – St Gabriel – that's about a block away. Look up the telephone number, Maurice. We can call through from downstairs.'

They went out and took the lift to the hotel foyer, and while Kesler slipped into the half cubicle and dialled the presbytery of the first church they had chosen, Maurice pretended to read a copy of *Die Süddeutsche Zeitung*, and watched the reception to see if the woman clerk was taking any notice of them. She wasn't.

Kesler came out and shook his head. 'No,' he said. 'They don't serve the convent. Give me the next number.'

'I'll try,' Franconi said. 'I'm feeling lucky today.'

When he came to join Kesler a few minutes later, he was grinning. 'You got it?' Kesler asked.

'They don't go to the convent either,' he said. 'But they told me who did. He's a retired priest, and all he does now is say Mass for the nuns and hear confessions. He lives in a hostel on the Burgstrasse.'

'How did you get all that?' Kesler asked. He was genuinely pleased when Maurice showed initiative and skill in his work.

'I said I had a sister who wanted to become a nun. I wanted to talk to a priest with experience of convent life, because the family was worried. The man I talked to went out of his way to be helpful. I had a feeling he wasn't too fond of nuns and convents. Probably one of the new "progressive" priests –'

'Huh,' Kesler snorted. 'I know the kind. Folksongs and guitars on the altar, and no celibacy. I don't know what's got into the Church these days.'

'I quite agree,' Franconi said. 'No wonder we don't go any more.'

They went out of the hotel into the morning sunshine, and took a bus to the Burgstrasse and the hostel for retired and aged Catholic priests.

Albert Kramer got the telephone call at seven in the morning. He was shaving; in spite of being fair he grew a tough beard, and he preferred the old-fashioned method of lather and blade to the electric razor. He wiped the soap off his face and picked up the phone in his bathroom. There was no preamble from the caller. 'Two comrades are going to have visitors,' the voice said. 'The day after tomorrow.'

'Who are they?' Kramer said.

'Josef Franke and Günther Mühlhauser. The Chief and a CIA visitor; very senior, all stops being pulled out for him.'

'Thank you,' Kramer said. 'I'll warn our friends.' He hung up. He went back to the mirror and resoaped his chin and shaved himself. The old ties of loyalty still operated, even in the heart of Holler's Intelligence kingdom. A schedule had been seen and the warning phoned through. Kramer had been an active member of the Odessa organization since the end of the war. He had run messages for them during the early days of the Occupation; his house had been used as a refuge for fugitives, and he himself enrolled under the most solemn oaths when he was eighteen and a student.

He had helped Odessa channel wanted Nazi officials of the SS through to Italy and Spain, where they took ship for South America, and in return Odessa had financed his education and his first business venture, as an importer of copper from Chile. That early business had been a cover for the activities of the underground SS escape route, but his natural flair for making money expanded it and added to it, until he was doing Odessa a favour rather than the other way round. Then he had married the nymphomaniac daughter of one of post-war Germany's most important industrialists, ignored her activities and made all possible use of his father-in-law. Now he was free of all but his old associations, and he held fast to them. His belief in the ideology of National Socialism was absolute; it had never wavered at any time throughout his boyhood or his adult life. He believed in the supremacy of the Aryan people and the truth of Adolf Hitler's political creed that Germany was destined to overcome her enemies and rule the world. He hated the English, the Americans and the Russians, and he had a profound physical revulsion from the Jews.

The core of his personality had not altered since his indoctrination in the Hitler Jugend; it was concealed so effectively that no one suspected him of being anything but a contemporary German of the best kind: brilliantly successful in business and widely consulted on government financial policy. A sportsman who sponsored promising young athletes, a patron of the arts, a close friend of one of Germany's most liberal politicians, Sigmund Walther. He was all these things because they were the hard shell that concealed the crab. He was a Nazi and he was waiting for the rebirth of National Socialism in another guise. And because the old links still existed and were strong, the information passed to Sigmund Walther by Heinrich Holler had been whispered to him. Eva Braun had borne the Führer a child. Walther was trying to find it. So he had set out to win the politician's confidence and become his friend. When Sigmund suggested that he join the Social Democratic Party as a candidate he had refused. He didn't want political office; he had enough power as an outside adviser. He wanted Sigmund to tell him about Janus, but Sigmund never did. So he had gone to see the widow, to offer his help and insinuate himself into her trust.

He didn't think Walther would have confided in her, because he personally considered women inferior, and took it for granted that Walther felt the same. He wanted to go to bed with Minna Walther very badly; she was the cool, Nordic type that appealed to him. He suspected that she was very sexual; he had an instinct for women and a lot of success with them. He wasn't deceived by the well-bred airs and graces of that Prussian lady, with her five children, and a husband like Sigmund who hadn't even been unfaithful to her once in nineteen years. He wanted Minna but he wanted to lock himself up with Sigmund's investigatory notes, and when she spoke of a successor to her husband, he had grasped the opportunity and offered himself.

He was confident of success. Not immediately; she might take a little time to convince. And seduce into sleeping with him. Once she had done that, she would be quite amenable to the rest of his desires. He had ordered flowers to be sent the morning after he had called on her. He didn't expect her to telephone; he was prepared to make a second approach, more personal than the first. He patted the aftershave on his cheeks and jaw; it stung pleasantly, and he liked the musky smell.

Mühlhauser and Josef Franke. Fifteen years in a Soviet labour camp for Mühlhauser and he was still being persecuted. Kramer didn't know him personally; he had merely given him a job when he was asked to do so. The same for Franke, who applied to the security service; the personnel officer had been given notice of his application and asked to view it favourably. He got the job through the network, although he didn't know it. Kramer kept a special diary with names and addresses and telephone numbers. He unlocked his dressing-table drawer and took it out, looking for Günther Mühlhauser's phone number. He dialled it, and waited. It rang for some time, before a woman answered. Kramer asked for Herr Mühlhauser and the former Obergruppenführer came to the phone. Kramer didn't give his name.

'You're going to have a visit, the day after tomorrow. The top man and an American. Be ready for them.'

'Yes,' the voice said. 'I will.'

'Contact a Josef Franke, security services. Warn him.'

'I will do that. Anything else?'

'Just be careful,' Kramer said; 'I'll call you after they've been. Try and find out what they want.' He hung up. Why would Holler and some senior CIA operator bother with a played-out old war criminal like Günther Mühlhauser? He'd been debriefed until there was nothing left to analyse but the dirt under his fingernails. Fifteen years in Soviet hands had made him less of a wreck than most, but he couldn't be of any use to any Intelligence service after all this time.

Kramer frowned, locked the little diary away, and began to dress. What did the CIA hope to gain from talking to Günther Mühlhauser? Least of all, why bother with a former SS man more renowned for his brawn than his brains? And then, as he got into the back of his car and directed his chauffeur to drive him to his office in the city centre, Albert Kramer saw the connection. He knew the records of the two men in every detail, though he had never met them face to face. The personal aide to Heinrich Himmler and the noncommissioned sergeant had one thing in common. They were both in the Bunker at the end. Sigmund Walther's murder had stirred up the ashes of the Führer's funeral pyre and that meant that the phoenix of National Socialist Germany was stirring in the flames which the world had thought put out for ever.

The child of Hitler and Eva Braun was still alive, and the reason the CIA had sent one of their top men to Heinrich Holler was to try and find him. Albert Kramer swore under his breath. If Mühlhauser or that numbskull Josef knew anything, Holler and the American would get it out of them. Nobody could have interrogated Mühlhauser about something which nobody in the Western alliance knew. If he had any knowledge of Hitler's heir, he had kept it from the principals of Odessa as well.

Kramer had made a mistake in alerting Mühlhauser and the other man. Neither must be allowed to talk to Holler, who was a traitor and a renegade, in Kramer's eyes, or to the highly skilled and ruthless operators employed by the United States Central Intelligence Agency. He picked up the telephone in his car and began to make arrangements.

Minna woke while it was still dark. She lay quietly, listening, and then reached out with her hand. He had gone to his own room. She switched on the bedside light, blinking against it, and then sat up. Her hair was loose and tangled, cold sweat had dried on her naked body. She leaned her head back, and a tear seeped under the closed eyelids and ran down her face and neck. She didn't blame Max Steiner; she blamed herself, and she cried with shame and self-disgust. He was different from Sigmund, rougher, less sentimental. He had made her aware of passions which her husband hadn't aroused, and she had loved her sex life with him and been deeply satisfied. Now a new man had come, and, instead of easing the pain and the loss, he had created new longings which she couldn't sublimate in grief.

She threw back the sheet and went to the bathroom; her

reflection in the glass was wild looking; she stared at herself and called the woman in the mirror bitter names. He was a stranger, a man who had come into her life because of Sigmund's death, and in the moment of self-knowledge, Minna admitted that from the first meeting she had felt powerfully attracted to him. And known that he felt the same about her. She had been able to stave off men while her husband was alive; she had never even been tempted, and opportunities to be unfaithful were always presenting themselves. Albert Kramer's hungry stare was easy to ignore; the tentative moves from friends and other women's husbands had been shrugged off with tact and determination. Her vanity had been satisfied because she knew she was still very desirable to men and this was important to her, but she had all she needed in her marriage. What had happened was not adultery, because she was a widow and her body was her own. But it was crude and disloyal, and she didn't love the man. She said that aloud. 'I don't love him. I don't even know him.' It wasn't possible to feel love for someone else so soon after her husband's death. . . .

And he hadn't said he loved her. She was grateful for that: hypocrisy would have made it worse. She stepped into the shower and soaked herself, as if she were carrying out a cleansing ritual. She dried herself, and rubbed her wet hair.

The bed looked cold and uninviting; half the bedclothes were on the floor. It was six o'clock and light was showing through the curtains. She put on a dressing gown and went downstairs through the silent house to the kitchen. There was a gleam of electric light under the door. He was making coffee. He turned quickly and saw her there. 'I couldn't sleep after I left you,' he said. 'Do you want a cup?'

'Yes,' Minna said. 'No sugar.' They sat on opposite sides of the table, and he lit two cigarettes and handed one to her.

'I'm not going to say I'm sorry it happened,' he said abruptly, 'because I'm not. And you shouldn't be either. We're very good together.'

'Yes, we are. But I've never felt ashamed before.'

'He's dead,' Max said gently. 'And you need to be loved.'

He held his hand out to her, palm upward, and after a moment she put her hand in it. Their fingers locked tightly. 'Drink your coffee,' Max said. 'It'll get cold.' Lying beside him in bed afterwards, Minna thought that he had said he loved her at one stage, but she was too close to sleep to be sure.

'I have been thinking of becoming a Catholic for some time,' Stanislaus Kesler said. The elderly priest looked surprised. He was a round, bespectacled little man, with a circlet of white hair round his bald head. He had come down to the priests' parlour to see the unexpected visitor. It was a bare little room, sparsely furnished with hard-backed chairs and a polished table. The floors were polished wood and they were as slippery as glass. There was a strong smell of beeswax. A garish statue of the Sacred Heart rested on a plinth in one corner, with a little red devotional lamp gleaming at its foot. The place reminded Kesler of his youth in Poland. He had been to a convent school as a child, and he recognized the smell and the spartan surroundings. He smiled encouragingly at the priest.

Father Grunwald had been retired for five years; he was nearing his seventieth birthday, and he had a peaceful life after his years as a parish priest during the turbulence of the post-war period. He said Mass for the nuns in the Convent of the Immaculate Conception, heard their confessions and acted as spiritual adviser to the Reverend Mother, who frightened him to death. He suppressed a most un-Christian resentment at being called in at this late stage to instruct a stranger in the Faith.

'That's very good,' he said. 'But I think you should go to your local parish priest. He is the proper person to instruct you. May I ask why you came to see me? I'm retired now, you know.'

Kesler took a gamble; 'Reverend Mother suggested it,' he said. 'Her family and mine were old friends.'

'Really?' Father Grunwald's white eyebrows lifted; the tufts peeking above the horn-rimmed spectacles made him look

123

like a little barn owl. 'Yes, well, that's very kind of her. . . .'

'I gather she thinks a great deal of you, Father,' Kesler said. 'It must make quite a change, looking after nuns. How often do you visit the convent?'

'I say Mass three times a week, and on Sundays, of course.'

'Do you hear confessions?' Kesler asked. 'That's the one thing about the Church that worries me. What would a nun have to confess, for instance?'

'They're not all saints by any means,' the priest said. 'People tend to forget that nuns are human beings with human weaknesses. You mustn't worry about confession; most non-Catholics find it difficult to accept at first.'

'I would very much like to talk to you about it, and about the Catholic Faith in general,' Kesler said. 'But you might not have much time to give me. When do you go to the convent, Father?'

'Tuesdays, Thursdays and Saturdays. And Sunday, of course. I'm there all day Sunday with Mass and Benediction, and most of Saturday morning, hearing confessions before Mass.' He grasped quickly at the excuse Kesler had offered him. 'I don't think I could possibly instruct you; you really need to visit a priest every day and it usually takes at least three to four weeks before you could make up your mind to the preliminary stage. Becoming a Catholic takes time, you know. I really think you'd do better to go to your local parish priest.' He heaved himself up from the uncomfortable chair, and Kesler stood, with his hand held out. Father Grunwald shook it briefly. He had never been happy with middle-aged converts; he believed that the Faith took a stronger root in the young.

'May God bless you,' he said, 'and guide you. I'll remember you in my prayers.'

'Thank you,' Kesler said. 'I shall need the gift of Faith. Goodbye, Father.'

Outside in the street he walked to the car where Franconi was waiting. He slipped into the passenger seat. 'Tuesday, Thursday, Saturday and Sunday,' he said. Franconi started the engine.

'Good,' he said. 'Which day will you go?'

'Thursday,' Kesler answered. 'I don't want him talking to the Reverend Mother about me. I said she recommended me.'

'That's tomorrow,' Franconi said. They were cruising along the street, and he turned right towards the centre of the city. 'You'll have to get some clothes.'

Kesler frowned. 'Not clerical clothes,' he said. 'The first thing the police will do, if they suspect anything, is go to the clerical tailors and the theatrical costumiers. That could give them a lead. I've got a dark suit, and I'll buy a black silk muffler and a black homburg. That'll get me into the convent.' Franconi looked at him, and then back to the road ahead.

'You don't think you can make it look like an accident?' he said. 'That's worrying.'

'I'll do my best,' Kesler said. 'I'll use the pen again, but you've got to get right up close to them. If there's any difficulty, I'll just have to do what I can. Don't worry,' he added. 'I won't take any risks. If I could persuade her to leave the building, all the better.'

'I don't like this at all,' Franconi said. He shuddered suddenly, as a nervous *frisson* quivered up his spine. 'You're quite sure she's not a nun?'

'Frau Gretl Fegelein; works as a lay helper. That's what it said on the paper,' Kesler reassured him. 'And you're not to be superstitious. Nothing will happen to me just because it's done in a convent. Let's go out and treat ourselves to a nice lunch. That'll take our minds off it. Bear left here; there's a very good restaurant down the next street. I looked it up in the Michelin guide last night.'

Günther Mühlhauser had come back from a labour camp in what was later known to the world as the Gulag Archipelago. The camps were full of Germans, prisoners of war, civilians captured during the Russian advance into Germany, SS criminals who had escaped the death sentence. Like himself. Mühlhauser hadn't expected to survive when he saw the conditions in which the prisoners were condemned to live and do hard manual labour.

They froze and they starved, and they died in their tens of thousands. The suicide rate was nearly as high as that for deaths from hunger and mistreatment. Men went mad, and were shot down like dogs; others died at their tasks, breaking the iron-hard earth to build roads which never ended, or mumbled their lives away in delirium. Mühlhauser was a very strong man and physically fit. He determined to live, because his sentence had a limit. That was the deal he had concluded with his Soviet interrogators. They wouldn't hang him, but they would send him to the slow death of the labour camp and it was up to him to survive if he could. He became a model prisoner; he co-operated with the guards and made it easier for them to supervise the other prisoners. He informed on three escape attempts, and consequently his rations were improved. He became so useful that the commandant withdrew him from work on the roads, and gave him an administrative job in the records offices of the camp. There Mühlhauser kept a tally of the dead, and of the pitiful few who managed to escape and were brought back and shot. He was gaunt and cold and underfed, but by comparison with those who resisted or failed to grovel to their guards, he lived well enough. At the end of fourteen years he was suddenly summoned to the commandant's office and told that he was being sent south. They shook hands, and the Russian gave him some cigarettes for the journey. He packed his few rags of clothing into a bundle, and marched for two days with a group of Russian civilians who were going to the railhead. Nobody told him anything.

The journey took a week, and four people died of cold. Mühlhauser divided up their clothing between himself and the remaining five men; he persuaded the guards to continue the original ration. Otherwise, as he pointed out in fluent Russian, they would have nothing but corpses to deliver at the end of the journey. They arrived in Moscow, and all but Mühlhauser disembarked from the train. He was locked into the compartment, and it was the following day before they moved out of the station. Nobody would tell him where he was going, but he was given more food, and a change of clothes, including a heavy army greatcoat, and boots. Mühlhauser had tried hard to forget his experiences in the years that followed his arrival in what was now East Germany, but he couldn't stop odd incidents floating like jetsam to the surface of his mind. Most persistent of all was the meeting face to face with his principal interrogator when the train crossed the Polish frontier. He had opened the compartment door, and the two soldiers guarding him had jumped to their feet at the sight of the red flashes on the colonel's collar.

He hadn't changed much, except that his cropped hair had tinges of grey in it. Mühlhauser knew by his expression that he himself was almost unrecognizable. The Soviet colonel had sat opposite to him, given him a cigarette and said simply, 'So you survived. I thought you would.'

'Yes,' Mühlhauser mumbled. 'Where am I going?'

'Home,' the Russian said. 'As I promised you. I always keep my promises.'

That was when Mühlhauser broke down and began to cry for the first time in fifteen bitter years. The colonel had got up and gone out of the compartment. He said nothing, and Mühlhauser never saw him again. He wondered whether the Russian knew that he was crying for shame as well as relief. He knew why he had been released. And the oath he had sworn, and violated to save himself, haunted him for many years. Until he married a second time, and his young wife had a daughter. He was settled in Hamburg; his name and background and his sufferings in Russia brought financial help and he knew very well where it came from. Also the offer of a job in a firm of textile importers.

His second wife was fifteen years younger, a secretary in the Customs and Excise; she knew nothing about his past. She accepted him as a returned German prisoner of war, and he married her within a year of meeting her. He loved her and she was an excellent wife. He liked her gay spirits; they made him feel young again. When she gave birth to Beatrix, he was so overcome with happiness and gratitude that he felt tempted to confide his past in her. But fortunately he resisted the temptation. The less was known about his capture in Berlin and what followed afterwards, the safer he would be. He gave himself up to his happy life and his infant daughter, and began to forget about the old days. Sometimes his memory was rudely jogged. Newspaper articles, books, discussions on TV.... They wouldn't let the past die. The Jews were hunting for his old comrades. He read of the trial and execution of Adolf Eichmann; there were other trials in West Germany of men he had known and served with. He was safe, but only just. His association with Himmler was known, but he had been purely an administrator; he had never been involved in the camps, or the liquidation of Jews in Russia. He had served his sentence in the snow-white hell of Northern Siberia, and he was left alone.

When he received the telephone call warning him about a visit from the police and an agent from the CIA, he had felt sick with apprehension. He couldn't eat his breakfast, and he snapped irritably at his innocent wife. He kissed Beatrix good-bye with extra tenderness and wondered what he could do, how he could avoid seeing anyone.

He remembered there was someone else he had to warn, and he did so from his office; he was trying to decide whether to pick up his wife and daughter and take the first train to her grandparents in Bavaria, when his secretary announced that a man was in the outer office demanding to see him, and refusing to give his name. Mühlhauser went grey with fear. He came out, and there was a man in a belted mackintosh and a brown felt hat, his hands stuck aggressively into his pockets. Mühlhauser had never seen him before. 'Yes? What can I do for you?' He heard the tremor in his own voice. 'You can go, Fräulein Huber.'

He was a young man, and suddenly he took off his hat. 'I'm afraid I have bad news for you, Herr Mühlhauser,' he said. 'I'm from the police. Your daughter had an accident at school this morning. You'd better come with me.' Mühlhauser gave a choked cry of anguish. He didn't ask to see the man's identity; he followed him blindly out of the building and down into the street. He got into the car which was waiting, and was taken to a house in the suburbs.

They let him see Beatrix through a crack in the door. She was sitting reading a comic book. There was a man in the room; Mühlhauser could just see his trouser legs. Then the door closed and he was facing the two men who had abducted him and a third who was sitting in an armchair. It was an unusual setting for kidnap and interrogation. The room was on the ground floor, and it was an ordinary sitting room, with a sofa and chairs, a TV set, ornaments and a plant in bloom on the table. Mühlhauser tried to swallow; fear had dried up the saliva in his mouth and he couldn't do it. The young man who had come to his office was standing a few feet away, with a gun pointing at him. The gun moved whenever Mühlhauser did. Albert Kramer looked up at him; he leaned forward in the armchair.

'We want some questions answered,' he said. Mühlhauser nodded. They hadn't hurt him or threatened him.

'Why is Beatrix ... why have you –' he stammered and stopped. Kramer's eyes were as fixed and malevolent as a snake's, about to strike. Mühlhauser knew what it meant when a man looked like that.

'Your child hasn't been hurt, or frightened. And she won't be, if you tell the truth.' Kramer paused deliberately. When he spoke again his voice was empty of emotion. 'If you don't co-operate, you'll never see her again. We won't do anything to you, Gunther Mühlhauser. We will kill Beatrix instead. Sit down.'

Mühlhauser felt his legs giving way. A tide of blind fury swept over him, and then receded before an even wilder panic. He knew the blond man in the chair meant what he said. Beatrix....

'Let her go,' he said. 'I beg of you, let her go home. I'll do anything you want.'

'She goes home with you, if we're satisfied.' Kramer answered. 'Or not at all.'

Mühlhauser bowed his head. 'What do you want from me?'

'You were in the Bunker at the end, weren't you?' Mühlhauser sensed the other two men, the one with the gun and the driver, leaning closer towards him.

'Yes,' he said. 'I was captured; I spent fifteen years in a Soviet labour camp.'

'We know that,' Kramer said. 'We looked after you, when you came home. You must have realized that?'

'I suspected,' Mühlhauser muttered. 'I was very grateful.' Now he knew whom he was facing. Certainly they would kill Beatrix.

'Why didn't they hang you, Mühlhauser? They hanged or shot everyone in the SS. Why not you?'

'I was an administrator,' Mühlhauser said. 'I had no part in the Einsatzgruppen, or the selection of foreign labour. . . . I hadn't been involved in action against Russian troops or civilians. You know all this already. I don't understand wha you want from me. . . .'

'The truth,' Kramer said. 'I want you to tell me what you told the Russians, that they let you live. Because you bought your life, didn't you, Mühlhauser? You saved your neck by betraying something to them. What was it?'

The room was very quiet; Kramer sat motionless, waiting. A car droned past the house. They'll kill me, Mühlhauser thought. But I don't care. So long as they let Beatrix go. . . . He raised his head slowly and squared his shoulders. He had betrayed his sacred oath. 'Blood and Honour' – the words floated through his mind. He wasn't afraid for himself.

He spoke to Kramer. 'I told them about the Führer's son.'

Minna placed one hand over the telephone and spoke to Max.

'It's Heinrich Holler,' she said. 'He wants to come and see me this afternoon.'

'We're going to Munich,' Max reminded her.

She spoke into the phone. 'I was going away this morning,' she said. 'Is it very urgent, Herr Holler? I see. Yes, of course I'll postpone it. At three o'clock then. Good-bye.'

Max put down the overnight case. The car was outside, waiting to take them to the airport.

'We can go this evening,' he said. 'I'd like to meet him. If you don't mind.'

'It won't be up to me,' Minna answered. 'He may want to talk to me alone, or he may talk to you too. You can be sure he knows you're staying here.'

Max put the cases in a corner; she had gone into the sitting room. He hesitated; a few hours earlier they had made love with feverish intensity. He knew everything about her body; he had explored it like a map. And he had lost his head completely at one moment and told her that he loved her. She had said nothing. The greater their physical intimacy, the more it disturbed him that he knew even less about her as a person. The woman in his bed was a separate entity from Minna Walther. It was almost impossible to connect the cool, self-contained person that had come down and said good morning to him with the passionate, demanding creature he had held in his arms through the night. He had said he loved her; she had said she hated him and herself. . . . He had a feeling of emptiness, standing there in the hall. He wanted to go to Munich to be alone with her, away from the house and the bed she had shared with Sigmund Walther. Perhaps then he could break through the barrier which restricted her response to sexuality alone. He went out and put the car into the garage.

He walked round the garden, as it was a beautiful morning, and there was nothing else for him to do. It was colourful with flowers and shrubs. He lit a cigarette and wandered through the paths between the flowerbeds. There was a tennis court and a swimming pool. He could imagine the parties given in the summer, with barbecues and iced drinks. Liberals and journalists and politicians. And Albert Kramer.

He came to the edge of the pool and stopped. His own reflection shivered in the bright blue water. He had a wife and two children. He hardly remembered their existence. He found it difficult to visualize their faces; he couldn't think of their Paris apartment in connection with his home. He should have telephoned Ellie, reassured her and talked to the children. The truth was he didn't want to; his disinclination was stronger than his guilt. He was in love with Minna Walther, that was part of the reason, but not the whole of it. His life pattern was changing even before he met her. The past kept coming up like a boil, plaguing him with the nightmare; his sex life with Ellie was stale, his children irritated him or bored him, and he felt increasingly restless. He didn't dream any more, because he was facing the implications of the dream in real life. He had stopped running away from himself. The time would come when he and Minna would come to terms with their relationship; when she would have to choose between her contempt for her own weakness and her dependence upon him. And he would have to choose too. But first their search had to be concluded. He began to walk back to the house.

Heinrich Holler was ten minutes late; he came in apologizing to Minna. 'I'm so sorry, but I had to make a call and it took longer than I expected. How are you, Frau Walther? You're looking well.'

Max got up, and stood waiting until Minna introduced him. Holler and he shook hands. 'Ah, yes,' Holler said. 'I always read your articles, Herr Steiner. They often tell me things I ought to have known and didn't!' He had a charming smile; he chatted to Minna for a few minutes, accepted a cigarette, and asked Max how long he was staying in Germany. 'You're writing an article on my friend Sigmund, I believe?' he said. Max didn't look at Minna; he hadn't discussed what he should say with her because, until he met Holler, he hadn't been certain himself. He made up his mind.

'That's what I'm supposed to be doing,' he said. 'But in fact I'm looking for the same thing that Sigmund Walther was looking for, and which he tried to tell me about before he died. I want to find Janus.'

Holler examined his cigarette and then glanced at Minna. 'You've given him access to Sigmund's papers?'

'Yes,' she said. 'He knows everything. And he had something very important to contribute.' Holler turned back to Max.

'I hope you'll confide in me,' he said. He listened without

interrupting while Max talked. At the mention of Fegelein's dying words, he looked up quickly, but he said nothing. When Max had finished he let out a deep breath.

'Thank God I got rid of my American colleague,' he said. 'He was trying to come with me today. You wouldn't know, of course, but the CIA are also investigating Sigmund's murder. They believe it was Russian-inspired. But they don't know, and I pray they never find out, that he was involved in the search for Janus. They have given that up; there was a lot of activity when we first heard of the child's existence, but there were as many people here who *didn't* want to help the Americans as there were like Sigmund and myself, who felt it was a German problem and should be solved by us.'

'Why did they stop searching?' Max asked.

'Because they believed the Russians had found the boy and killed him,' Holler said.

'And you don't think so?' Max said.

'No. Because we believe that they're still looking,' Holler answered.

'And that's why they killed Sigmund.' Minna spoke for the first time. 'Because he was getting close. But if they were searching for the same person, why not *let* Sigmund find him and then step in!'

'I've tried answering that point, and I can't,' Holler admitted. 'Except that they couldn't risk the man's identity coming out; rather than chance Sigmund succeeding and alerting me, they preferred to go on looking themselves.'

'I keep forgetting,' Max said. 'We're looking for a grown man.'

'You have a list of names,' Holler said. 'How many people have you seen?'

Max hid his surprise. Of course Holler knew about the list. The West Berlin police would have passed it on.

'Otto Helm, Herbert Schmidt, Josef Franke. We're going down to Munich to try and see Gretl Fegelein this evening.'

'Helm and Schmidt are dead,' Holler said. 'The deaths were meant to look like accidents, and if they hadn't been on your list, nobody would have questioned it. But I did, and both men were murdered. So it seems that someone else is treading in your footprints, Herr Steiner. Or else, by some incredible coincidence, these people are on *another* list. So far, nothing has happened to Josef Franke.'

Minna had been standing by the fireplace while they talked; she often leaned against the marble chimneypiece, one foot on the fender. Max remembered the erotic effect of her long thigh under the skirt. She came and sat down facing both of them. She had lost colour, but her composure was like a mask through which no feeling of alarm or even surprise was evident.

'If nothing *does* happen to him,' she said. 'Then there is another list. Probably my husband was the first name on it. Max seeing the other two may have been sheer, incredible coincidence, as you said.'

'And if it is, and someone is killing off the people who were in the Bunker,' Max said slowly, 'they're going to get to Minna and me, because we've talked to them.'

Holler didn't answer. He changed the subject. 'What did Franke tell you?'

'He told me that Fegelein was shot for betraying the future of Germany. He didn't understand the significance of it. But I did. And that led to Günther Mühlhauser, who was Himmler's confidant and liaison with the Bunker. Fegelein told him about Janus. And my guess is, Herr Holler, that Mühlhauser told the secret to the Russians.'

'Who had it confirmed by the autopsy report on Eva Braun,' Holler said. 'But if he only knew of the child's existence, that wouldn't be much use to them. He had to know where it was hidden. And he can't have known, because they're still looking ... I don't want to depress you, but you won't see Gretl Fegelein.'

'Why not?' Minna asked. 'Why is she so immune? I've never understood how that convent has been able to defy someone like you, Herr Holler, and refuse to let you or Sigmund talk to her. That woman was with Eva when she had the baby; her husband knew where it was being hidden, and she must have known it too!'

'You underestimate the power of the Vatican,' Heinrich Holler said. 'Gretl Fegelein went through the denazification courts and was acquitted. She took refuge in that convent as soon as she was released from custody, and I have it on the best authority that the Vatican undertook to protect her for the rest of her life. It was made clear to me, and to others, notably the CIA in the early days, that any violation of Gretl Fegelein's sanctuary in the convent would cause a major diplomatic rupture with the Papacy. So she cannot be made to answer any question. And she certainly won't be persuaded. We've tried, as you know very well, Frau Walther.'

'This time, I'm going to try,' Minna said.

It was Curt Andrews who discovered that Günther Mühlhauser was missing. Holler had politely but firmly refused to introduce him to Sigmund Walther's widow; as a sop to the American's professional pride he suggested that he arrange a meeting with Mühlhauser. And Andrews, aware that he was being sidetracked, decided to pay Heinrich Holler back in kind. Instead of telephoning and making an appointment for himself and Holler, he went direct to Mühlhauser's office. His secretary seemed flustered, and Andrews detected uncertainty when she said he had left his office. He could be very engaging when he chose and he asked his questions so gently that she answered without realizing that it was none of his business where Mühlhauser had gone.

'I don't know,' she said. 'Someone called here this morning, a young man, not very pleasant looking – he refused to give his name – he was quite rude to me, in fact, and when Herr Mühlhauser came out to see him, he sent me away. The next thing I knew Herr Mühlhauser was rushing out after this man – he didn't even put his hat on – and when I tried to ask him when he'd be back, he didn't answer! He looked terribly upset. He hasn't phoned in or anything. I did telephone his wife, but he hadn't come home. I really don't know what can have happened.'

'Well, don't worry,' Andrews said kindly. She was a woman

in her middle fifties, plain and efficient, but unused to coping with the unexpected. So a young, tough-mannered man had called on him, and Mühlhauser had gone rushing out – Andrews smelled conspiracy; whether on the part of Heinrich Holler, whom he didn't trust an inch, or someone else he wasn't sure. But he was sure that Mühlhauser wasn't going to be around to be asked questions. Whoever had killed Otto Helm and the ex-valet Schmidt wasn't going to make the same mistake and get to his victim too late.

'I think I'd better go and see Frau Mühlhauser,' he said. 'Could you give me the address?'

The secretary hesitated: 'I'm sorry, but I'm not supposed to give Herr Mühlhauser's private address or telephone number to anyone, sir.'

'I do understand,' Curt Andrews said. 'But I think you can give it to me.' He took an ID card out of his pocket and handed it to her. It appeared to be issued by the West German police in Bonn. Curt Andrews always carried ID cards when he travelled; he had British, French, Italian and West German cards, and even one from East Germany. The secretary looked at it, and said, 'Oh, oh dear. Yes, of course. I'll get the address for you.' Andrews put the card back in his pocket. Languages were another of his talents. His German was fautless, so was his French; Italian was more difficult but he could manage well in the regions, where local dialects made every outsider sound different. He had never mastered the long English vowels; the forged Scotland Yard Special Branch ID had never been used.

'Here, I've written it down, and the telephone number,' she said. He took the piece of paper, and thanked her. 'Don't worry,' he said again. 'I'm sure everything is all right. I'll get Herr Mühlhauser to call you, when I see him.'

Holler had given him a car and a driver; Andrews swung his big body into the back seat, and gave the driver Mühlhauser's address.

Albert Kramer was back in his office. He told his secretary he was taking no calls and didn't want to be disturbed for the next half-hour. He needed time to think; he lit a cigarettte and noticed that his hand was unsteady. He wasn't surprised. He couldn't imagine anyone who would have been unmoved at the end of Günther Mühlhauser's interrogation.

He smoked rapidly, staring ahead of him through the cigarette haze, not seeing his surroundings. The others had wanted to kill Mühlhauser and the child. One of them, Brandt, who was too hotheaded and rough for his own good, had smashed the old man in the face and knocked him to the ground. Kramer had stopped them hurting him. His brain was working at top level, clear and calculating, refusing to be hurried into anything that might prove to be a mistake. And murdering Günther and Beatrix Mühlhauser was exactly the kind of unpremeditated act of vengeance which could destroy them all. He would have liked to shoot Mühlhauser; it was the little girl, calmly reading comic books in the next room, who saved her father's life. A vanished father and daughter would entail the biggest manhunt West Germany had seen for years.

She had been taken from school on the same pretext as Günther; an accident at home. The man who was amusing her had got her out of school. His face would be remembered; so would Brandt, who had tricked Mühlhauser into going with him. Albert made his decision, and Mühlhauser, who had been expecting death, burst into tears.

He had walked out of the house, holding his daughter by the hand, bound by Kramer's final threat. Beatrix was the hostage for his silence.

Kramer opened his cupboard and poured himself a drink of cognac. It was incredible; he kept going over the facts to himself, trying to see any way in which Mühlhauser could have lied. But he hadn't been able to fault him. And instinctively he knew that what he heard was the truth. A truth so fortuitous that it was no wonder his hard hands were shaking. With excitement. With a fierce joy and expectation. Now, more than ever, he needed to get hold of Sigmund Walther's papers.

'Günther! What have you done to yourself?' He saw the expression on his wife's face and put a hand to his cheek. It was throbbing and obviously the bruise was coming out. He said gently to his daughter, 'Go and play, darling. I want to talk to Mummy.'

Hilde Mühlhauser put her arm round him protectively. 'What happened? Did you fall – and why have you brought Beatrix home so early –'

'Come into the kitchen,' he said. 'I've got things to tell you.'

She didn't interrupt him; he watched in anguish the horror in her eyes, and felt her draw away from him.

'You –' she said, 'you were one of *them* – oh, my God!' Hilde had been terribly distressed by a recent television programme about the extermination of the Jews. He had tried to dissuade her from watching. Now he saw his wife's love shrivel and die as he told her what he had been and why he was sent to Siberia. He blinked back tears, but he didn't falter. He told her everything except the secret which had bought his life from the Russians. And done the same for Beatrix and himself that afternoon. The blow had shaken him badly; his face throbbed and pain scorched up and down his neck and shoulder, where he had fallen on the floor.

'Something happened today,' he said. 'It involved Beatrix.'

She gave an angry cry and started up. He said, 'It's all right, she didn't know anything about it.' Then he told her about the men from Odessa.

'I'll never forgive you,' Hilde Mühlhauser said. 'Never. You brought your child into this filthy business – I want to know exactly what happened. Otherwise,' she looked at him and he saw real hatred in her eyes this time, 'otherwise I'm going to the police!'

'You can't,' he said. 'The people who threatened us were Nazi sympathizers. They're very powerful still. One word about this afternoon and they'll harm Beatrix.' He didn't dare say 'kill' although that was the word Kramer had used.

'Oh, you swine,' Hilde said. 'You swine!' She suddenly began to cry. He tried to put his arm round her but she jerked away.

138

'We've got to decide what to do,' he said slowly. 'I was thinking about it on the way home.'

'I don't care what you do,' his wife said. 'I'm taking Beatrix home with me. You can do what you like. I'll get a divorce.' She sobbed into her hands.

That was when the doorbell rang. Beatrix was nearest the hall; she put down her doll and opened the door. Then she went to the kitchen door. She saw her mother crying and her father standing looking oddly helpless, with a horrible blue and yellow mark on his face. Behind her stood Curt Andrews.

'Take my advice, Frau Mühlhauser,' he said a little later. 'Don't do anything in a hurry.' He had listened to the almost hysterical accusations of the young woman against her husband. Andrews didn't sympathize with either of them. To him the human tragedy of broken trust and fear was merely a nuisance, because it took up time. He pacified the wife and defended the husband, not because he believed his own arguments, but to defuse a potentially dangerous situation. He didn't want Hilde Mühlhauser grabbing her child and running off to Bavaria. He didn't want any attention drawn to the family.

'You mustn't judge your husband,' he said. 'If you'd been born a few years earlier you might have had to face the same decisions as he did. A lot of patriotic Germans joined the SS because they believed they were fighting for the survival of their country.'

'Don't tell me *he* didn't know what they were doing? About the concentration camps, and the gas chambers!' She swung round on Mühlhauser, her face contorted. 'I feel sick to my stomach,' she said. 'The thought of touching you makes me sick!'

Andrews saw Günther Mühlhauser flinch and sag; a young wife had certainly got him by the balls, he thought. But not as much as the kid had got them both.

'You may be angry with your husband,' he said, 'but you don't want to risk anything happening to your child, do you?' That cut her short, he noted. She went a ghastly grey colour. 'I thought she looked pretty upset when she saw you and her father quarrelling in the kitchen,' he said coldly. 'That kind of thing is very bad for young children. And, after all, it's her safety we're really worried about; not whether your husband was a member of the S S administrative staff a hundred years ago. I should take a hold on yourself, Frau Mühlhauser, and go and calm her down, while I talk to your husband.'

Mühlhauser poured him some beer; the sitting room was stuffy and full of cigarette smoke.

'You're in a mess, aren't you?' Andrews said. 'Your Nazi friends have caught up with you, and you've nowhere to run. They've found out you talked to the Russians, and you're scared they'll fix a nice accident for you.' He watched Mühlhauser as he spoke. He hadn't believed the story and he was just waiting to smash it to pieces. Mühlhauser didn't answer. He had recovered himself while he talked to the American; he put his wife's reactions aside, because there was nothing he could do about them. It would take a lot of time and patience to win her back. If he ever could, after what she had learned. He had been thinking rapidly while he talked to Curt Andrews. This was the C I A man he had been warned about; luckily the West German counterpart was not with him. The more he remembered Kramer's voice, the more sure he became that it was he who had telephoned the warning. So the man sitting opposite was one of the C I A's top men. A man with authority, able to carry out promises if he made them. . . .

To Mühlhauser his release from the interrogation had seemed a miracle at first, but while he travelled home with Beatrix he recognized it was only a reprieve. They wouldn't kill him without killing Beatrix too. He would be punished for his betrayal later, when he imagined himself safe. Or, worse still, the threat to murder his child would be carried out, in the guise of an accident, if they thought he had betrayed his oath a second time. . . . Even if it wasn't true, there was no guarantee for Beatrix and none for him. He made up his mind at the same moment as Andrews exposed his story as a lie.

'How do you explain your release from Siberia?' he asked. 'You say you gave details of the events in the Bunker to the Russians and they let you off hanging?' He didn't give

Mühlhauser time to answer. 'And you say the people in Odessa didn't figure this out until now? *Now* they reckon you betrayed them and they're out to get you –'

'I wasn't a war criminal,' Mühlhauser said. 'They knew that – the Russians couldn't find anything against me.'

'Except membership of the SS and intimate friendship with Himmler,' Andrews sneered. 'That hanged lesser men than you, Mühlhauser, right here in the West!' He snapped his fingers contemptuously. 'Your life wasn't worth that! You made a deal, and it's just catching up on you –'

'Yes,' Mühlhauser answered. 'Yes, I did. And I want to make one with you, Herr Andrews. But I want to know whether you can protect me and my family.'

Curt Andrews didn't show surprise. 'I can protect you,' he said. 'But only if it's worth my while.'

Mühlhauser tried to smile; it hurt his face and became a grimace. He had survived once, when all the odds were against him. He had survived Soviet Intelligence, the labour camps and, today, the merciless vengeance of his own kind. And now that his daughter's life was at stake, survival was all that mattered.

He faced Curt Andrews steadily.

'I can tell you,' he said. 'Not just what I told the Russians, but what I didn't tell them. And that's what I'll give in exchange for a refuge in the United States and the protection of the CIA.'

'Tell it then,' Andrews said.

Mühlhauser shook his head. 'No. I've got one card and it's an ace, Herr Andrews. I'll put it on the table for you, when Hilde and Beatrix and I are safe in the American Consulate.'

Andrews didn't hesitate. 'Good enough,' he said. 'Call your wife and daughter. I have a car outside.'

6

It was easy to waylay Father Grunwald on his way to the convent. He kept an ancient car at the rear of the hostel in the Burgstrasse and, as he walked towards it, Maurice came up behind him, and rabbit-punched him in the back of the neck. He toppled and fell without a sound. 'Take the wallet,' Kesler said. Franconi turned the priest over, and robbed him in seconds of his money and pocket watch. They left him there and hurried to their own car which was parked some fifty yards away, near the main road. Franconi took out a few marks from the wallet and put them in his pocket; the watch was stainless steel and worth nothing to anyone. They drove to the nearest street litter-bin, and dropped the empty wallet and the watch inside.

'Good,' Kesler said. 'We'll go to the convent now.'

Franconi parked at the side of the building; it was an ugly red brick, with a short flight of steps leading up to the entrance porch. 'Be careful,' he said to Kesler.

'Don't worry, I will.' He got out and walked to the convent. He wore his dark grey suit and a black homburg; a black silk scarf concealed his ordinary collar and tie. He carried a small black leather attaché case.

He rang the bell and waited. He felt very calm and alert; he always reacted to a difficult job with extra coolness. Danger steadied his nerves. The door was opened by a woman in a grey skirt and blouse; she wore a grey nun's headdress.

He knew he was going to succeed when she said immediately, 'Good morning, Father. Come in, please.'

He glanced quickly round the large bare entrance hall, taking stock of the doors and the staircase to the upper floors. The smell of wax was overpowering. He wondered for a second why the holy orders had such an obsession with polished floors. His leather-soled shoes skidded on the glassy linoleum.

He spoke to the nun. 'I've come in place of Father Grunwald,' he said. 'I'm afraid he had a nasty accident this morning. He was robbed in the street.'

'Oh,' she said. 'How dreadful. Is he hurt? The Community will be so upset.'

'I'm Father Rittermann,' Kesler said. 'I was asked to come and say Mass for you. He's all right, just shaken. There's nothing to worry about. You'll have to show me where the chapel is, and the vestry.'

'Yes, of course, Father,' the nun said.

'But first,' Kesler said,' I'd like to go into the parlour, Sister. I've got a message for one of your lay helpers.'

'Certainly.' The nun walked across to a door on the right, and held it open. 'This is the parlour. Whom do you want to see, Father?'

He gave a gentle smile, and removed his hat, placing it on the table. 'Frau Fegelein,' he said. 'It concerns one of her family. If she could come quickly, so that we don't start the Mass late...?'

The nun nodded, and went out, closing the door. Kesler took the pen out of his pocket and checked its mechanism. He had a sheet of paper prepared; it was a printed will form, and it looked official enough to deceive anyone for the necessary minute or two while he produced the lethal pen. He had his story well rehearsed. A man named Philip Fegelein, the brother of one of his former parishioners, had left a will and he was helping to trace the beneficiaries. If Frau Fegelein would be good enough to read through it and see whether she was in fact one of the persons named ... and then to sign....

The door opened and he turned round. A tall woman came into the room. He saw with surprise that she was dressed like the nun who had let him in. Franconi was right; their victim had taken the veil.

'Frau Fegelein?' he asked, and he stepped forward to shake hands.

'I am Reverend Mother Katherine,' she said. 'Sister Aloysius told me the horrible thing which had happened to poor Father Grunwald. I gather he isn't hurt?'

'No,' Kesler's smile had faded, 'just very shaken. He'll be quite himself in a day or two.'

'And you are Father Rittermann,' the tall nun said. 'You're going to say Mass for us. We shall all offer it up for Father Grunwald.'

'Yes, indeed,' Kesler nodded. It was not going right and he knew it. Adrenalin was flowing through him, sharpening his responses, making him bold.

'I asked to see a Frau Fegelein,' he said. 'I have a family matter to discuss with her. Is it possible for her to come, Reverend Mother? This is very important.' He drew himself upright, exerting the authority he remembered of the priests in his youth.

The nun had dark eyes; they were very penetrating, and they considered Kesler without any trace of the deference nuns normally showed towards a priest.

'I'm afraid it is quite impossible, Father,' she said, 'because there is no such person here. We have half a dozen lay helpers, and they've all been with us a long time. There is no Frau Fegelein. I'm sorry, but you've been misinformed.'

Kesler knew that she was lying. He knew that the nun who had let him in had gone straight to the Reverend Mother with his request, when she would herself have known if there was no woman called Fegelein among the six lay helpers. He had no alternative but to bluff it through, and get out of the convent as quickly as possible.

He shook his head. 'Well, that's very odd. I had this letter from one of my old parishioners, his name was Fegelein, and he told me he had this cousin who was living in your convent.'

He shrugged. 'What a mystery – I suppose I did read the address right.' He frowned. 'Anyway, Reverend Mother, there must be other houses in Munich.'

'Not of our order,' the nun said. 'If you'll come with me, Father, I'll show you the vestry and the chapel.' He thanked her, and they went out into the hall.

There he stopped, clapped his hand to his head and said, 'Oh dear, how forgetful of me – I've left the keys in my car. Excuse me, Reverend Mother, but in these days when everything gets stolen – I shan't be a moment!'

'What can we do now?' Franconi asked. They were driving back to their hotel. Kesler had taken off the black scarf; he had left the homburg behind in the convent but that couldn't be helped. There was nothing to identify him with it.

'I don't know,' he answered Maurice. 'I'm sure the woman's being hidden there, but there's no way we can get to her. Not unless we go in and stage a massacre and we're certainly not doing that!'

'What about the money?' Franconi said. 'They can make this an excuse not to pay –'

'I'll put a call through to that wretched Paul,' Kesler said. 'I'll tell him she's not in the convent, and that's that. If they cut the fee, I don't mind. I have a very nasty feeling over this one; I think it's much more complicated than they let us know. Besides, I've been seen in the convent and by the priest. They're going to connect my appearance with his being robbed, and link it up with this woman Fegelein. Whoever or whatever she is, those nuns are standing guard, and they'll know that an attempt has been made to get to her.'

'You're not going to tell Paul this,' Franconi interrupted. 'Let him find out for himself. . . .'

'Leave Paul to me,' Kesler said. 'I know how to manage him. We'll ring through at once. I'm going to suggest we go ahead and finish the contract with the man in Bonn.'

'I never liked this business,' Franconi said. 'Nuns are unlucky to me. You go and book the call through, and I'll park the car. I can start packing.'

'Yes,' Kesler said. 'I want to get away from here as soon as possible. I'll ask about the trains to Frankfurt. We can go on to Bonn from there.'

Heinrich Holler looked at Curt Andrews. He made no attempt to conceal his anger.

'You've overstepped the bounds this time,' he said. 'I'm going to demand that Mühlhauser and his family are handed over to us. You had absolutely no right to take charge of German nationals.'

'It happened so fast I had no alternative,' Andrews explained. He had scored heavily in the game Intelligence services play with each other, ostensibly on the same side, and he could afford to be conciliatory. He had come back to meet Holler after two hours spent taping Mühlhauser's account of the interrogation by the Russians, and he had already sent a telex prefixed *most urgent* to his Director in Washington. But he didn't want an official row with Holler's West German Intelligence Service, and he had prepared himself for accusations and demands to give Mühlhauser back.

'I was bored, and I thought I'd see Mühlhauser while you were busy with Frau Walther. Okay, I should have waited and gone with you, but I didn't, and it was just as well. He was scared out of his mind, and getting ready to run. He *asked* for American protection because he was convinced he was going to be murdered. And he convinced me. So I drove the family to our Consulate. He's quite ready to see you, and answer any questions, but he won't come out. He wants to get to the States where he feels he'll be safe.'

'You realize that we could have caught the men who abducted him, if you'd called in our police? By now, they've disappeared.' Holler glared at him. 'Neo-Nazi thugs prepared to kidnap a child, and threaten her life! But you don't care about that, do you.' He made such a gesture of disgust that Andrews reddened. He called the German a string of obscene names in his mind, but beyond the slight colour his face showed nothing. 'We'll go to the Consulate,' Holler snapped.

'Immediately. I hope we'll get some line on these people, but thanks to you, I doubt it!'

They drove to the Consulate in silence; the atmosphere was hostile, and when Andrews offered him a cigarette, Holler just said, 'No,' and looked out of the window. Andrews's presence, however, secured Holler an interview with Mühlhauser.

'Now,' Heinrich Holler said, 'you've given me all the details of the men who held you this afternoon? There's nothing else about them you can remember? No detail you've overlooked – I want you to think very carefully.'

Günther Mühlhauser shook his head. 'I've told you all I can,' he said. Andrews was not in the room; only Holler and a police stenographer taking notes. Holler didn't use tape-machines; they could be falsified, but the notes were transcribed and signed and on the record.

'The house was probably broken into,' Holler said. 'Finding it won't lead anywhere unless they left fingerprints we can match up.' He seemed to be musing, rather than talking to Günther Mühlhauser. To the stenographer he said, 'I think that's all then. Transcribe that stuff and bring it back for Herr Mühlhauser to read and sign, will you?'

He took out a cigarette packet, offered it to Mühlhauser, who refused, and then lit one for himself. He seemed quiet, reflective; Günther watched him anxiously. He knew all about Holler, who had been one of the Abwehr's brightest young men, before the service got involved in the plot to kill Hitler.... He wasn't lulled by the other man's calm. Holler puffed smoke into the air; it formed a neat circle and then gradually enlarged until it lost its shape and disappeared.

'I want the truth, Günther,' he said. 'Otherwise I'll apply for you officially on a criminal charge, and they'll have to hand you back.'

'What criminal charge?' Mühlhauser started up. 'I've done nothing –'

'I'll think of something,' Holler murmered. 'Don't worry about that. Are you going to answer my questions? Truthfully, just as I'm sure you answered everything the American

147

asked you. . . . You'll never get to the United States unless I let you go. Andrews knows that perfectly well. And when I get you out, I'll release you, so your Nazi friends will have plenty of opportunity to find you.'

'I thought you were a man of honour,' Mühlhauser said. He had sunk back into his chair. He looked old and very tired.

'I am,' Holler answered. 'Where ordinary people are concerned. But not people like you, Günther. You're a special breed of men, remember? The Black Knights of the Third Reich. "Blood and honour." The concentration camps, the extermination squads, the guardians of the gas chambers and the execution yards. I spent some time with your people; they broke my right leg in three places, and then made me try and walk on it. . . . It would be ironical, wouldn't it, if they were to kill you? One of their own kind who betrayed them? What did you betray, Günther? Why did they come after you when you've been home for so many years?'

'Can I change my mind,' Mühlhauser said, 'and have a cigarette?'

'No,' Holler said. 'You can't. You can just answer my question.'

'If I tell you everything,' Mühlhauser said, 'will you promise to let us go to America? Andrews gave his assurance we'd be protected there.'

'Yes,' Holler nodded. He stubbed out his own cigarette. 'Yes, the CIA can have you. I wouldn't want anything to happen to your little girl. Or your wife; I saw her outside. She's a pretty girl. Begin from the beginning, Gunther. Take your time.'

He sat and listened.

'I was caught by the Friedrichstrasse bridge over the river Spree,' Mühlhauser said. 'A few of us had changed out of our SS uniforms, and we were dressed as civilians and hoping to escape through the Russian line to the north. We didn't have a chance. The Russians took the bridge and there was no way through. I was picked up, and taken to an interrogation centre they'd set up near the Wilhelmstrasse. I couldn't produce papers or a story to cover myself. There was a Soviet colonel in

148

charge. He accused me of being an SS officer and said I was going to be shot. So I played for time. I told him who I was and that I'd been in the Bunker. They sent me to the rear, to a special camp, and the proper interrogation began. The same man was in charge. I told them everything I knew about the suicide of the Führer and Eva Braun, I gave them names of people who were with us in the Bunker, I told them Himmler was trying to negotiate a separate peace with the Western Allies, but it wasn't enough and I knew they were going to hang me.'

He looked at Holler and then at his own hands as if he expected to find something had changed in them.

'So I made a deal with the colonel,' he said. 'I told him what Fegelein had told me, for Himmler's use. Eva Braun had a child by Hitler. It was a boy, and it was two years old. I told him where it was being kept. They sent me to a labour camp as a reward.'

'Where was the child?' Heinrich Holler asked.

'With a foster-mother in Munich. Her name was Brandt, and Eva's sister Gretl Fegelein had made the arrangements. Brandt thought it was the bastard of a high Party official. It was called Frederick, after Frederick the Great, Hitler's hero.'

'And what do you think they did with this information?'

Günther Mühlhauser clasped his hands together and looked up. 'I think they killed the boy,' he said. 'Just as they took the Führer's body out of Berlin. They wanted to wipe out all trace of him. To leave nothing, not even a grave. They would have seized the child and murdered it.'

'Munich was occupied by the Allies,' Holler said.

'That wouldn't stop the KGB,' Mühlhauser said.

Heinrich Holler nodded slowly. 'No,' he said, 'it wouldn't. And you didn't cheat, did you, Günther? You didn't give them the name and address of someone else so they could murder the wrong child?'

'I wished I had,' Mühlhauser confessed. 'I wished I'd been cunning enough to make up a story, but I didn't. I told them the truth. Otherwise I wouldn't be alive now.'

'Yes,' Holler said, 'that seems to make sense. And this is

what you admitted to the men from Odessa today?'

'I didn't tell them I knew where the boy was hidden,' Mühlhauser muttered. 'I kept that back. I just admitted telling the Russians he existed.'

'And they let you go free? I find that very hard to understand.'

'Not really,' Gunther Mühlhauser sounded bitter. 'They couldn't have killed Beatrix and me without causing a huge police hunt. They didn't want that. They pretended to let me go. I would have been punished later; maybe through Beatrix. Some accident would have happened to her and I'd have known but never been able to prove anything – That's why I must get her and my wife to the States. You couldn't protect us, Herr Holler, even if you wanted to.'

There was a knock on the door, and the stenographer came in.

'Here's the transcript, sir,' she said. Holler glanced at the pages and then handed them to Mühlhauser. 'Read those, and sign them if they're what you said.'

Mühlhauser did so, and handed them back. Holler stood up, and limped across to the door. He turned to face Mühlhauser before he opened it.

'So the mystery of Janus is solved,' he said. Gunther answered firmly, 'Yes. And you'll let us go?'

'The CIA are welcome to you, Gunther,' he said. 'Just remember to tell them the same lies that you've told me.' He opened the door and went out.

In Geneva the man known to Kesler and Franconi as Paul put down the telephone at the end of the call from Munich. He sat and tapped a pencil against the edge of the table. So far they had disposed of two of the four people designated with expertise and speed. Helm and Schmidt were dead. But the woman Gretl Fegelein had eluded them. The convent denied all knowledge of her, but the men who employed Paul and professionals like Kesler and Franconi didn't make mistakes. He didn't know what to do; he had told Kesler to call back in three hours, and he hoped to have fresh instructions for them. Kesler had sounded irritable and on edge; Paul guessed that his attempt to get to Gretl Fegelein had involved him in some risk of being recognized. He was leaving Munich in the hour, and couldn't guarantee to make the call until the evening.

There was nothing Paul could do but contact his superior and relay whatever orders he was given. He got up and locked the room behind him; it was a dingy office at the back of a shop selling cheap men's shoes. He told his assistant, an elderly man who helped him three afternoons a week, that he was going out for an hour, and then made his way on foot to the bus stop. He bought a ticket to the Rue du Rhone. It was only a hundred yards to one of Geneva's smartest hotels. He went round to the service entrance in the basement, and asked to see the undermanager, M. Huber. He was kept waiting for ten minutes, and then shown up in a lift to the ground floor and into a bright, well-furnished office. Huber came forward and shook hands. He was a man in his mid-forties, with sleek fair hair and an ingratiating smile. 'Good afternoon, Raymond,' Paul said.

'Good afternoon, Paul. Sit down, and have a drink. What would you like?'

'Nothing, thank you.' Paul had never got over his nervousness of the smiling Raymond Huber. His courtesy was full of menace. There was nothing Paul needed more than a drink at that moment.'

'What's your news?' Huber asked.

Paul told him. He nodded when the names of Helm and Schmidt were mentioned, and murmured, 'Excellent, very good,' as if he were praising a member of his staff. The smile was gone when Paul had told him about Kesler's failure to reach Gretl Fegelein. 'He says she's not at the convent,' Paul finished; he hesitated and then said, 'There couldn't be a mistake, could there, Raymond – it's certain she's at that address?'

'We don't make mistakes,' Raymond said. 'She's never left that place in more than twenty years. He blundered, that's all and he's trying to cover it up.'

'What shall I tell them to do?' Paul asked. 'They're calling back tonight for instructions – do you want them to try again? It could be dangerous; I got the impression Kesler would be recognized. He seemed very anxious to leave Munich.'

'Then he certainly did blunder,' Raymond said crisply. He walked over to his desk, lit a cigarette and pulled out a bottle of cognac from the drawer, with a little glass. He poured himself a drink, sat down behind the desk and sipped it. Paul didn't interrupt him. He had been working for them for five years; like Kesler and Franconi he had begun with the rackets in Marseilles and graduated through the school of narcotics, blackmail and murder to the rarefied heights of political assassination.

The money was very big; Paul had two large bank accounts in Switzerland, one in Zurich and the second in Berne. He was a rich man, and if Raymond ever allowed him to retire he owned a luxury villa in the beautiful Seychelles Islands, far enough away from his old life and associates. He had a woman he had been living with for years, and two teenage children. She only knew him as the owner of the shoe shop. She was not part of his plans for retirement to the Indian Ocean.

'I shall have to take instructions from higher up,' Raymond said suddenly. He frowned and Paul quailed inside; the blue eyes were like dull stones and he knew that meant Raymond was angry. 'She was the most important target. I hope those two are not getting past it.' He didn't address his remarks to Paul, more to himself. 'You say they're leaving Munich? Where are they going?'

'Frankfurt and then to Bonn,' Paul answered. 'The last name on the list. What shall I tell them to do?'

'Carry out the assignment,' Raymond said. 'And no mistakes this time! This has become very important. Emphasize that. At all costs this man must be eliminated as quickly as possible. Tell Kesler if he completes this part of the contract satisfactorily we may overlook his failure in Munich.'

'Shall I mention the fee?' Paul said.

'Yes; it's what motivates them, after all. Say they shall get the full payment. Good afternoon, Paul. Thank you for coming.' He walked over and shook hands with the older man; the bright smile was back and the eyes were no longer opaque and dangerous. Paul hurried out of the room and down through the service entrance.

Raymond Huber went back to his desk and picked up the house·telephone. 'I'm not to be disturbed for the next hour,' he said. 'Reception can deal with complaints, and please don't let them ring through and say somebody has made a double booking and will I come down and sort it out. Thank you, Janine.'

He was a restless thinker; he roamed round the office, looking out of the window, and back to his desk, lighting cigarettes and occasionally sipping brandy. He had worked at the hotel for ten years. First as a trainee, then through the various departments, and now as under-manager. It was the perfect cover: no one who was welcomed by him would connect the charming young Swiss in his formal jacket and striped trousers, a fresh flower in his buttonhole, with the man who had been born in a village on the Russo-Polish border and served several years in the foreign sector training department of what was then the N K V D in Leningrad. Raymond had lost both parents during the war; he had memories of burning villages and corpses, and a sky which was darkened by smoke and burning ash that floated on the wind. He had been taken with the refugees into central Russia to escape the German advance; his brilliance at school was noted, and he was sent for higher education to Moscow. His progress was steady; he left Moscow University after only two terms to study at what was said to be a technical institute in Leningrad. Here he was enrolled in the Soviet Intelligence Service. When he arrived in Switzerland he was bilingual in both French and Schweizerdeutsch, and was equipped with the identity of a genuine Franco-Swiss who had died after a motor accident. Raymond Huber was the key controller for the assassination department of the Service in Western Europe. The higher power to which he intended referring the problem of Gretl Fegelein was visiting Lake Lucerne on a Norwegian passport.

Huber had used Kesler and Franconi for a number of

political murders, and this was the first time they had not accounted for their target. Their killing of Sigmund Walther was a classic. There was not a clue left for Interpol or the Sûreté; the newspapers had ceased to speculate, and interest was already fading. That was why it was so important that the others should appear as accidents. There must be no chain of connection to alert someone like Heinrich Holler, for instance. And yet Raymond knew, because a trusted agent had told him, that Holler was involved.

He had received the news over his private telephone line only a few hours ago; it was the last information that particular agent would impart for some time, but it contained another and even more disturbing revelation. Time was running short for Kesler and Franconi's contract. The last person on it could have been killed at their leisure, but not now. He damned the Convent of the Immaculate Conception to a place in their own hell. One bastion too strong for the inquisitors of Western Europe, too secure for his expert killers, protected by a power which he personally resented because it was not based on a political reality. Fegelein's wife had sought sanctuary with the Roman Catholic Church, and the power of that Church had protected her and her secret as effectively from his agents as from those of Holler and the CIA. Something very drastic would have to be done about the Convent of the Immaculate Conception.

He locked his office, and went through to the main foyer; he paused at the reception desk. 'I'm going out for a few minutes,' he said to the clerk. He pulled on a light raincoat to hide his formal clothes and buttonhole, and was soon one of the crowd wandering along the Rue du Rhone. Raymond went to the nearest post office and entered a telephone booth. He dialled the number in Lucerne direct and spoke to his superior officer. The conversation was short and mostly one-sided. Raymond came out of the post office and strolled back to the hotel. It was a beautiful evening, with the sun still spreading a pink and purple haze over the sky, in which the stars were twinkling prematurely.

He went back to his office; there had been no crisis, no

messages. He asked for an outside line and telephoned Paul at his home number. 'Has our friend called yet? No? Good. Now listen. Tell him to forget Munich, you understand. But there are two more people I want him to visit. Yes, take a note of the names.' He spelt them out clearly, and gave the city, but not an address. At the other end, Paul copied them out. His common-law wife was watching television, and his two sons were arguing over the programme.

'I've got that,' Paul said. 'I'll give the instructions. Right, yes, I'll tell them to get it done as quickly as possible.'

He hung up and went back to his chair. He memorized what was written on the piece of paper, and then crushed it into a little ball and burnt it in the ashtray. His elder son sniffed and made a face. 'What are you burning, Pa? It stinks.'

Paul was fond of his children. He had made handsome provision for them when he retired to his villa. 'Just a bit of scrap paper,' he said. 'An old bill.'

The boys' mother looked round at him without interest. She had been pretty when young, but she had lost her looks and her figure after the second baby was born. She cooked well and was a careful housekeeper, but he hadn't slept with her for years.

'Do stop talking a minute,' she complained. 'I can't hear what's going on. . . .'

'Turn up the volume, then,' Paul said. At that moment the telephone rang again. He had refused to have an extension, pleading the extra cost. But with only one phone, nobody could pick up the second and listen in.

'Oh, for God's sake,' the woman grumbled. 'It's never stopped all evening! Just when this quiz programme is on, it rings and rings. . . .'

Paul got up and answered it. It was Kesler. 'Oh,' Paul said. 'Yes, I've got the orders for you. Don't bother sending any to Munich, but take two extra samples. Yes, that's what I said. Two. I'll give you the names they're to go to – are you ready?'

'I'm ready,' Kesler said. Franconi was by his elbow. 'Pencil, quick,' Kesler hissed at him. 'Write it down.'

'Wind up the business as quickly as you can,' Paul

instructed. 'The profit is just the same without the Munich sale. But you've got to hurry. And don't be too particular about your sales methods. It's the results that count. Call through when you've got the final figures.'

Franconi leaned over Kesler's shoulder and read what he had written. He looked at Kesler. 'Walther's widow, and isn't that the journalist who was with him?'

'Yes,' Stanislaus Kesler answered. 'We've got a contract for them both. And this original one. He says we're to leave the convent alone.'

'Thank God for that,' Franconi said. 'The same money?'

'Yes. He said so. He wants it all done as soon as possible. Come on, Maurice dear, let's start getting the plan worked out. We must decide which one to go for first and then make our travel arrangements. One thing that makes it easier, they don't mind whether it's accidental or not.'

'That puts the contract into the high-risk category.' Franconi frowned. 'We should have asked for more.'

'Don't be greedy,' Kesler admonished. 'It'll be fast and easy. Then we're retiring. Just be content with that. Now, get out the schedules and the map and let's make up our minds where we go first.'

'It's funny,' Max said, 'to think that it all started here. Munich's such a gay place.'

Minna smiled at him. 'You sound like a tourist,' she said. 'Light-hearted Bavaria, all drinking songs and *lederhosen*. There's more rubbish talked about South Germans than there is about Prussia. We're all militaristic brutes, and the Bavarians and the Austrians are delightful. The irony of it is that the Nazi Party really started in the South.'

'You've really studied the subject, haven't you?' he said. They were dining at the Künstlerhaus, with its courtyard garden. She wore a pale green dress which suited her, and he almost told her how beautiful she was. He said many extravagant things when they made love but she maintained her aloofness outside the bedroom. The duality of her nature confused him; he was deeply in love with her, but no closer to understanding her than when they first met. They had arrived in Munich, booked into a quiet hotel on the outer perimeter of the city centre, and he had resisted the urge to go to bed and stay there. While he hesitated, Minna suggested they dined at the Künstlerhaus. 'It's wonderful food,' she said. 'And I love the atmosphere. Sigmund and I always went there when we came to Munich.'

He watched her now across the table; she was smiling at him over her glass of wine. He loved her so much that it was as much pain as joy when they were together. She spoke quite freely about her husband, as if he and his memory were on a different plane from her relationship with Max. He had begun to feel jealous of Sigmund Walther. 'Yes, I suppose I have become quite an expert,' she said. 'When I was very young, nobody mentioned the Nazis. It was just as if they hadn't existed as far as my family and our friends were concerned. I had quite a shock when Sigmund told me what they were really like.'

'I think we all wanted to forget it,' Max said. 'That's why I left Germany; I wanted to escape the war and everything that went with it. Looking back, I think I deliberately tried to shed being German. You know, neither my wife nor my children speak a word? We talked French or English at home.'

'Where are your family? You've never mentioned them before.'

'There didn't seem to be much point,' he said. 'They've gone to stay with friends in England. I ought to telephone; I just haven't got round to doing it.'

Minna Walther said quietly, 'Tell me about your wife, Max. And your children.'

'Why?' he asked her.

'Because I'm curious,' she said. 'I knew you were married, but it was all quite vague. What's your wife like?'

'Ellie?' He was surprised by his own reluctance to discuss Ellie with Minna Walther. He was suddenly on the defensive about his silly, irritating wife, and the way he was neglecting her. 'She's American,' he said. 'We met in London, and we've got two children, a boy and a girl. We've been married almost seventeen years.'

'Is she pretty?' Minna asked. 'I'm sure she is.'

'Yes,' Max said, and there in his mind's eye was Ellie as he had last seen her, hurt and chillingly aloof as she took their children to the plane. 'She's very attractive indeed,' he said. 'Now let's talk about something else, shall we?'

'You mustn't feel guilty,' Minna said gently. 'So long as she never knows what's happened, it won't matter.'

Max leaned back in his chair; candlelight enhanced her beauty, softening the Prussian bone structure. Her eyes reflected the green of her dress. Ellie and his children. It was the wrong moment, but he couldn't help himself. What had to be said would have no meaning if it was just part of their sexual relationship. 'I'm in love with you, Minna,' he said. 'And my marriage is finished. You didn't break it up, it was over anyway before I met you. That's why I don't want to talk about my wife, or my children. And if I feel guilty, that's too bad.' He reached down to the ice bucket and poured wine into her glass.

She didn't look at him. 'You mustn't love me, Max,' she said suddenly.

'No? Then what the hell am I doing with you every night?'

'Making love,' she said. 'That's different.'

'Different for you, you mean.' They were facing each other now, and he was very angry. He thought for a moment that there were tears in her eyes and then dismissed it as a trick of the candlelight.

'I'm sorry,' she said. 'I didn't mean to hurt you. I need you so much, and everything we have together is very valuable to me. But I don't want to interfere in your life. I don't want to involve you too deeply. Please, don't be angry.'

'You don't want to involve me? Minna, from the first moment we met, we were *both* involved. I don't know what you're running away from but it's time you stopped. You're trying to be two people: the woman I make love to, and the wife of the hero Sigmund Walther. You're his widow, darling; he's not there any more. You couldn't sleep with his memory, could you?'

158

'That's cruel,' she said. 'But I deserve it.'

He nodded. 'Yes,' he said, 'you do. You need to be loved, and you need a man who loves you. Otherwise what we're doing is having a marvellous screw.' He saw her wince at the crudity, and he went on, 'That's what you're pretending, isn't it? That's why you put up the barriers with me as soon as you step out of bed. I didn't mean to force the issue now; I wanted to get the other business settled first and then say all this. But it's done, so we may as well face it. I love you, and I want to know if you love me.'

She wanted to cry out to him to stop, stop before it all went wrong....

'I can't tell you that,' she said. 'I don't know the answer myself.'

'All right,' Max said. 'That's honest, for a start. I'll be satisfied with that. It's up to me to make you love me, isn't it?'

She shook her head, and the lights danced in her hair, 'I wish you wouldn't,' she said. 'I wish you'd leave well alone.'

He laughed, but it was not a happy sound. 'It isn't well for me,' he said. 'Do you want coffee, or shall I get the bill?'

'The bill,' she said. She took a mirror and looked at herself; it was the first time he had seen her do so, and he knew it was a ruse to avoid saying any more.

They found a cruising taxi and went back to the hotel. He took her hand and she didn't resist. They didn't say anything until he brought her to her bedroom door. He turned her towards him. 'Do you want me to come in?'

He saw the defeat in her face, and then the lowered eyelids and the parted lips. Her arms went round his neck.

'You know I do,' she said.

Curt Andrews got a reply to his telex late that night. Gunther Mühlhauser was safe in the Consulate, with his wife and child. The wife had tried to leave, taking Beatrix with her, but without actually putting her under guard Andrews managed to dissuade her from doing anything in a hurry. She had looked at him with hatred, her eyes red from crying.

'I don't want to stay with that murderer,' she said. 'I'm going back to my mother and I'm taking Beatrix with me.'

'You've no right to accuse your husband, Frau Mühlhauser,' Andrews reproached her. Inwardly he damned the vehemence of the young German conscience. If she was going to be a nuisance then he would get really tough.... 'You haven't heard his side of the story. I can promise you, many of the SS were perfectly decent men. They've all been painted as sadists and killers by persistent Jewish propaganda. You owe it to your daughter to give her father a chance to explain himself.' He had sounded sanctimonious enough to turn his own stomach, but at least it quietened her for the time. His Director's telex was terse; typical of the man's economy of mind: *Congratulations on discovery of extreme importance. Deal with it personally.*

Deal with it personally. That was the kind of instruction Andrews liked. He could tell Heinrich Holler to take a running jump at himself with that telex in his pocket. He made arrangements for Mühlhauser to be flown out with his wife and child on the first flight available the next morning, then he checked out of the hotel without telling Holler, and set out for Munich. There was no internal flight till the morning and he didn't want to wait that long. He hired a car and began the long journey by road.

But if he was anxious to avoid Holler, the chief of West German Intelligence was equally determined not to be found by him. After leaving the Consulate, Holler had driven back to his hotel, and there to the city police headquarters where there was a series of messages waiting for him. One posed an urgent question about the influx of terrorists from France in the guise of students: two had already been detained as a result of information, and were found to be carrying grenades and plastic explosive. The target was an Israeli orchestra making a tour of the major towns. Holler dealt with that quickly, and skimmed through the rest; a leak through Norway which was bringing one of the Embassy staff under suspicion, and armed robbery which became his province because one the criminals had been linked to the Baader-Meinhof . . . and a report from Munich concerning an incident at the Convent of the Immaculate Conception. Holler stopped leafing through the reports and began to concentrate. Munich police were instructed to contact his department if that particular convent was involved in anything out of the ordinary. He was reading very carefully; the priest attached to the convent had been knocked out and robbed; he was recovering in hospital. The Reverend Mother had reported a priest arriving in his place, who simply walked out and disappeared. Holler knew the reputation of the Reverend Mother of the Convent of the Immaculate Conception. If she had felt the need to go to the police, then there was something seriously wrong. . . .

Unlike Andrews, who was busy making arrangements for the reception of Mühlhauser in New York, Heinrich Holler caught the evening plane to Munich.

Early the next morning he was going through the reports in a private office in the central police station. He listened quietly as a nervous officer gave an account of his interview with the Reverend Mother. The black homburg hat lay on his desk with a tag stapled to it.

'Father Rittermann, eh? And you've checked with all the Catholic parishes on any priest of that name?'

'Yes, sir. We did that straight away. There were two Rittermanns, but neither corresponded with the man who went to the convent. One was about twenty-five, and the other was in hospital after an operation. There was no trace of any priest called Rittermann or anyone knowing about the attack on Father Grunwald and being sent as his replacement. In fact, the timing makes it impossible, unless the so-called priest was responsible for the assault and robbery.' Holler looked down at the typed page. 'I see you found a wallet and a watch belonging to Grunwald. No fingerprints?'

'Nothing, sir, just a lot of smudges. He wore gloves.'

'Very professional for a backstreet mugger,' Holler said. 'And of course the priest didn't see who hit him. Is he well enough to interview? Check with the hospital. And telephone

Reverend Mother Katherine. I'd like to see her. And don't take any nonsense; this is a criminal charge.'

He went to see Father Grunwald first. The older man was in a side ward in the Augsburg Hospital; he looked pinched and grey. Holler sat down with a police inspector to take notes. He recognized the signs of shock in the bad colour and the quick breathing. He apologized very gently to the priest for troubling him with questions, but the convent was also concerned. He did hope the Father would be able to help.

'You didn't see your attacker, or notice anyone near before you were struck down?'

'I don't think so,' Father Grunwald muttered. 'I was just going round to my car to go to the convent as usual, when the next thing I felt was a terrible blow and then I knew nothin₁ till I woke up in the ambulance. . . .'

'And there was nobody about before it happened? Try to think, Father.'

The old man's forehead creased in the effort to concentrate. 'I think there was someone getting out of a car . . . I can't be sure. . . . But there was no one else in the street.'

'What sort of car – did you notice the colour or the make?'

Father Grunwald picked fretfully at the top sheet. 'Yes, I did. I'm interested in cars, you know. I've had mine for ten years and there's never been a thing wrong with it. . . . It's a Volkswagen, and they're so reliable'

'They are indeed,' Holler nodded. 'Was this car you saw a VW?'

'Oh, no. It was an Opel; dark green.'

'And a man got out of it?'

'Yes, he did, I'm sure he did.'

'And what impression did you get of him – old, young, fat, thin – anything that struck you?'

'I don't know,' the priest mumbled. 'I didn't look at them properly, you see. I just noticed the car.'

'You said, "them",' Holler reminded him. 'Were there two men, perhaps?'

'Yes, one on the street and one inside,' Father Grunwald

answered. 'I couldn't see the one in the car . . . I didn't look at them, I was in a hurry.'

'Yes, of course you were. But you've been a great help already. You noticed the car, and the colour and the make, and now we are sure you were attacked by two men, not one. Don't you see how much that helps us?'

'I hope so,' the priest said. 'This has been a dreadful experience. I'm not able to stand shocks like this. Why would anyone want to rob *me*? I'd nothing but a few marks and my old watch. . . .'

'I don't think they did want to rob you,' Holler said quietly. 'I think they wanted to get someone into the convent in your place. The theft of your wallet and your watch were just done to hide the true motive.'

'Why?' Father Grunwald's eyes rolled from Holler to the inspector, who hadn't spoken. 'Why would anyone want to go to the convent instead of me? Maybe they wanted the chapel plate – there are some very valuable silver-gilt candlesticks and a chalice . . . How did they know I went to the convent on Thursdays?'

'Perhaps you told them,' Holler suggested, 'without realizing there was any harm. Who did you see that week, apart from the people you see normally? Did anyone telephone you, or call on you –'

The old man frowned again; he had been sedated to take the edge off the shock. He didn't know but his blood pressure had dived as a result. He felt sleepy and frightened at the same time. But also angry. Very angry with whoever had knocked him down and taken his few marks. . . .

'Only a man wanting instruction,' he said at last. 'I sent him away; I'm too old for converts now. I told him to go to his own parish priest.'

'Do you get many inquiries like that?'

He looked at Holler's grave, sympathetic face. 'Why, no. No, I don't think it's happened to me since I retired there. . . . But this man said Reverend Mother had recommended him. . . .' He didn't finish the sentence and his eyes opened wide with alarm. 'You don't think it was him who –'

'I think it's very likely,' Holler said. 'Now you can really help us. What did he say to you. Did he ask questions about the convent?'

'Yes, yes,' the old man nodded. 'I didn't think about it, but he asked me when I went there and whether I'd have enough time to look after his instruction and I saw I could make an excuse and I told him. . . .'

'Now tell me what he looked like?' Holler said.

'He had grey hair,' Father Grunwald said. 'He was rather ordinary, middle-aged and he could have come from the East. He wasn't a Bavarian, not with that accent. . . . I didn't like him much. I didn't want to instruct him. People have made up their minds about religion by that age, I think. . . . Glasses? No, he didn't have glasses – or a moustache or anything. Rather a heavy man, and quite tall. . . .'

'But not the man you half noticed in the street, getting out of the Opel?'

'No, no, I'd have remembered him. That one was young with fair hair.'

Holler stood up. 'Thank you, Father Grunwald,' he said. 'I won't tire you any more. You've given us a great deal to go on. I'm sure we'll find whoever did this to you. Take care and get well soon. Good-bye.'

The Munich police started with the cheap boarding houses and then the commercial hotels; they were looking for two men, one grey-haired, well-built and tall, his companion young and blond. The registers revealed nothing, until they came to a modest *pension*. The detective found two names on the register, both having left on the day of the attack on Father Grunwald. The proprietor, a middle-aged woman who ran the place with her married daughter, described the two men.

'Very nice gentlemen, both of them. They kept to themselves and they only ate breakfast with us. I told them we did a nice evening meal, but they always went out. Then the older one paid the bill on Thursday and they left about – oh, four o'clock, I think.' The register was made out in the names of Kesler and Franconi. Nationality Swiss, with two addresses in Geneva. The detective produced a small folder and laid it on the reception desk. There were sections of the human face, all interchangeable. 'I'll put one together and you tell me what's wrong with it,' he said. The woman shook her head. 'No, the nose is wrong. It wasn't hooked, it was a bit blunt.'

Twenty minutes later the Munich detective had assembled two identikit pictures of the men who had stayed at the *pension*. Holler set off with them to see Father Grunwald. When he came into the ward he stopped; there were screens round the bed. A young doctor came out and Holler went up to him. 'Is anything wrong with the priest? Here's my card.' The doctor glanced at the police ID with its photograph of Holler in a little plastic window. He shook his head. 'He had a heart attack about half an hour ago. We've tried everything, but I'm afraid it's no use. He's dead.'

'I'm sorry,' Holler said. He spoke to the Munich inspector who accompanied him as they ran down the steps into the street. 'That was our best witness. Now the only person who can really identify him is Reverend Mother Katherine.'

'She'll be better than poor old Father Grunwald,' the policeman said.

'I'm not so sure,' Holler said. 'But at least I'll get a chance to see her and ask some of the questions. . . . Let's get back to the office.'

He settled himself behind a borrowed desk, lit a cigarette and began to make notes. He wrote at random, setting down whatever came into his mind. He made no attempt yet to arrange the interview with the Reverend Mother. There were other points he wanted to clear first. The cigarette burnt down to its filter in an ashtray. The page became crowded with items, and names. Holler read them, adding here and there or sometimes crossing out. Herbert Schmidt. Otto Helm. Two men had visited Schmidt, and one of them had killed him. One man had been seen in the vicinity of Helm's house before it was set on fire. He reached for the telephone , and spoke to his office in West Berlin.

'Give me a description of the man seen walking his dog – that's right, three separate people came forward. Yes.' He listened, writing it down. Young. Fair-haired. Medium height. His pen scored underneath each word. 'Good, now get the Schmidt file. The two men who were with him when he died.... No, I'll hold on.' The minutes went by; he sat with his eyes closed, thinking.

'Hello – yes, you have. Good. Give it to me.' There followed a description of the two German gentlemen, said to be army officers, that Herbert Schmidt's cousin had let in to see him. Grey-haired, heavy-built. Younger, blond hair.

He hung up. In Berchtesgaden they had passed themselves off as Germans. In Munich they registered as Swiss. The old priest had detected an accent in his caller which placed him well to the east of Germany. The picture was taking shape, like a finished section of a larger jigsaw puzzle. They had identified Father Grunwald and the older one had substituted himself to get into the convent. From what Heinrich Holler knew of the Reverend Mother, she would never have called the police unless she felt her community was threatened. The chain of coincidence was too long to be credible except for the one, vital link between the men who had murdered two survivors of the Bunker and the imposter who had run out of the convent. Gretl Fegelein. Holler had a feeling of exhilaration when he wrote that name down and read it aloud. The men who had killed Helm and Schmidt were also trying to get to Eva Braun's sister.

And so were Max Steiner and Minna Walther. He had the address of their hotel, which Minna had given him. He put a call through and asked to speak to Max.

'This is Holler speaking. I'm in Munich. Listen, I haven't time to explain but I don't want Frau Walther going to the convent. What? She has! Damnation – No. Never mind. Call me when she comes back later.'

A shaft of sunlight had settled on the picture hanging above the fireplace; it was a sentimental reproduction of the Sacred Heart. Minna studied it while she waited in the convent parlour. The Christ was a beautiful Aryan, with blue eyes and softly waving chestnut hair, one sensitive hand pointing to the allegory of his love and suffering on account of mankind, a heart surrounded by a crown of thorns, enclosed in a nimbus of light. She wondered whether the artist had realized how anti-Semitic he was being when he painted the original. Jesus, of the House of David, had never looked like that. She heard the door behind her open and she turned. The nun came towards her, one hand resting lightly on the silver cross she wore round her neck. She wasn't as tall as Minna but she gave the impression of height.

'Frau Walther?' The accent was the twin of Minna's East German pronunciation, with the clipped Prussian vowels. Minna stared at her; at last she found words. The formality gave her time to recover from the shock of recognition.

'Reverend Mother Katherine. It's very kind of you to see me.'

The nun smiled and sat down on one of the stiff little chairs. 'I'm only too delighted to see General Ahrenburg's daughter,' she said.

Minna thanked her. The two women were facing each other across the polished table where Kesler had left his hat.

'But you wouldn't see my husband,' she said. 'He wrote to you many times.'

'I know he did,' Mother Katherine nodded. 'But there was no way I could help him. I don't think I will be able to help you either. Before you come to the point of your visit, how are your family?'

'My mother is very well; my father died four years ago. And you know what happened to my husband.'

'I do. We had a special Mass said for him.'

'That was very kind,' Minna answered. 'But you could have seen him and helped him, Mother Katherine. He was a good and brave man, and he loved Germany. As the daughter of Baron von Stein, don't you feel responsibility towards your country any more?'

'I have another identity,' the nun answered. 'I have a new name, and new loyalties. What happened to my father is perhaps a little worse than what happened to your husband. If I have come to terms with that, I know the real meaning of

patriotism. You're not a Catholic, but I'm sure you understand the principle of obedience to a higher power.'

'There is no higher power in this convent than you,' Minna
said. 'I know enough about Catholics to know that. Why are
you protecting Gretl Fegelein? You, of all the people in the
world.'

'I have never heard of Gretl Fegelein,' the Reverend
Mother said.

'You're not supposed to lie,' Minna said. 'It's a sin, isn't it?
And you can't lie to me, Freda, because we've known each
other too long.'

'Don't call me that,' she interrupted. 'My name is
Katherine Ignatius; there is no such person as Freda von
Stein.' She made a movement as if she were going to get up,
and Minna leaned towards her quickly.

'We were friends once,' she reminded her. 'When we were
children – you remember how my mother and father comforted you and your mother? You stayed with us until the
Russian advance, didn't you – then we all fled together. Your
father and mine were close friends. So close that he wouldn't
involve Papa in the bomb plot because he felt it was going to
fail, and he knew the penalty.'

She paused; Mother Katherine had stayed in her chair;
under the grey nun's veil, her face was very pale.

'I remember your father very well,' Minna went on. 'He
was always so kind to me. They strangled him with piano
wire, hung up on a meat hook. Hitler watched the cine film.
Maybe Gretl Fegelein was there. Have you asked her, Freda?'

'What do you want?' The nun's voice was low. 'Why does
anyone want to bring up the past?'

'Why do you and your Church want to hide it?' Minna
countered. 'Other people are looking for that woman, not
Germans, but our enemies.'

'I know they are,' Mother Katherine answered. 'One of
them came here, posing as a priest. He asked for her, and I told
him I'd never heard of her. Then I knew that there was danger.
Danger to my community. That's why I agreed to see you,
Minna. I can't have my nuns put at risk. Why, after all these

years, should Eva Braun's sister be of interest to anyone?'

'If you'll let me see her,' Minna said. 'I'll tell you. Or she can tell you.'

The Reverend Mother stood up. 'Come with me,' she said.

Albert Kramer poured himself a Steinhaeger. He liked a schnapps when he came back from his office, and he experimented; he decided that the old favourite, a Manhattan, was the one he liked the best. He was in a buoyant mood; he examined himself in the mirror above the fireplace in his drawing room, and felt satisfied.

He had spent a long afternoon with certain members of the Bundestag discussing his proposal to stand for election; he dropped hints that Frau Walther would endorse him as a candidate to take her husband's place. The idea was very well received. He was encouraged and assured of support. He had remembered to send flowers to Minna, as part of the campaign, but he was surprised when she didn't acknowledge them.

He wasn't a man to be rebuffed easily. He rang the house in Hamburg and was told she had gone away. Yes, the flowers had arrived, and Frau Walther had been there, but the housekeeper didn't know the date of her return. She had gone to Munich. Kramer felt annoyed, and then dismissed it. Minna would come round; it added spice to his pursuit of her. She was unaware that she was his quarry in more than a personal sense. She didn't know that he knew what was in those papers of her dead husband and, thanks to Mühlhauser, he had information of his own.

The immensity of the secret had made him reckless. He dreamed dreams of power and greatness, and the echoes of salutes shouted from ten thousand voices in one uniform cry rang through his memory and brought a flush of excitement to his face. He felt tuned and fit like an athlete before a race, and his sexuality was at a high pitch. He needed women regularly, but he had been careful not to get involved in an affair in his own social circle. He didn't want scandal or attachments. He used a reputable agency to supply him with girls. He had found one in particular very pleasing; she matched his exultant mood. He had made a call when he got home, and arranged for her to come. His staff were discreet; they knew when he entertained a lady to dinner, that they were not to gossip if she stayed the night. Or left in the small hours. Kramer didn't usually give the girls dinner until he was sure they were amusing companions. Then he liked to play the host. It made the sex more enjoyable if he could dominate the girl as a person, rather than an object who took her clothes off, pocketed her fee, and left. That annoyed Kramer because it was impersonal, and he felt it a reflection upon his masculinity. He liked to play with the girls over the dining table, miming the seduction agreed beforehand. The girl he had booked for that night was ideal for the purpose. He had showered and changed, ordered a good dinner with some of his better wine, and was drinking his cocktail in self-admiration before she arrived.

When the door opened he came forward, and as his manservant withdrew, he lightly kissed the prostitute's hand.

'Fraulein – this is a pleasure.'

'Herr Kramer,' the girl responded, 'how kind of you to invite me.'

She was a well-educated girl, who worked during the day in the sociology department of the Ministry of the Interior. She had brown hair and large blue eyes, with a delightful smile; she was expensively dressed in navy silk, with pearls round her neck and in her small lobes. She had big breasts, which made her slim body look top-heavy, but Kramer found the imbalance exciting.

He offered her a schnapps, and she pleased him by accepting. They talked and drank, and she played her part so well he almost forgot she would cost him three hundred marks at the end. He wanted to touch her, but it would have spoiled the charade. He wondered how much he would have to pay if he ripped her dress later, and decided it would be worth the money. He allowed himself the titillation of stroking her hand. She smiled delightfully into his eyes.

Outside in the tree-lined avenue Kesler and Franconi walked past the entrance. Franconi looked at his watch.

'No one else has come,' he said. 'She's been there over an hour.'

'I'll drive the car round,' Kesler said. 'You keep strolling along on the opposite side, and make sure no one else goes in or the girl comes out.'

Franconi nodded. It was a mild evening, dark but warm. He wore a hat, which was unusual, but Kesler insisted. He had become quite nervous after the debacle in the convent. Franconi did as he was told. He strolled, very slowly, along the opposite side of the road from Kramer's house. There were lights on the first and ground floors. He had seen a man open the door when the girl arrived, and it wasn't their target. There was no kiss or handshake. So there was a male servant in the house. Kesler didn't want to confront him; he was trying, in spite of their last set of instructions, to keep the accidental aspect of their contract. Franconi saw the car nose ahead of him and pull up. He walked to it and slipped inside.

'Nothing,' he reported. 'It's past nine. They must be having dinner.'

'We'll wait,' Kesler said. 'I don't think he'll come out tonight. If we're clever we'll catch them in bed.'

Franconi made a grimace. He had a real horror of heterosexuality. 'Supposing they don't go to bed?' he said. 'They may be going on somewhere else.'

Kesler lit a cigarette. 'Then we'll follow them. We'll get him one way or the other, don't worry, Maurice. I have instinct for a job that's going to go well. I'm very confident about tonight. We'll take this turning and come back up again. We can park near those trees; we can see the front door perfectly from there.'

He smiled encouragingly at Franconi. His own nerves had been shaken by having to run from the convent. That nun was no fool; she'd give a very crisp description of him. But Munich was far enough away from Bonn, and Bonn in turn from Hamburg, where the last two on their contract lived. Then a flight to Geneva, to collect the money, and afterwards

Tangier ... He switched on the radio, and tuned into some disco music, because he knew Maurice liked it. He preferred classical himself.

Kramer's companion was called Heidi; she was twenty-four and she had been supplementing her income since she was twenty. Her family lived in the country some hundred kilometres from the capital city itself; her father had retired from medical practice after a heart attack, and he and her mother lived a quiet rural life. Heidi was their only daughter, and the family were very close. She was educated and a proficient typist, but the job with the Ministry was only adequately paid.

Heidi enjoyed good clothes, skiing holidays, and was saving for the day when she got married. She had always known she was attractive to men, and being a practical girl, when she heard that it was possible to make a lot of money doing what she had so far done for nothing, she didn't hesitate. She looked at Albert Kramer across the dining table, and toasted him in his own champagne. He wasn't her type, and she didn't particularly enjoy the ugly display of masculine aggression which he called making love. But she obviously suited him and the money was exceptionally good. He leaned across and ran his hand down her arm. She responded with a sensuous giggle. His eyes were slightly red from drink, but it didn't impair his performance.

'Coffee?' he asked her. 'Here, or upstairs?'

Heidi played her part perfectly. She wet her lips with her tongue, and said, 'Upstairs.'

It was a quarter to midnight when Kesler and Franconi opened the door into the entrance hall. Franconi's early criminal background included picking locks, and this one had been easy. The security lock had not been used, in view of Herr Kramer's lady friend upstairs. The servant had gone to bed. There was a single light on in the hall.

Kesler went first; although he was the heavier of the two, he never touched a loose board. On the first floor they paused; there were no lights under the doors. Kesler beckoned Franconi and they started up the stairs again. There was a light on the landing. They switched it off. A streak of dim light showed under one of the three doors on the landing. The two men stood side by side, absolutely still and quiet, listening. It was a thick door; the house was well built. It was a little while before they could distinguish the muted sounds of a male voice. Kesler looked at Franconi in the gloom and nodded. 'I'll deal with him,' he whispered. 'You see to her.' He slipped a gun out of his pocket; Franconi did the same. Then Kesler closed his gloved hand round the doorknob and very slowly eased it round until the door was open.

Kramer didn't see them. He had his back to the door, and the girl was kneeling in front of him; they were both naked. She saw nothing either; her eyes were closed and she was concluding the first part of the ritual dictated by the client.

Kesler came up behind them, and laid a hand on Kramer's shoulder. Kramer gasped and swung round; the girl toppled over, caught off-balance. Kesler shot him through the right side of his head, close to the eye. The girl Heidi managed one sharp cry of fear before Franconi cut it off. He dragged her to her feet, one hand round her mouth; her eyes rolled upwards in terror. Franconi changed his hold on her, and Kesler stepped close and shot her twice in the heart. Maurice let her fall quickly; she sprawled on her stomach, blood collecting on the carpet underneath. Kesler needed help with Kramer's body. Together they managed to lift it on to the bed, and the big mirror on the opposite wall reflected the scene of death as it had done the gymnastics of sex. Kesler fitted the gun into Kramer's right hand, crooking the index finger round the trigger; he brought it up level with the bullet wound and then let the arm fall naturally. The gun slipped out of the dead hand on to the floor. Kesler looked round him quickly.

'Murder and suicide,' he whispered to Franconi. 'Come on, don't forget to shut the door. Hurry!' They flitted down the stairs, into the hallway and out through the front door. The porch was in shadow and for a few seconds both men sheltered, making sure no one was in the street. They left at the same time, keeping close to a line of ornamental bushes, slipped through the gate and were in their car in less than a minute. Kesler switched on, and took care not to gun the engine. They moved off silently and without undue speed. Franconi lit a cigarette and passed it to Kesler. Kesler smiled; he was in excellent spirits. Release from tension after a job always made him elated.

'Wasn't that a classic?' he asked Franconi. 'Perfect. Now we're on the autobahn. We can pick up a bit of speed.'

'You think anyone heard the shots?' Franconi asked.

'No,' Kesler said. 'Very unlikely. The servants would be on the top floor. They won't be found till the morning. And we'll be having a nice big breakfast in Hamburg by then.'

'She's dead,' Minna Walther said. 'I saw the grave.'

Max didn't say anything; he felt numbed with disappointment. The feeling changed to anger and he swore.

'That was our banker,' he said. 'The one person who could have told us where that child was, and what had happened to it!'

'She was buried in the crypt under the chapel,' Minna said slowly. 'I just stood there and knew we'd failed. We've come to the end, I'm afraid. My God, I feel exhausted suddenly.' He came and put his arms round her; she leaned against him.

'Holler's waiting for us to call him,' he said. 'I'll do that, darling. But I'm going to get you a drink first.'

She surprised him by shaking her head. 'I don't feel like anything,' she said. 'You talk to Holler; tell him what I found out.'

'I will,' Max stroked the top of her head; the hair was very fine and soft. She sat on the sofa in their hotel sitting room, with her eyes closed. She heard Max go into the bedroom and ask for Holler's number at Munich police headquarters. She opened her eyes and turned her head to listen. He came back and said, 'He's coming over right away. Albert Kramer's been found dead. Holler thinks it's another murder.'

He saw the colour rush up into her face, and wondered why she should blush rather than turn pale.

'Albert? It's not possible – oh, my God!'

'It looks like suicide,' Max said. 'There was a girl with him; she'd been shot and apparently he'd killed himself. Holler's certain it was a double murder.'

'But why? Why Albert?'

'God knows,' Max said. 'Except he was a Nazi. And he'd headed the firing squad in the Bunker.' He looked up at her. 'But nobody knew about that – except ourselves and Heinrich Holler.' A few minutes later reception phoned to tell them Holler was on his way up.

'So Gretl Fegelein is dead,' he said, looking at Minna and puffing jerkily at his cigarette. 'Five years ago, is that right?'

Minna nodded. 'Yes,' she said. 'There was a date on the stone.'

Holler nodded. 'Five years, I see. So that source of information has gone for ever. Taking the secret of Janus with her, we must presume.' He glanced at Max.

He liked Max Steiner; he recognized the type, and saw a little of himself so many years ago in the younger man. Brave without being flamboyant, independent minded; not a man who gave up easily. He was so much in love with Minna Walther that Holler didn't even speculate whether they were lovers. He had always admired her; she had dignity and composure as well as good looks. He admired her a lot less for taking Max into her bed so soon after Sigmund Walther's death.

'Are you sure Albert Kramer was murdered?' Minna asked the question.

'Not sure,' Holler answered. 'Certain. We knew Kramer; he used a call-girl agency, and the one who was killed with him was a regular. There was no motive for her murder and less still for him to commit suicide. His manservant says he was in great spirits that evening; his secretary confirmed that the day was just as usual: he made appointments for the rest of the week – he was exceptionally cheerful. Nothing about his actions or appearance point to a man who is going to murder a prostitute and then kill himself. Besides, we Germans don't go in for that kind of crime. Kramer was murdered, with the girl, and then set up to look like a suicide.'

'But why?' Max asked.

'For the same reason as Helm and Schmidt,' Holler answered. 'Because he knew something connected with Janus and the Bunker. I believe the same people tried to get to Gretl Fegelein in the convent. Not knowing she was dead, of course. The point is, where will they go next?' He stubbed out his cigarette, rubbing the butt to fragments of paper and tobacco. He spoke to Minna. 'I believe something else,' he said. 'I believe the men who killed Sigmund are picking off a list of people. Herr Steiner – you told me a man came to see your wife in Paris, and frightened her so much she left the country. Posing as a Sûreté man, isn't that right?'

'Yes,' Max said. 'He wasn't; as I told you, I checked. It could have been a crank, but I didn't think so.'

'Did your wife describe him to you?'

'Yes, she did. I passed the description on to the Sûreté. It didn't fit any of their men.'

'Tell me what he was like,' Holler said.

'Medium height, thin, very dark hair, blue eyes. Certainly French.'

'Not the same as the one at the convent, then, but undoubtedly connected. The object was not to threaten your wife particularly, but to find out if you had told her anything Sigmund had told you. Fortunately for you, Herr Steiner, your wife knew nothing, because you hadn't had time to tell her.'

'I wouldn't have told her anyway,' Max said. 'I never discussed my work with her; she didn't take much interest in what I was doing.' He didn't look near Minna when he said it. He banished the memory of Ellie's frightened face, because his conscience was stirring while Holler talked. His family had been threatened, and he had sent them to friends while he pursued his own objective, and then fell in love with another woman.

'The question is,' Holler went on, 'why anyone is bothering to kill these people if the Russians actually found and disposed of Hitler's child?'

There was a moment of silence and then Max said, 'But you said it wasn't true, they never found him. . . .'

176

'I didn't think they did,' Holler answered. 'But in the last twenty-four hours I've changed my mind.'

'Why?' Minna had got up; now she was pale, unlike the moment when she blushed at the news of Kramer's death. 'Why have you changed your mind – you've got to tell us!''

'I don't have to tell you anything,' Holler replied gently.

'Yes, you do,' Minna said. 'You got Sigmund to do your work for you, looking for the child. That's why he was killed. You owe it to him to tell me why you think Hitler's child was found and murdered.'

Holler didn't answer. He hadn't visualized her as an opponent. He got up and stretched himself, buttoning his jacket. 'What I owe Sigmund,' he said quietly, 'is to protect you. Your visit to the convent and what you've discovered makes you as dangerous to these people as any of the others they've murdered. You're to forget about Janus, Minna and you too, Herr Steiner. From now on, it's a matter for my department. For your own safety, I would like you to get out of the country, and stay out until this business is over.'

He held out his hand to Max. 'You can't get any further,' he said. 'Take her away till it's safe.' He took Minna's hand and bowed over it.

'I'm not going,' she said.

'You may change your mind,' Holler answered. 'I hope so. For both your sakes.' Then he was gone.

Curt Andrews found what he was looking for in the files of the *Munchener Merkur*. They were old and yellow, and the newspaper was dated September 1945. It was a small item low down on an inside page devoted to unimportant home news of a non-political nature. The paper operated under the guidance of the Control Commission. It was headed TRAGIC ACCIDENT. Andrews read it, and took down the name and address supplied. 1945. It was a very long time ago, but there was just a chance that the family were still living there.... He drove to the modest suburb, and his hopes began to fade as he saw the new houses and the evidence of extensive rebuilding. But the street name hadn't been changed, and there it was, right at the end of the road on the corner, a double-fronted house with a small garden. He parked the car, went to the door and pressed the bell. It chimed instead of ringing. Nobody came and he pressed again, longer and harder so that the maddening little tune repeated itself. The door opened so quickly that he was taken by surprise. He put on his ingratiating smile and said, 'I'm looking for a Frau Inge Brandt. Does she still live here?'

The woman was in her early forties, her dress was neat but drab and she wore no make-up. 'You didn't have to ring like that,' she said aggressively. 'I was round the back. Yes, my mother's still here. Who are you?'

'I'm a reporter from the American *Daily News*,' he said. 'I'm doing a story on your city and its growth since the war. Seen from the human angle. I'd like to get some impressions from your mother of what it was like after the war. I was told she'd been in Munich right through. We're paying very well for information,' he added.

She didn't hesitate. 'Come in,' she said. 'My mother's in the back garden. She's old, you understand, but her mind's very clear. We could do with some extra cash – everything's got so expensive these days!'

The old woman was sitting in a garden chair with a rug spread over her knees; she had white hair done up in a bun, and a wrinkled, sharp featured face which made Andrews think of a bird with spectacles balanced on its beak. Her daughter bent down and spoke quickly to her; the mother glanced over to him, and nodded. 'There's a chair over there,' the daugher said. 'I'll bring out some coffee. My mother wants to know what you're prepared to pay.'

'Two hundred marks,' Andrews said. Inge Brandt had the broken voice of old age; it was throaty and masculine. She was very clear in her mind, just as her daughter said. Andrews guessed that she must be close to eighty. He spent the first fifteen minutes asking questions about the wartime conditions she had lived through, making notes, meaningless scribbles masquerading as shorthand. He was sympathetic and interested as she described the hardships of the last years of the war. Bombing, food shortages, living in shelters, the terrible casualties on the Russian front.

'And then,' he said. 'I heard you lost your little boy. Was that due to the war in any way?' The eyes were bright and they darted a shrewd look at him.

'No,' she said. 'It was a terrible thing; we were out shopping and he got knocked down by a man running past him; there were crowds everywhere, it was so quick I never even saw what happened. But my boy fell over, and when I picked him up he was dead. He'd broken his neck in some way. They never found the man who bumped into him.'

'How terrible for you,' Curt Andrews said. He knew exactly the blow the Russian agent had used to kill the child.

'In fact,' the old woman said, 'he wasn't really mine. Irma is, and I've a son living in America now, but Frederick was a foster-child. I took him in, you see, during the war. I think he was the son of someone high up in the Nazi Party. Not that I had anything to do with them myself. You must be sure to say that.'

'Oh, I will,' Andrews assured her. 'Of course.'

'I was sorry for the little fellow,' she said. 'People had no morals in those days. Children were being born all over the place. He was a lovely child, big blue eyes, and very bright. Quite a mischievious little boy. . . . I was very upset over it.'

Curt Andrews put his notepad in his pocket and pulled out his wallet.

'I'm sure you were,' he said. The bright little eyes were fixed on his wallet, and the withered lips moved as he counted the notes. 'Thank you, Frau Brandt,' he said. He laid the money on her knee, and she fastened a hand like a claw over the notes. 'This will make excellent copy. Especially the part about you taking in children. People love the human interest. Did you have any others besides Frederick?'

'No,' she said. 'He was the only one. A lady brought him to me when he was a few weeks old. I don't think he was hers, though. You can tell a mother when she handles her own child. Very well dressed, she was, I remember. She had a lot of fox furs.'

'And you never saw her again?' Andrews was on his feet. He shook hands without waiting for the negative answer. 'Good-bye, and thanks again. I'll send you a copy when it comes out.'

'She'd like that,' her daughter Irma said. 'She reads a lot.'

He waved good-bye to her as she stood at the front door. He got into his car and drove to his hotel; he was whistling. The first part of Günther Mühlhauser's story was true. He had to decide what to do next, and he rejected the idea that he could handle the problem alone. Or even with CIA assistants, who could be sent to join him. He needed Heinrich Holler. He went upstairs to his room, opened the fridge and took out two miniature bourbons, and mixed them with ice and soda. He kicked off his shoes and stretched out on the bed, sipping the drink. It was all so obvious once you knew where to look. A monument of lies marked the grave of truth. The phrase appealed to him, and he couldn't remember where he'd heard it. He was a trader in lies, as adept as any of his colleagues in the game of secrets. He saw no moral dilemma in twisting facts into fiction, any more than in killing a human being to achieve a political end. It was the idealists he disliked, with their moral overtones intact; they could be bloody to the elbows, and still look down upon the pragmatists like himself. He hadn't forgotten the jibe of Heinrich Holler that he, Andrews, didn't care about the life of Mühlhauser's daughter Beatrix. He was going to enjoy squeezing the German until it was *his* finger on the trigger this time.

In his office Heinrich Holler issued instructions.

'I want copies of those indentiphotos given to every hotel and boardinghouse in the city. And the same in Hamburg. All proprietors are to report to this office if anyone answering the descriptions takes a room. Circulate to Immigration at the airports.' He put down the phone. It was possible that the killers calling themselves Kesler and Franconi had already left the country, but he didn't think it likely.

The pieces were fitting together but the picture was not

complete. The murder of Albert Kramer proved that. He was not even known as a former member of the Hitler Jugend; there was nothing to connect him with the Bunker, or with the mystery of Eva Braun's child. Unless he had been one of the men who kidnapped Mühlhauser, and spared his life because of the information Mühlhauser gave him. That information had sentenced him to death. But who knew that he was in possession of it, except the betrayer himself? And the betrayer had betrayed again, and sent a warning to his Russian masters. No wonder they had freed Günther Mühlhauser from the labour camp. And now, by some brilliant opportunism, he had settled himself in Washington, the protégé of Curt Andrews and the CIA. He was going to enjoy telling Andrews that he had actually put a Soviet agent into place.

The pattern that was emerging made sense to Holler now; he had been quicker to follow the lead given him by Mühlhauser than Curt Andrews. He had checked the accident to Inge Brandt's foster-son with the Munich police, and the details were hall-marked Soviet Intelligence. So Hitler's son was dead. Janus was solved. He had said that to Mühlhauser and known by the readiness of his agreement that he was lying. Minna Walther had seen Gretl Fegelein's grave in the Convent of the Immaculate Conception. She believed it was the end of the search. No doubt the Reverend Mother intended her to think so. He lit another cigarette; smoking was bad for him. He was always told to stop when he had his regular medical check-up. Unfortunately it helped him to concentrate; also he enjoyed it. There was nothing he could do about his crippled leg, the result of Gestapo beatings, or the scars left on his mind by what he had suffered. At least his lungs were his own affair.

He drew a pad towards him and began to drawn a circle. He added details and the circle changed its shape. When he finished he sat and looked at it. Two heads, back to back, united. Janus, one of the oldest gods of mythology ... Janus ... Janus.... And suddenly he understood. He pushed his chair back in excitement and struggled awkwardly to his feet. 'My God,' he said out loud. 'My God, that's what it means – not Hitler himself, but the twin forms of Janus and Jana!'

Not one child, but two. Eva Braun had given birth to twins. The boy was dead, but there was a daughter that Gretl Fegelein had separated from her brother as a precaution. And she was still alive.

That was what Mühlhauser had told Kramer and his undercover Nazis; because of this they had forgiven him his betrayal of the boy to the Russians. And then Mühlhauser had warned his Russian contact that he had been forced to reveal the boy's death. Kramer's knowledge of that was the reason for his elimination. And that meant that the chain of murders beginning with Sigmund Walther and anyone else who might have known what Janus represented had been a Soviet operation aimed at concealment, not discovery. Men and women had been killed, not to find the heir Hitler had left behind him, but to hide the fact that he had already been found and was dead.

Holler sat down again; he crumpled the drawing of Janus into a ball. Now the puzzle was coming into frightening focus. The Russians had a candidate of their own, primed and ready to step on to the stage of European politics as the puppet of the Soviet Union who had manufactured him. The evidence they had suppressed all those years ago would be produced as proof of his authenticity.

They weren't trying to find Eva Braun's daughter by the Führer, because Mühlhauser had withheld that last piece of information. He had bought his life by telling them about the boy, holding the girl in reserve for just the emergency which arose when Kramer questioned him. Very clever; Holler had underestimated the man's cunning and will to survive. Now the knowledge of Hitler's daughter was possessed by the neo-Nazi movement in West Germany.... Mühlhauser had lied to him, passing the information of the boy's fate as if it were the only secret left. He had withheld the truth not only from the Russians, to whom he was bound by treachery, but also from the democracy of Western Germany. Holler could follow the twisted motives of a man who had been the friend of

Heinrich Himmler; he knew from terrible experience, the power of the Black Knights' oath. Mühlhauser had tried to keep faith with it by hiding the daughter of his Führer until she could be of use to those who were working for a resurgence of National Socialism. The threat to his own child Beatrix had forced him to protect her at all costs, and by making a deal with Curt Andrews he had placed himself and his family in safety, and averted Russian vengeance by giving them Kramer as a victim. He would be very valuable to his controller when he was established in Washington as the protégé of the CIA.

The Vatican had taken Eva Braun's sister under its protection because she was seeking shelter for Eva Braun's child; the significance of a direct descendant of Adolf Hitler had brought the considerable diplomatic power of the Papacy into operation. They wanted to keep her hidden from the world, and the solution was so obvious that Holler couldn't forgive himself for being blind to it.

The girl was never coming out; the Reverend Mother of the Munich convent and her predecessor had instructions to keep her beyond the reach of outside contact. She could never be allowed to marry, produce children – it didn't need much imagination to see that she had been persuaded to become a nun.

Holler sighed in relief. The political acumen of the Vatican had seen the problems many years before they could become reality, and found a wise solution. He couldn't have wished for a better one himself. Let her stay in peaceful anonymity; nuns were happy people, possessed by a childlike trust in God and His goodness. He didn't need to fear her any more. His duty was to inform his Chancellor of her existence; it might be advisable to approach the Vatican with the object of moving her to a less vulnerable place and obliterating the links between her and the convent. Kramer's people could search for her in vain. The possibility of a Russian imposter posing as her brother was far more serious. Only the highest authority in Bonn could authorize the action Holler wanted to take to frustrate the Soviet manoeuvre. He would have to consult with his government about the plans he had in mind. There was plenty of time; evidence had to be collected and prepared for public scrutiny; the timing was vital.

He thought of his old friend Sigmund Walther, murdered to perpetuate a lie that had still to be told, and he remembered Minna and the journalist. Their danger was acute. They had followed the killers without knowing it, and their involvement with the search for Janus must sentence them to death. He reached for the phone to call their hotel and order them to leave, when there was a knock at his door. It opened and he saw Curt Andrews; the American looked bigger and more menacing. Holler put the phone down.

'Curt? I thought you were in Hamburg, nursing the Mühlhauser family.'

'And so I was,' Andrews said. He walked to the desk and stood looking down at Holler. 'But I felt it was time you and I had a meaningful discussion about the special relationship between our Agency and your Service. Before it gets to a higher level.' He pulled a chair forward and sat down without being asked.

'You've been holding out on us, Holler,' he said. 'Washington isn't going to like that.'

7

It was Kesler who made the call to the Walthers' house in Hamburg.

'My name is Aaron Levy,' he said. 'May I speak with Frau Walther, please?' Franconi was beside him in the public booth. He saw Kesler frown. 'Oh, she's not? Oh, dear. She told me to call her about some jewellery. Can you please tell me where I can get in touch with her? It's very important, I have a client who won't wait.'

At the other end of the line, Minna's housekeeper hesitated. Jewellery – surely her lady wasn't selling anything? But Levy was a Jewish name and all the dealers were members of the Chosen Race, as she described them to herself.

'Hello, hello,' Kesler shouted into the phone; he grimaced and whispered an aside to Franconi: 'She's not there. I think we've been cut off – oh, yes, yes, I thought we'd been disconnected. Thank you. Hotel Kaiserhof – you don't know when she'll be back – I'll contact her there then. Thank you. Good day.' He turned to Franconi. 'She's in Munich – the last place I wanted to go. The woman didn't know when she was coming back.'

'What about Steiner?' asked Franconi.

'Paul said he'd be with her,' Kesler scowled, and shouldered his way out of the booth. 'I want to get everything finished as quickly as possible,' he went on. 'But I don't fancy going back to Munich. I've been seen and I could be recognized.'

They began to walk along the sunny street, two sober-suited men in earnest conversation. Franconi still wore the hat, which bothered him. He hated having his head covered. They drove their rented car out of the public car park, and set out for a drive. It was a warm day, and they took a route that brought them in sight of the sea. They stopped and watched the shipping in the Elbe.

'I'll go,' Maurice said. 'I'm not known. I'll settle the two of them and get out on the first flight. We'll meet in Geneva.'

'No, no, I won't do it like that,' Kesler said. 'I wouldn't have a moment's peace worrying about you. We'll go together and I'll stay low and wait for you. And promise me you won't take any risks.' He put his hand on Franconi's shoulder. 'Remember how much you mean to me.'

'I will,' Maurice Franconi said. 'Don't worry, Stanis. We're going to have our money and our house in Tangier. Leave the two of them to me.'

They decided not to check into a hotel together in Munich. Kesler went to a guest-house, and Franconi, armed with his briefcase and hand luggage, booked into a businessman's hotel where he merged perfectly into the background. Both used aliases and forged passports. The boarding house registered Mr Levy, resident in Antwerp, and the hotel accepted Maurice as an Italian from Milan. They didn't meet for dinner that night, and neither slept properly for worrying about the other. In the morning, Maurice telephoned Kesler. 'I've checked with the Kaiserhof. They're both there.'

'What are you going to do?' Kesler asked.

'Go in tonight. They have rooms on the same corridor.'

There was nothing Max could do about it; Minna had refused to go to West Berlin. He had tried persuasion, even resorted to the ruse of making love to her. She had surprised him by the vehemence of her refusal to listen to his arguments or to let him touch her. 'I'm not leaving Munich now,' she said.

'Holler knows something, that's why he wants to get rid of us. I said it and I meant it. He used Sigmund to do his investigating for him, and Sigmund died because of it. He's not going to fob me off now. I have as much right to know whether the child was really murdered or not – and if he was, why isn't the investigation over? You have a right, too; you came here to find out the truth and you're being frightened off because Holler wants to keep it to himself.'

'I'm not being frightened off,' Max interrupted angrily, 'because I believe Holler when he says we're in danger. He told me to take you away for your own safety. And it makes sense. Sigmund, Helm, Schmidt, Kramer – they can't leave us alive if they had to kill the others. We know too much, darling, don't you see? We've been following Sigmund's lead, and we've got even further than he did, because you found out that Gretl Fegelein was dead. It's the end of the road – you said that yourself, when you came back.'

'You want to give up?' she asked him. 'You've had your question answered, so now you'll sleep in peace – is that all it meant to you?'

'Stop trying to needle me, Minna,' he said. 'I'm not worrying about myself. I'm ready to stay behind and get what I can out of Holler, if only you'll go. I don't care if bloody Eva Braun had triplets, if it means you're in danger!'

He stopped and they stared at each other; he realized what he had said a few seconds later than she did.

'Not triplets.' She came and caught hold of him. 'Not Hitler and Eva Braun,' she said. 'But a son and a daughter, Janus and Jana, That's what the code Janus means.'

They stood locked together. He felt her tremble, as if from excitement. 'And the girl is still alive,' Max said.

'She must be,' Minna said slowly. 'That's why Holler has taken the initiative.' There was something in her eyes which Max had never seen before. 'I've got to find her,' she said. 'Sigmund gave his life for this. I've got to carry it through for him.'

'I thought you loved me,' he said. 'But it's still him, isn't it?'

'No.' She shook her head, then reached out and touched his

cheek. 'But what I feel about you doesn't change my love for him and what he tried to do for Germany. There's been so much treachery, so many lies. Albert Kramer, his great friend – the people Holler knew would try to stop him finding anything detrimental to the Nazis, the men who killed him and the people who sent them. If you really love me, you'll help me now.'

'Oh, Christ,' Max said desperately, 'I'd go to hell and back if you asked me. But think, my darling. What good is a girl to anyone? She'd never be a focal point for people like Kramer – they wouldn't follow a woman.'

'She could have a child,' Minna said. 'And the world has changed; you're thinking of the old Germany, but the Nazi attitude to women doesn't apply any more. Children, Church and Kitchen. What kind of a woman is she? What kind of monster does a monster breed?'

He didn't answer. He put his arm around her and tried to draw her close again. Her body was stiff, unresponsive.

'Will you help me find her?' she asked him.

Max Steiner had never believed in premonitions. He was impervious to superstition. But fear swept over him as he looked at Minna and knew that because he loved her so much, he was going to act against his instincts.

'If that's what you want,' he said. She put her arms round his neck and kissed him. They made love, and for a time he slept. When he woke she had gone to her own room. He had a feeling that what she had done was a reward.

Maurice Franconi had booked a table for dinner in the hotel restaurant. He had a drink in the bar first; he seated himself in a corner where he could see the doors. He felt unaccountably nervous, infected by the alarm of Kesler. He had worked out his plan, taking care of the smallest detail. He had gone up in the lift to the second floor and marked out the rooms numbered 47, 48. There was no one in the corridor; it was the hour when most people were in their rooms before going down to the bar or going out. He had noted the type of lock, and felt confident of picking it without any difficulty. And the weapon he carried was Kesler's deadly cyanide pen. He had come down by the stairs, so that route was familiar to him; washed his hands in the cloakroom, and bought a newspaper from the bookstall in the foyer.

He drank one vodka and lime, making it last; he watched the couples who came into the bar, looking for a tall blonde woman and a dark man. He saw several who might have been his target, but didn't quite fit the description. He recognized Minna Walther and Max Steiner in the dining room. They had a table by the window, and he was across the room from them, sitting close to the serving door at a table allotted to non-residents when the restaurant was full. He ordered a light dinner; drank some white wine, and watched the man and woman he was going to murder. His observation was completely impersonal. As human beings they held no dimension for him beyond a target that had to be assessed and sighted correctly. He didn't form an opinion of Minna as a woman; he didn't like women on any level, even the most superficial. Max he judged in terms of strength and alertness, should anything go wrong. Their relationship was obvious; he saw the way the man reached out for her hand, and lit her cigarettes. They might well be in the same bed when he broke in.

'I've cabled my Director,' Curt Andrews said, 'so there's no way you can keep this under wraps. It's not a West German problem any more.'

Holler had hardly spoken; Andrews found his silence disconcerting. The air was hazy with cigarette smoke, and the ashtray in front of him was full of stubs.

At last he looked at Andrews. 'The daughter of Adolf Hitler is a world problem, not an exclusive for your department to use for American advantage. That is, if she really exists.'

'Don't try and bullshit me,' Andrews snapped. 'Mühlhauser told me the boy was killed, but nobody's found the girl. Or even knew she existed. It's my guess Gretl Fegelein kept her with her and took her to the convent?'

'And what possible problem can she represent if that is true?' Holler asked. 'I believe she's become a nun, and that, Herr Andrews, is the best possible solution for us all.'

'Oh, sure,' Andrews sneered. 'A bride of Christ, eh? What happens if she jumps over the wall sometime – maybe she doesn't know who she is, and she finds out and decides she's had enough of convent life. . . . If we've figured out what Janus means, then so will the Russians. And just how long do you think she'll stay behind that wall?'

'As long as I decide to keep her there,' Holler said. 'I give you my word, and I'll say the same to your Director, that the woman will never come out into the world. As for the Russians – you can leave that to me.'

Andrews shifted one big leg over the other. 'I might be content to do that,' he said flatly, 'but my Director won't. Nor will the Intelligence services of the other NATO countries. And we're duty-bound to inform them of what we've discovered. Just as you should have informed me, Holler, under the terms of our mutual aid agreement.' He shook his head. 'You withheld information, and that's an official complaint. I have an instruction from Washington. You'd better see it.'

Holler picked up the telex. He read it, folded it and handed it back. 'And will this satisfy you?'

'I won't know until I can judge the situation for myself,' Andrews said.

'And supposing,' Holler said quiety, 'I tell you to mind your own business and get the hell back to Washington?'

Andrews grinned contemptuously. 'You can try, my friend, but I don't think your Chancellor will be very happy when he hears about it. You're tied up pretty tight with us, Holler. Either you go along with the official request in that telex or I take the first plane to Bonn. I personally don't mind which way it plays.'

Holler appeared to be considering. He watched Curt Andrews's foot, in its polished slip-on shoe, swing backwards and forwards while he waited. He was trapped and he knew it. He would have to accede to the request made in the telex. Andrews had played it very cleverly. But not as cleverly as

Holler intended to do. No trace of resentment showed on his face as he looked at the American.

'You have a right to the information; but I'll have to get authorization from my government to protect myself.' He stood up in dismissal. Andrews didn't move.

'How long will that take?'

'I should have an answer within twenty-four hours, maybe sooner,' Holler said.

Andrews got to his feet. 'Just so long as we don't find the lady's disappeared,' he said.

'We haven't yet established that she's there,' Holler reminded him.

'Then the sooner we find out the better,' Andrews said. 'I'll call you tomorrow.'

They didn't shake hands; Holler came to the door and opened it for him, and they nodded to each other like adversaries. Holler came back to his desk and sat down. He reached for the telephone and made the call to Max Steiner which Andrews had interrupted. There was no reply from his room or from Minna's; Holler checked with reception. Yes, they were still in the hotel and hadn't given notice they were leaving. Holler murmured a rare obscenity to himself. He knew who had refused to take his warning and his advice. Minna Walther wouldn't leave; he remembered her determination and the reminder of how he had used her husband, and how as a result Sigmund had died. There was no mistaking the loyalty and the strength of purpose in her; stronger than fear for her own safety and for the safety of the man she had taken as a lover. Yet not strong enough to keep her faithful to her husband's memory for a decent interval. Holler had married when he was in his twenties. His wife had saved herself when he was arrested by applying immediately for a divorce. He had never trusted a woman enough to marry for a second time.

He made an internal call. He had to protect Minna Walther and Max Steiner in spite of themselves. Then he put through a call to the Chancellor's office in Bonn and activated the scrambler.

The community of the Immaculate Conception were in the chapel for Benediction when the message came through for Reverend Mother Katherine. She knelt in the front pew, with two senior sisters on either side of her; the twenty-two sisters and three novices were ranged at her back, the six lay helpers last of all. The replacement for Father Grunwald was slightly older, and much less agile. He went through the service very slowly and reverently, and the morning Mass took ten minutes longer. Mother Katherine bowed her head in adoration at the Elevation of the Host, and the silvery tones of the nuns rose in the traditional hymn of praise. O Sacrament most Holy, O Sacrament Divine. For the first time in many years, Mother Katherine was unable to stop the tears filling her eyes. Love of God had blotted out pain and softened hatred into understanding; in time it would finally emerge as forgiveness. The penance she had chosen for herself had become harder as time passed; she tried to repress the memories awakened by the visit of her childhood friend that morning. No one had spoken her real name or reminded her of her father for many years. His image swam through the tears; a stern but gentle man, a tender husband and father; her mother had adored him, her elder brothers had both been killed with Rommel's Afrika Corps, and the family, reduced to three, had clung closer together in their grief. She was said to resemble her father; in the days when she looked in a mirror, she had tried hard to find him in her own reflection, but without success. And if she searched too long, then that other image would surface in her imagination, as it had done in nightmares as she was growing up. The struggling figure on the end of a wire noose.... Hatred had nearly unbalanced her mind; the Roman Catholic faith had offered sanctuary against a world where materialism was the new religion. The doctrine of reparation for the sins of others by a life of prayer and service showed Freda von Stein where sanity and purpose lay. She had taken her final vows in the Mother House in Salzburg. Ten years later she was sent to Munich and found that the past she had tried to escape was locked in with her. She blinked back the tears and concentrated on the hymn.

God was the arbiter of her fate; she had made Him a gift of her life when she became a nun. It was His will that she should find herself protecting what she hated most. When the moment came that she could look on the face of a certain novice and feel pure sisterly love in Christ, then her vocation was fulfilled. She prayed for that moment, as she did every day of her life. When Benediction was over and the last hymn sung, she led the way out of the chapel. In spite of herself she glanced at the back row of nuns, and then as quickly looked away. She could feel those other eyes upon her, watching, the head turning slightly till she was out of sight.

Sister Aloysius hurried up to her as she came out of the chapel into the main hall. 'Reverend Mother, excuse me, there was a telephone message. A Herr Holler called. He asked you to telephone him as soon as you came out of chapel. He said it was most important. I've written the number down and put it on your desk.'

'Thank you, Sister.' She went into her private room, closing the door.

The scrap of paper with the number of the Munich police headquarters lay like a white feather on the wooden desk. The Sister's rounded writing looked as if a child had taken down the message. Heinrich Holler. She knew well who he was, and what the message meant. The convent had kept him out, shielded by the power of diplomatic relations with the Vatican. She had been a young woman when she first came to the convent in Munich; she hadn't known who the woman and the child were; that secret was entrusted to her when she became the Reverend Mother.

And it was she who kept vigil beside the deathbed of Eva Braun's sister and promised to protect the girl from the evils of the world outside. Her hand had closed Gretl Fegelein's eyes when she was dead. But now the walls were breached. Poor, aged Father Grunwald had been struck down, and a man posing as a priest had got into the convent, asking for a woman who was dead. She had known then that the outside world couldn't be held back any longer. She had sent a message to Rome, and taken her childhood friend Minna

193

down to the little crypt where the sister-in-law of Adolf Hitler had been buried. It was Mother Katherine's only hope of keeping the promise made by her Church, and when Holler telephoned she knew that it had failed. Gretl Fegelein's grave had not been proof enough that there was nothing left to hide. She dialled the number and asked to speak to Holler. He had known her father well.

He didn't ask for an appointment; she noticed that, in spite of his courtesy. He arranged a time to call upon her. He was bringing a representative from the United States security services with him. She sat quietly after the conversation, one hand plying with the silver crucifix on its chain round her neck. Rome had given her instructions. She would obey and carry them out, but above all she must resist the cry of her own heart to be relieved of her responsibility. She had no right to hope for that, because the love Christ asked of her had still to conquer antipathy and fear. She closed her mind to everything but prayer. When she went to join the community for supper, she was serene. She had placed tomorrow in God's keeping.

'I'm tired tonight,' Minna said. 'Would you mind, Max?'

'Of course I mind,' he answered. They were holding hands, and he squeezed her fingers gently. 'I like making love to you, or haven't you noticed – don't be silly, darling – of course you're tired. That damned bed's too narrow for two to sleep comfortably. Let's have something with our coffee, and then we can go upstairs. Brandy?'

'No, not tonight. You're very good to me, Max. Why can't you be a pig sometimes?'

'Why should I be?' He played with her fingers; they were long and thin, with pale varnished nails. He found her hands exciting.

'Because then I wouldn't love you so much,' she said. The waiter came and took the order for coffee in the lounge. Max pulled back her chair and followed her out of the restaurant. He saw a man watching her as she passed his table; he was young and good-looking, and Max glared at him. She chose a corner table. He lit a cigarette and gave it to her.

'You know you've never said that to me before, out of bed.'

'That I loved you? How funny; I thought I had, many times.'

'No,' Max insisted. 'Never. Tonight was the first time. That makes tonight rather special, doesn't it?'

'Yes,' she said gently, 'I think it does. And you still don't mind if we don't sleep together – maybe I'm not as tired as I thought.'

'Oh yes, you are,' he said. 'A good night's sleep for you, and who knows I might just wake you early in the morning. I've been thinking about something. Here's our coffee.'

'What have you been thinking about?' He saw the intense look that changed her face and made it watchful.

'About ourselves,' he said. 'You and me, for a change. Relax, my darling, we're not going to think or talk about anything else.'

'All right,' she said. She sighed. 'Just about us. Tell me what it was you were thinking.'

'Only that if you married me we wouldn't have to take separate rooms in hotels,' he said.

'Max,' Minna said, 'Max, please. You *are* married. You're not a man who can throw his responsibilities aside and be happy. I can't think of anything permanent yet; it's too soon after losing Sigmund. And I keep thinking how unhappy your wife must be.'

He leaned back in the chair, cradling the glass of brandy in his hands. He didn't feel angry because he felt she was evading the issue. She had said she loved him. After that, in his mind, the other obstacles simply melted away.

'Minna,' he said firmly, 'let me tell you about my wife and family. And before I start I want you to understand one thing. If I'd never met you, I don't think I would have gone back. I've been unhappy and frustrated for years, and I haven't been faithful to my wife either. You imagine a sad, neglected woman, and fretful kids worrying because they haven't heard from Daddy.' He surprised her by laughing; it was mocking and angry. 'I married Ellie in England in the fifties. It wasn't exactly pleasant being a German in London at that time. The English hated us; I was very lonely and very guilty because of being German. It was a time of national self-disgust for most of us who were abroad. The concentration camps, the Gestapo, the murder of millions of Jews. I didn't know where to hide myself. Ellie wasn't just a pretty girl, she was friendly and understanding, and she loved me. We had a son and then a daughter and by this time I was with *Newsworld* and doing very well. I had my job. And Ellie had the children. She didn't need to mother me any more because there were Peter and Francine to look after, and her whole life revolved around them. They're not nice children, Minna. Maybe it's because she spoiled them, or maybe the mixture of her and me doesn't work very well. My son is a lout who's never thought of anything or anyone but himself since he was old enough to think at all. Francine whines and wheedles because he's a bully to her, but she's as selfish in her way as he is. My wife thinks that Freud and Spock rule the world, and the only function she and I have is to pamper and pander to our children. My work doesn't interest her; I don't interest her, except as Peter and Francine's father. Maybe I'm being unfair but that's the kind of marriage we have, and I don't want any more of it.'

He offered her the glass of brandy. 'I promise you one thing. If you walked out on me tomorrow, I wouldn't go back to Ellie.'

Minna sipped the brandy and handed it back; the glass was warm from his hands.

'My son Helmut,' she said. 'He's not selfish or anything like that. And he worshipped his father. He doesn't like me very much. And if I'm honest, I don't really like him. I've never admitted that before.'

'It's not an easy thing to face,' Max said. 'The world is full of misconceptions; one of the biggest is that you automatically love your blood relations.'

'Sigmund did,' she said. 'He loved me and his children and it didn't matter how different we were from each other. He

196

loved his friends, and they loved him. I'm making him sound like a prig, aren't I – but that's not true. He was very much a man.'

'He must have been,' Max said, 'for you to be what you are. He wouldn't grudge you happiness – not the man I talked to in the Crillon. I've interviewed a lot of men and women with façades that fooled the outside world. I know what's real and what's fake. Your husband was the real thing. I wouldn't want to take his place, because I'm not like him. I'm just an ordinary man who loves you and wants to spend the rest of his life with you. Think of it like that.'

She smiled, and he thought she was truly beautiful at such a moment.

'I will,' she said. 'But you're not ordinary, not in the least. I'll go upstairs now. You finish your brandy. I won't lock the door – if you do wake early. . . .' She leaned across and kissed him lightly on the mouth.

He sat on in the lounge, drinking slowly; the good-looking man with sleek blond hair who had ogled her in the restaurant was sitting at a table on the left. He was reading a newspaper, and it lowered for a moment as Minna walked past him. He left the lounge not long after she did, but Max Steiner didn't notice. He had made up his mind to so something that night which had been nagging at his conscience, and which his talk with Minna had made imperative. He went to reception and asked them to put in a call to Ellie in London.

Minna had undressed and, following a lifelong routine, she was brushing her hair. It was fine hair that crackled with static electricity and flew out in fine gold strands under the brush strokes. It soothed her when it was done by someone else. Sigmund used to brush it for her before she went to bed. It was often a prelude to making love. He liked her hair long, and she compromised to please him. It swept down past her shoulders when it wasn't held in place. She watched herself in the dressing-table mirror; how familiar and yet how alien the woman looked, gazing back at her. It was a young face, and the long hair was deceptive. She had always been tall, even as a child, with long limbs and an athletic body which rounded as she grew up. Rather like a boy, some of her aunts had said, not with approval. She had been dressed in an old suit of her brother's with her hair hidden under a cap when they were refugees from the Russians. The advance guard of the Soviet army were picked troops; picked for their savagery and Asiatic origins. Women in their eighties had been raped and left for dead by them. They had never seen a woman in a short skirt; the stories of atrocity and horror harassed the thousands fleeing to the safety of the Western Allied armies, their homes and possessions abandoned to the Russians. Be brave, her mother and father had told Minna, be a brave girl, whatever happens. How brave was she now, she asked herself. . . . The brush was laid aside. Her son didn't see the courage in her, only repressed emotions. He reproached her for being Prussian, as if it were her fault. But Sigmund often told her she was brave, and kissed her on account of it. And Max Steiner loved her. She had told the truth when she said she loved him. She wanted him to know and remember that.

She switched out the dressing-table light and left the latch up on her bedroom door. She lay with the bedside light on for a few minutes, then she reached out and turned it off. She had said she was tired, too tired to take him into her bed. It wasn't the truth. She was restless and she wanted him. It was a deliberate act of self-denial. She was coming close to Sigmund, lying alone in the dark. She repeated the words spoken by her mother as they fled through bombed and burning villages with the noise of battle close behind them. 'Be brave, Minna. Be brave whatever happens.'

At last she fell asleep.

Franconi took the lift to the second floor; two women went up with him, a mother and daughter, overweight and well dressed, chattering in Dutch. He stood back to let them pass out at the first floor, and the younger woman gave him an interested smile. He ignored it, and continued up. When the doors opened three people were waiting. He hurried out into the corridor and they got inside; the red eye on the lift indicator travelled downwards. There was no one in the corridor as he walked along it, and he opened the door to the stairs and lightly ran down to the floor below. Room 47. Adjoining Room 48. The woman had gone upstairs early and alone. He checked his watch. It was still only eleven. She could be having a bath, reading, waiting for the journalist to come and join her. It was too early to do anything. He knew there was a cubbyhole on every floor where the laundry baskets and cleaning materials were stored. He slipped inside and perched on a basket lid with the door just ajar. It gave him a clear view of the corridor and the two rooms.

In the next hour people came up and went to their bedrooms; there was a lot of talk and closing of doors, the lift was busy. It grew quieter and his watch said it was after midnight. Max Steiner had not appeared. Franconi had slight cramp in one calf, and he got down and moved outside the cubbyhole. It was very quiet. The red eye of the lift was stationary on the indicator for the ground floor.

She must be asleep by now. But what was the lover doing? A quarrel, perhaps – he didn't think so. He had seen her kiss him good night. It was twelve twenty-five.

He looked up and down the corridor once more and again to make sure that the lift was still at rest. Then he slipped the piece of cellophane out of his pocket to pick the lock of room 47, and moved towards the door.

Max was not quite sober when the call came through; he had ordered two more brandies, making the tedium of waiting an excuse. He heard the operator on the line. 'Mrs Max Steiner take a personal call from Munich....' And then Ellie's voice, sounding higher than normal, her Midwest accent stronger.

'Is that you, Max?'

'Yes,' he said. 'How are you? How are the children?'

'We're just fine,' came the answer quickly. 'How are you?'

'I'm fine too.' The stilted exchange continued while she told him about Peter and Francine. They liked London; their friends had taken them sightseeing, to the Tower and the waxworks at Madame Tussaud's. They were going to take a picnic and visit Windsor Castle the next day. He had a vision of the family party going down in the car with sandwiches and flasks of coffee, and the inevitable cans of Coke for his son and daughter. Ellie driving them before her on the tour, determined to improve their minds, while they squabbled and she refereed, being as always scrupulously fair.... It was like a scene from somebody else's boring home movie. He cut it short because the brandy had made him tactless.

'Ellie – listen, never mind the children for a minute. I want to talk to you about something important.'

'So far as I'm concerned, the children *are* important.' The reply was curt.

'I know they are,' he despised himself for placating her, but he wanted to tell her and get it over. 'It concerns them too. Ellie, I've been thinking while we've been apart.'

'Funny, so have I.'

'I think we're in a mess,' he said. 'It's probably my fault, but I can't just go back and take up the old life.' There was a pause, and then she said,

'I can't either, Max. That's what I've been thinking too. I've talked it over with Tim and Angela and they agree with me. Peter and Francine are so much happier than they were in Paris.'

He didn't mean to lose his temper but he did. 'To hell with Peter and Francine! That's all you ever think about – the children, the children – I'll bet they're happy, doing just what they like and running circles round you. I called you to tell you something.' He took a deep breath to calm himself, and wished he hadn't lost control.

'You've met someone else,' his wife said. 'That's it, isn't it? That's why you've rung exactly once since we left, and now you have the gall to wake me up and disturb my friends at this hour – you're drunk, too, I can tell –'

'Ellie, please,' he begged in desperation; it shouldn't have developed into a row. If he hadn't said what he did about the children she wouldn't be so angry.... 'Ellie, I'm terribly sorry. I should have called or written but I couldn't. Can't you see I didn't want to spring this on you, when you came home? I wanted to warn you about the way I felt. . . .'

'You didn't have to warn me. I knew it was over when you walked out on us and went off on your own. I hope you do a great piece for your magazine. I hope you'll find it's worth losing your family. I'm going to get a divorce. If you can't be a father to the children, I'll find someone else who can!'

He felt a horrible mixture of anguish and relief.

'If that's what you want,' he said. 'Don't be angry, Ellie, please. . . .'

'Oh, go to hell! Go back to your Kraut girlfriend!' The line went clear.

Kraut. She had never used that word before, even when they quarrelled seriously. Kraut. Hun. Boche. The scornful epithets of enemies; he was more drunk than he realized, because he looked furiously at the telephone and said loudly in English, 'To hell with you, too.' The lounge was empty; or nearly so; two men were still sitting drinking beer in a corner table. He supposed they were residents. Reception was closed, and a night porter sat in a cubicle reading a paperback. Max began to walk to the lift. His anger had disappeared, leaving a sick unhappy feeling in which there was more guilt than regret. He'd done it so badly, so crudely, just because he wanted to make sure of Minna and tear down the last obstacle to full possession of her. Because he had never possessed her, except in sexual climax. She had eluded him, keeping some part of herself in reserve. Even when she said she loved him, he sensed an area of privacy that excluded him. He weaved a little on his way to the lift, and one of the two residents in the lounge watched him and frowned. Max went into the lift, and the man hurried across to go up with him. 'Which floor?' he asked.

'Second.' Max scowled at him. He wanted to go to Minna, to take her in his arms and tell her his wife wanted a divorce, there was nothing to stop them – but she hadn't wanted him to come. She was tired, she said. In the early morning if he woke. . . .

The lift stopped, and the doors opened. He stepped out. The lights were dimmed slightly in the long corridor during the night. The man watched him walk towards his bedroom door and, satisfied, pressed the button to descend. Room 43, room 44, 45, 46, Minna's room, 47. Max stopped suddenly. The door was ajar.

Maurice Franconi found that the bedroom door was not locked. The latch had been put up; all he had to do was turn the handle. He wore cotton gloves, easy to pull on and off. Very gently he eased the door open a crack, and saw there was no light inside. A glance over his shoulder showed the corridor empty. He pushed the door and eased himself inside. It took a minute or more before he became accustomed to the faint light showing from inside, and could distinguish objects in the darkened room and move towards the bed. He had a very acute sense of another human being's presence; he could tell in the pitch dark if a place was occupied, like an animal prowling for prey. He didn't hear Minna Walther breathing, but he knew she was there before he could see the outline of her body in the bed.

He walked carefully across the floor, testing it for loose boards at every step; there was one creak and he froze. Nothing changed; the woman didn't stir. Franconi reached the side of the bed. He could see perfectly by now; her head was dark against the white pillow. She was lying on her side, one arm outside the covers. He smelt gardenias, and recognized the scent she was wearing. He made a little grimace of disgust. Sickly, cloying smell. Women turned him over; much more than they did Kesler, who didn't seem to mind them. He put his right hand in his pocket and found the pen. He brought it out slowly. He would have to lean across to get it close to her face. Then he heard the sound of the lift doors opening in the corridor. He hesitated; he had left the door of the room wide enough to give himself light. If anyone passed and saw it – it only needed a few seconds to puff the deadly gas into the sleeping woman's face, a few more to close the door and keep it shut till the latecomer had gone. If it were the journalist come to visit his lover, Franconi would be ready for him. The pen would dispose of him too. He moved very quickly, leaning over and towards Minna, and that was when she brought her arm up to rest above her head.

Franconi started back and dropped the pen. He saw the door push open and knew that he had no chance to hide. He didn't carry a gun, and the pen was gone. He was across the floor in seconds, and as Max Steiner stepped into the room, Franconi crashed against him, and sent him reeling sideways with a savage elbow chop. He didn't wait to strike again and kill him, because he heard Minna's scream behind him. He swerved into the corridor, and ran for the stairs. He cursed in breathless Italian, skipping down the flights to the ground floor, and there he stopped and waited. He had to get out of the hotel, but not to be seen. To be seen would identify him as the attacker. He had to walk out unobserved, or hide until he could slip out in the morning.

He opened the door leading into the lounge and heard the telephone at the porter's desk ringing. He saw two men in the lounge race towards the lift, and he flattened himself in the shadows. From the office behind the reception desk, two more men appeared, and Franconi broke out into a sweat of fear. They were detectives; the hotel was staked out, and he had walked into the trap set for him. The exits would be closed; he couldn't get away. He opened the door again and peered out. He couldn't stay where he was, the stairs would be searched immediately. He had to place himself somewhere that didn't excite suspicion. His initial panic was fading; his sharp intelligence raced through every possibility and settled on the one that Kesler had always taught him to use in an emergency. Never run. Never draw attention to yourself. Blend into the scenery.

The scenery was the residents' TV lounge, which was in semi-darkness and close enough to the stairs exit for him to slip through to it. He bent low and hurried across the little space to the big, dimly lit area with its sofas and tables and chairs. He made his way to a far corner, and stretched himself out in a deep armchair in front of the set. He peeled off the cotton gloves, cursing them for their loose fit and the loss of the cyanide pen. But leather gloves were difficult to use delicately, and a man wearing them in a hotel at night would be instantly suspicious. He rammed the gloves down the side of the chair. There, with his hands folded across his chest, and his mouth ajar snoring, he was found by Holler's security men twenty minutes later.

In the bedroom upstairs Max held Minna in his arms. She was trembling; he could feel it, but apart from her extreme paleness, she was calm. Holler was expected at any moment; a detective was on guard outside the door. The hotel was being searched and the registers checked for anyone resembling Max's muddled description. He had the vaguest impression of a man, glimpsed as he lay half dazed on the ground. Not too tall and not very big. Dark or fair, old or young – he couldn't tell them anything more. No weapon had been found, nothing but a fountain pen which had rolled under the bed; it didn't belong to Minna but it could have been lost by the previous occupant of the room.

'Oh God,' Max kept saying, 'if I'd been a few minutes later –'

It was Minna who comforted him. 'But you weren't,' she said gently. 'And nothing happened to me. I'm quite all right, darling. I was just shaken, that's all. It might have been a rape – someone who'd seen the door wasn't locked, I may not have shut it properly, and they came in and saw a woman in bed –'

'It was the man who killed Kramer and the others,' Max said. 'He was going to kill you. Just like Holler said. I'll never forgive myself for letting you stay here and not taking his advice.'

'You couldn't have made me go,' Minna said. 'I make my own decisions, darling. And there's one thing we can be thankful for; they'll catch the man. Then we'll know we're safe.'

'We're leaving first thing in the morning,' Max insisted.

She shook her head. She disengaged herself and moved

away from him. 'No,' she said quietly. 'I'm staying to the end. Nothing can alter that.'

There was a knock on the door and, before Max could reply, Heinrich Holler came in.

In the sitting room of her friends' Putney house, Ellie Steiner sat and cried. There was a cup of tea beside her which she couldn't drink, and Angela had an arm round her shoulders and was trying to calm her.

'Try to be sensible,' she was saying. 'You said he was drunk – you can't take that call seriously. He'll probably ring tomorrow full of apologies.'

'Oh no, he won't.' Ellie blew her nose and wiped her eyes. 'He wasn't drunk when he wouldn't come with us after we'd been threatened. He's a bastard, Angela. The more I think of the way he's treated me and the children, the more I see what a bastard he is! I think he got drunk so he'd have the courage to tell me –'

'But you've been thinking on these lines yourself,' the other woman pointed out. She was a practical girl, and she had never seen Ellie's marriage to Max as a permanent relationship. He was too volatile, too obviously irritated by his family; she personally didn't like him much, whereas she was deeply fond of Ellie. She liked Ellie's earnestness and sense of responsibility; she shared the same enlightened views on child rearing and the priorities of motherhood. She would never have admitted to prejudice, but she didn't like Germans.

'You haven't been happy,' she said. 'Never mind him, think of yourself. Now face it, Ellie, you said so the other evening to Tim. That's what matters – how you and the children feel. I think this may be a blessing in disguise.'

'I don't want to lose him,' Ellie Steiner said. 'A broken home is terribly bad for children –'

'Not as bad as parents' quarrelling,' Angela said firmly. 'If he wants to go, then let him. Only you see that you get what's due to you and he provides properly for Peter and Francine. We'll find you a nice little flat, near us, and you'll meet lots of people –' She was working herself up to anger. 'You're a damn sight too good for him,' she said. 'You'll meet someone else, and be really happy. Now drink that tea, and come up to bed. I'll give you a Mogadon, and you'll sleep right through.'

Angela had a square little English face and her jaw set aggressively. 'If he rings again, you let me answer him. He won't do this sort of thing in a hurry when I've had my say. Come on, Ellie dear. Upstairs.'

She led Max's wife up to her room, and made her swallow a sleeping pill. Then she tucked her in solicitously, and went back to her own bed and her husband.

'Bloody Germans,' she said, settling down beside him. 'The sooner she gets rid of him, the better for all of them.' Her husband made a sound of agreement.

There were 218 people staying in the Kaiserhof; apart from the guests there were twelve men who were not registered and had been in bed with lady guests or were on their way out when they were stopped by the police, one drunk found snoring in the TV lounge, who turned out to be staying at another hotel, and the night staff of thirteen men.

Holler interviewed every male considered physically capable through age or proximity of making the attack upon Minna Walther. The married men registered with their wives were excluded. That left the twelve who had remained in the hotel surreptitiously, four homosexuals staying in adjoining rooms, who immediately attracted Holler's interest, the drunken Italian found in front of the TV, and the night staff. The thirteen night staff were all in their late middle age, all with *bona fide* backgrounds as residents of the city and established employees of the hotel. He interviewed the remaining suspects in the manager's office; the hotel remained closed and no one was allowed to leave.

The description of the two Swiss, Kesler and Franconi, did not fit any pair of individuals. The homosexuals were ruled out as soon as he saw them. An elderly businessman and a teenage pimp with a record of soliciting – the man's embarrassment was pitiful when he was questioned – and two antique dealers, both so effeminate and slight that from behind they could have passed as women. Neither could possibly have thrown Max Steiner off his feet. But there were five men of medium height with blond hair, and another three whose colouring didn't fit but whose age and physique did. Every one of them had identification which at first check seemed genuine. Of the eight suspects, Holler mentally reserved three. There was a Bavarian musician, who had picked up an elderly woman staying at the hotel and, according to the woman herself, had not gone to bed with her as he had indicated. He had sat up talking and suddenly excused himself. There was a young engineer from Basle who had booked in for the night en route to Prague. His papers were in order, but it seemed an expensive choice for a man of his age for one night, and there was something ill-disposed about him which alerted Holler. The last was the textile dealer from Milan who had gone to sleep in the TV lounge. His story checked out easily. His hotel confirmed that he was staying there; the Milan address was authenticated by a telephone call, and his passport was in order. What worried Holler was his eagerness to help. All the other suspects had complained in varying degrees; some became very abusive. But the fair Italian was complaisant about being kept in the hotel and investigated; he was a shade too co-operative, and Holler didn't equate that with the Italian temperament. He thanked everyone and dismissed them, promising to release them from the hotel as soon as possible, and when they had gone he began to think and chain-smoke.

The killer had not got out of the hotel. The time factor made it impossible for anyone to have left because the main exit in the front, the service exits and the fire escapes were guarded by his men, and as the alarm was raised all the doors were locked. This time it was one killer, not two, and from Max Steiner's vague impression it could be the younger and smaller of the two men who had killed Schmidt in Berchtesgaden and stayed in the *pension* together at the time Father Grunwald was attacked. And he was there, in the hotel, hidden behind a false identity and a well-documented background which would take more than a few days to break down. Holler had nothing on which to arrest any of them; unless he could find some piece of evidence or identification he would have to let them go in the next few hours. The man he was hunting would never be found again once he left the Kaiserhof and slipped into the Munich streets.

It was possible that a new assassin had been employed and the others withdrawn, since the Reverend Mother had seen one of them at close quarters. But Holler didn't think so; if his instinct was right and it was one of the original pair who had begun the chain of murders with the killing of Sigmund Walther then the proprietress of the *pension* would certainly be able to point him out. An identity parade could be held in the hotel, with Minna and Max Steiner to reinforce the principal witness. If she were unable to see one of her clients in the line-up then he would have to release the suspects.

He looked the number up in the telephone directory and dialled. It was very early in the morning and he had to wait some minutes before it was answered. The daughter took the call; no, her mother was not at home. Yes, she supposed she could come to an identity parade, but she didn't think she'd be much help. She sounded rather breathless, as if she had been running to catch the telephone before it stopped ringing. Really, she couldn't remember all that much about the Swiss gentlemen. They had a lot of guests staying a few nights and already she wasn't too sure what either of them had looked like. She didn't remember saying one of them had fair hair. . . . No, it didn't come back to her at all. . . . Holler put the telephone down. She wasn't going to get involved; he knew the type of person who regarded any contact with the police as a social stigma. If she or her mother did recognize the younger of the two men they wouldn't say so. Then he paused, the lighter aflame, the cigarette in his lips waiting to be lit. He made a second call.

At the other end of the telephone line the woman replaced the receiver with shaking hands. Her eyes were wide with terror, and she whimpered as Kesler brought the gun to her breast. 'I didn't tell, I didn't. . . .' He nodded at her encouragingly and shot her through the heart. Her mother lay dead in her bed upstairs. He looked at her as her body slid down, buckling from the knees, and collapsed in a ragdoll heap at his feet. 'You didn't,' he said softly, 'and you're not going to now.' He left her there and slipped out of the back entrance into the street.

When Franconi didn't contact him Kesler knew that the plan had gone wrong. He walked through the empty streets in the pre-dawn and passed the entrance to the Kaiserhof Hotel. He walked on past the police cars parked outside and closed his eyes against a rush of tears. Maurice had been caught. He didn't even think of his own safety. His lover wouldn't give him away; he didn't consider that as a risk. But if Maurice were cornered and alive then he, Kesler, had to protect him as much as he could. He caught an early bus, filled with workers on the first shift, and hurried to the *pension* where they had stayed before.

He got in through the rear door; he knew where the mother and daughter's bedrooms were; there were only ten bedrooms in the place. He shot the older woman as she slept, and caught the younger on her way down to answer the telephone. Nobody else would recognize Maurice. He went back to his small boarding house, let himself in and sat on the bed, his shoulders sagging, his head cradled in his hands. He wept for the man he loved, then he packed his clothes and left some Deutschmarks on the dressing table. He caught the first train out of the city travelling to Salzburg. From there he would fly to Zurich and then on to Geneva.

He bought a newspaper at the station and scanned it, sick with anxiety, and suddenly he began to hope. There had been an attempted assault on a woman staying at the Kaiserhof. No names were being issued for the time and a number of suspects were being questioned by the police. He hadn't got away, but he hadn't been caught outright. Maurice always kept his head; hope surged in him. As his plane took off and thrust upwards through the brilliant sky, Kesler said a prayer to the patroness of his youth in Poland, the Miraculous Virgin of Cracow, for Maurice Franconi's safe return to him. He would never have abjured his atheism and prayed for himself.

Everyone was informed of the identity parade; the hotel staff and the twelve men selected for the initial investigation, were politely asked to wait in the closed cocktail bar. Coffee and sandwiches were served, and Holler's chief subordinate apologized for the delay, and assured them that it was merely a routine. But the hotel remained closed, and nobody was allowed to leave. It was nearly lunchtime when Minna and Max Steiner saw Holler again. He had decided to hold the parade in the main hall, where his witnesses could watch from the lounge. 'I'm afraid it'll be a waste of time,' Max said to him. 'I didn't see anything but a shape in that half darkness. Minna saw nothing at all, she just woke up with the crash when I fell.'

'I know that,' Holler nodded. He knew that Steiner resented Minna being brought into the identification; he had tried to resist the suggestion, but Holler insisted. Holler sympathized with Max Steiner; he didn't want her to be upset by trying to pick out the man who had attempted to kill her. Holler had listened, and apologized, but Frau Walther was needed; someone would come and bring them both down to the lounge. Privately he thought that Minna Walther was not nearly as fragile as Max Steiner thought.

When they came downstairs Max had his arm round her, and Holler thought again: He's in love and he's a fool. She doesn't need protecting: she's not afraid of anything. . . .

'You stand here, please.' He positioned them in the archway leading to the lounge. They could be seen from the main hall.

In the cocktail bar Maurice Franconi tried to eat his sandwiches. The strain was affecting his stomach, which was revolted by food. He was glad of the coffee. He didn't join in the complaints of the others; he and the Swiss engineer kept themselves apart. The Swiss was taciturn, and to Franconi he seemed very nervous.

'What's the good of locking us up here?' somebody demanded loudly. 'It happened in the dark, didn't it? That's what I understood – so how could anyone be identified?'

'It's a police trick,' someone else answered, 'just to keep us here. I'm going to take this up with my lawyer when I go home. It's disgraceful; I've missed an important business meeting this morning.'

Franconi listened and said nothing. Who could they have found, apart from the woman who was asleep and the man he had flung aside in a dark room – it was all nonsense, just as that idiot had said, moaning about a business meeting – if only he could have got word to Kesler. He must know it had all gone wrong and be frantic with worry. Franconi wondered what Kesler would do. The sensible thing was to get out as fast as he could and go to ground in Switzerland. That was what he, Maurice, would have done, and yet part of him, which was afraid, hoped that perhaps Kesler was still in Munich. . . . He reproached himself for letting his imagination take a morbid trend; nobody could identify him, and the police would have to let them all go for lack of evidence.

They'd be asked to stay in the city for the next twenty-four hours, and they'd all give that assurance, before they started telephoning lawyers and making furious complaints. He'd be out of Munich within an hour of walking through the hotel doors. They couldn't prove anything against him, or the parade wouldn't have been necessary. He urged himself to keep calm and appear confident. It was funny how guilty some of the men were looking; Kesler always said most human beings had something to hide. . . .

Holler's assistant appeared at the door of the cocktail bar. He opened it and stood aside. 'So sorry to have kept you waiting, gentlemen. Come through this way, and line up over there. That's right. Thank you.'

Franconi saw them standing inside the archway; the tall blonde woman and the journalist. His heartbeat steadied. Just those two, as he'd expected. Neither of them had seen anything they could identify. He took his place in the line-up.

Holler had come to stand beside Max. 'Do you see the man who attacked you last night?'

'No,' Max said. 'It could have been any of them.'

Holler turned to Minna. She shook her head. Franconi had been watching them, and he gave a slight smile.

'That's what I was afraid of,' Heinrich Holler said. 'It was just too dark. But we have one more witness. Let's see what she thinks –' He turned and snapped his fingers. The little black and white terrier bitch was slipped free of her lead. She had been travelling on a special charter flight from Holler's home in West Berlin. Franconi stood rigid as the little dog scampered through into the main hall. His nerves were screaming as the terrier trotted forward and then stopped, her head cocked to one side, her bright eyes like buttons. He hadn't killed her because she'd looked at him and licked his hand. Suddenly she saw him, and she bounded forward with a happy bark of recognition and leapt round his legs, wagging her tail in delight and trying to jump up into his arms. He didn't kick her away; he just stood motionless, until Holler came towards him. He smiled at Franconi. 'The little dog seems to know you,' he said. 'I think I may have something else that belongs to you, too.' He brought his right hand up very quickly, and the gold pen was pointing its lethally charged tip an inch from Franconi's face. He reacted involuntarily, with the instinct for danger that had several times saved his life. He leaped backwards and shielded his face with his arm.

'Yes,' Holler murmured, 'it is your property. You will accompany the officers to police headquarters. The rest of you gentlemen may leave now.' He didn't see his men take Franconi. He swung round and turned his back on him.

8

'It sounds as if you're trying to blackmail me,' Heinrich Holler said. 'If so, Herr Steiner, you're making a stupid mistake.'

'I was sent here by my magazine to write an investigation of Sigmund Walther's murder. I'm living on an expense account, and doing an assignment I asked them to finance. I owe them the story. That's all I'm saying.'

'Not quite,' Holler interposed. 'You're suggesting that unless you and Minna see this woman for yourselves, you're going to write the story of Adolf Hitler's children for *Newsworld*. Which may-or may not be desirable from my government's point of view. If that isn't blackmail, what is it?'

It was Minna who answered him. 'It's a fair exchange,' she said. 'If you don't mind the story being printed, then there's nothing more to say. If you want Max to give up something which could make him the best-known political journalist in Europe, then you owe him a favour in return. And you know very well what you owe me. My husband's life.'

'Sigmund knew what he was doing,' Holler said. 'Now you're blackmailing, Minna. I told Sigmund that he was going into something dangerous, and that I couldn't protect him. He understood the risks and accepted them. Nobody regrets his death more than I do.' He stared at her and then at Max; his expression was contemptuous. 'What good will it do

Sigmund if you see a woman for a few minutes – she'll never be interviewed or seen by anyone again.'

'What harm is there in seeing her?' Max asked. 'Minna has suffered a lot; you may not approve of us, Herr Holler, but you've no right to judge. I'll give up the story if you'll show us what we've been looking for. And I'll give you a sworn undertaking that I won't mention anything that could embarrass you or the West German government.'

Holler didn't answer for some moments. They were silent, watching him. He couldn't let Steiner write the truth; premature exposure would forewarn the Russians. The revelation that Hitler's son was killed had to be made by Holler, and when it was authorized by Bonn. There would be no mention of a twin sister.

'If you do that,' he said at last, 'and I want the same from Minna, then you can be present when I see the woman. On the condition that neither of you attempts to talk to her. Is that understood?'

'Yes,' Max said. 'If you draw up what you want us to sign –'

'It'll be ready this afternoon. Come back here at three, and we'll go to the convent. I shall have an American colleague with me.'

'She's there?' Minna said. 'You're sure?'

Holler nodded. 'I can't think of a better place to hide a girl, can you? I'll see you at three o'clock.'

They began to walk back to the hotel; Max held her arm linked close to him. 'What's the matter, darling? You seem upset.'

'He thinks she's a nun,' Minna said. 'I can't believe it; it's too ironical. I am nervous, Max. I want to see her for myself, and at the same time' – she turned to him – 'I dread it.'

'But why? Don't you see it's the best possible solution? She'll never know who she is, and she'll never pose any threat to anyone. There won't be any legacy from Hitler now. The Catholic Church will have seen to that.'

'I can't imagine it,' she said. 'Do you suppose she'll look like him?'

'I don't think so,' Max replied. 'Probably take after Eva.'

'She was a very stupid woman,' Minna said slowly. 'Hysterical, neurotic.... Girls tend to be like their mothers, don't they – my daughters look more like me than Sigmund.... A nun – I just can't imagine it.'

'I bet she's a perfectly ordinary woman,' Max insisted. 'Convent-reared, pumped full of religion and living a nice celibate life. No grandchildren, darling, no chance for anyone to make political capital out of her. Come on, let's take a taxi and I'll buy us both a drink before lunch. You mustn't be worried about seeing her – it's what you wanted, isn't it?'

'Yes,' She managed to smile at him. 'Yes, of course it is. I'd like that drink. What are you going to write about, if you can't tell the truth? And do you mind too much – giving it up for me?'

'I don't give a damn,' he said. 'All I want is for you to be happy, and put everything behind you. So we can start afresh. As for the story, it's going to be all about Sigmund Walther and how he tried to unify and help his fellow Germans. I've thought of the heading: "Death of a patriot." Do you like it?'

'It's wonderful,' she said softly. 'And so are you.'

'Children,' Ellie Steiner said, 'we're going home.'

'Oh no! Why – we like it here! I don't want to go back to Paris –' Peter's face flushed, and he scowled. He noticed that his mother looked red round the eyes and seemed to be nervous.

Francine made a face. 'I don't want to go either,' she said. 'I like it better here. Why do we have to go back?'

'Don't you want to see Daddy?' Ellie asked.

'Not much,' her son said. 'Why can't he come here –'

'Peter, you don't mean that. I know you've missed him, just like I have, and Francine too. And he misses us.'

'He doesn't phone up and he doesn't write,' the boy pointed out. 'I don't call that missing us. I'm not going.' He threw himself backward into one of the chintz armchairs; his mother had explained how this would damage the springs, but he went on doing it.

'Ask Daddy to come here,' Francine insisted. 'Tell him we don't want to go back to Paris. I hate the *lycee* – they make you do so much homework – English schools are much better.' Ellie looked at them in turn, begging for co-operation. They were seldom united about anything, but she saw their resistance as a proof that Paris was perhaps not the best place for them, since they disliked it so much. It was their home, and surely if children were well orientated and secure they would want to go back to it. Admittedly they were temporarily going to a progressive school where there was less emphasis on work and more on personal initiative, and of course nobody frustrated them – but even so, it was an indication of how badly she and Max had failed to make them happy at home. . . .

'Please, Mummy,' Francine coaxed. 'Let's wait for a little while longer – wait till Daddy sends for us?'

Which he won't, was Peter's silent response. With any luck, he's left. He won't hit me again, anyway.

'I can't do that, darling,' Ellie said. Angela believed that absolute honesty was best with children. They only suffered through lies and treating them as inferiors. But Ellie couldn't tell them the truth because she had a miserable feeling that neither of them would care. Whereas she did, and nothing her friends could say could alter her unhappiness at losing Max. She felt bitter, and angry. If divorce was so bad for children –

'Don't you love Daddy?'

'No,' said Peter.

'Yes,' Francine hesitated. 'But I'd rather stay here.'

Then she began to cry; Peter, to his astonishment, felt like doing the same. He didn't love his father, he insisted to himself, biting his lips to stem the tears. He didn't, he didn't. . . . When Ellie put her arms round them both, she was crying too.

'All right, all right, darlings,' she murmured. 'Don't get upset, now, please . . . we won't go back then, we'll stay here –'

She didn't understand, and nor did he, why Peter suddenly wrenched himself free of her and raced upstairs to lock himself in his room. He had been fighting his father so long, and suddenly he was frightened and miserable because at last he'd won.

By teatime, their mother had recovered her composure. She was cheerful and made plans for the weekend. There was no mention of Paris or going home. She told Angela that evening that the children had decided for her what was best for all of them.

She would very much like Tim to handle the divorce.

Curt Andrews had put a call through to Washington the previous evening; he had gone to the American Consulate, and waited through until 1 a.m. to speak to his Director. It was a longer call than the Director normally tolerated with a subordinate; Andrews talked for most of the time. The Director listened, interposing a question or two, and then told Andrews to stay where he was and wait for a decision. Andrews dozed in the office, until the.call came through at 4 a.m. His instructions were brief; he was smiling when he hung up. He went back to his hotel, showered and went to bed, without any intention of sleeping. He rested physically, and began to work on his plan of action. He had been trained to present himself with likely problems and then set about solving them; so far as he could see, the real initiative didn't rest with him or Heinrich Holler. But the directive was clear, and it had come down from the White House. Nobody who could be used as a focal point for German unity must fall into the hands of the Soviet Union. Assurances from Heinrich Holler were not sufficient guarantee to allay American anxiety. Andrews could hardly wait for the coming confrontation. He fell asleep in the early morning, and woke at nine; the appointment Holler had made was for late afternoon. Andrews had a large breakfast, and went back to the Consulate. There were no further messages and he had lunch with the Consul and his family. An official car drove him to the Convent of the Immaculate Conception at exactly three forty-five; he waited in the parked car until he saw Holler arrive and get out. To his astonishment he saw that a man and a woman were with him.

'Reverend Mother?' Sister Aloysius came into the Superior's private room.

'Tell Sister Dominic that Sister Francis should come to the parlour at four o'clock.'

'Yes, Reverend Mother. I'll tell her so now. If she asks me why, what should I say?'

Mother Katherine smiled at the little nun; she was a sweet-natured, simple woman who had spent most of her adult life in the convent. If she had a fault it was curiosity. 'She won't ask you,' Mother Katherine said gently. 'Just give Sister Dominic the message. Thank you, Sister.'

The Mistress of the Novices was far from simple; long experience of the different types who either had, or believed that they had, a true vocation to the religious life, made her difficult to mislead. She had spent a long time talking to Reverend Mother Katherine about the novice Sister Francis. It had not been a happy conference. The Reverend Mother had never known the older nun to be so disturbed; several times she was near tears. 'I try to be fair, Mother, I try to see everything she does through Our Lord's eyes, but there's something so different about her – the other novices think she's a saint. But I . . . oh dear, even trying to describe it is so difficult.'

'I know it is,' Mother Katherine had said. 'I know exactly what you feel.' But she hadn't put that feeling into words. Sister Dominic was upset and confused for the first time in twenty years of guiding young women before they took their final vows. Mother Katherine reassured her and said nothing. She had deliberately delayed the girl's entry into her novitiate, on the grounds that she must be sure of her vocation and not misled by her convent breeding; but even her impeccable novice years had not relieved Mother Katherine's mind. She was waiting for Heinrich Holler to come that afternoon in the hope that he would have a solution to the problem of Sister

Francis which would relieve her and her community of the responsibility.

She heard the doorbell, and knew that he and the others had arrived. She didn't wait for Sister Aloysius to knock on the door; she went out into the hall. She saw the little nun's face bright with curiosity; so many questions and nobody to answer them; it was a true penance for her. Not like the one she had endured for so long. But then God made the back for the burden. They had an Irish nun in the community when she first came, and she had taught them that saying from her native land. It didn't translate well into German. She opened the parlour door and went in. Holler stood up, so did the man he introduced as Max Steiner and the big American. She came and took Minna's hand.

'I didn't expect to see you,' she said. 'But I'm very glad you're here.'

Max Steiner watched her; it was interesting to see how her personality dominated them. She radiated authority and self-assurance; even Curt Andrews seemed hesitant until she sat down and spoke to them.

'I assume that you all know we have a novice here called Sister Francis. She has been in the convent since she was a child. She took her novice's vows two years ago. I understand from Herr Holler that you wish to see her. She will be with us in a few minutes.'

'And she is the child that Gretl Fegelein brought into the convent?' Holler asked.

'Yes,' the nun answered. 'She is the same person.'

Curt Andrews cut across Holler's next question. 'And this Sister Francis is the daughter of Adolf Hitler and Eva Braun?'

Mother Katherine glanced at Holler, and he nodded. 'Yes,' she said to Andrews. 'That is what I understood when I was made Reverend Mother.'

'Before we see her,' Heinrich Holler said. 'I think that Herr Andrews, who is representing United States interests, would like to be reassured that Sister Francis will take her final vows and remain in the religious life?'

Max saw Minna leaning forward. She hadn't spoken since

they sat down; she had been watching the Reverend Mother with tense concentration.

'I can't answer for her,' the nun said. 'She can't be forced to remain with us.' Andrews's look of triumph was noted by Holler.

'Naturally,' he said quickly. 'But a person who has never known the outside world and is within three years of her final vows —'

'Does she know who she is?' Max asked.

The nun shook her head. 'No,' she said. 'Thank God.'

'Why do you say that?' Andrews said. 'What sort of a person is she?' Minna saw that suddenly the old Freda von Stein was looking at them under the nun's veil.

'That's very difficult for me to answer,' she said. 'All I can tell you is that we have lost three vocations since she became a novice herself; all of them were influenced by her. The nature of the influence is not exactly what it seems. She is devout, scrupulous in all observances of our Rule, faultless in her behaviour. Many in the community talk of her as a saint.'

'But you don't think so, Reverend Mother?' Andrews said.

'There is no sanctity that brings doubt and confusion to those in contact with it. Sister Francis pervades the community; her presence is felt even by those of us who are in authority. But if you asked me to accuse her of any act of disobedience or irreverence, I couldn't do it.'

'What would you say about her?' Minna asked the question. 'As a human being, what do you think of her?'

The Reverend Mother hesitated. 'In the name of charity I shouldn't say this; but equally I have to tell the truth. I have tried very hard not to be influenced by knowing who she is. But I felt it even when she was just a child. The Mistress of Novices, who is responsible for her, feels it too and is terribly distressed. I think she's wholly evil.'

Nobody spoke; Curt Andrews was crouching forward on the hard little wooden chair; he reminded Max of an animal in sight of its prey. There was a little tap at the door, followed immediately by another. Mother Katherine rose to her feet.

'Come in.' The door opened and a girl in the grey dress and white veil of the novice hesitated on the threshold.

'Come in, Sister Francis,' the nun said.

She was tall; that was Max's first impression, the second was the sweetness with which she turned to her Superior. 'You sent for me, Reverend Mother?' She had a deep, warm voice.

'Yes, Sister.' Mother Katherine turned to Holler, and asked a silent question. He gave a slight nod. She turned to the young nun. 'Thank you, Sister. You can go back to the community now.'

The girl's disappointment showed for a brief second, and then submission took its place; she bowed her head slightly. 'Thank you, Reverend Mother.' She gave them a look that seemed to touch on each of them personally; Max saw Holler's reaction. He recoiled, as if he had been given a shock. It was Curt Andrews who held the nun's gaze; she had large blue eyes, and they were brilliant, as if there was a light behind them. Max had never seen such eyes in anyone before. 'One moment, Reverend Mother,' he heard Andrews say. 'I'd like to hear Sister Francis answer that question – the one you said you couldn't answer for her.'

'I don't think that's advisable,' Holler interrupted sharply. He had turned very pale.

'You promised me a guarantee,' Andrews said. 'The young lady is the only person who can give it. I have the President's authority to speak to her myself.'

Minna had got up; Max saw her move slowly out of her chair, and step back, as if she didn't want to be part of what was happening. And he knew now what Andrews was going to do, and he also saw from Holler's face that the Intelligence Chief had been taken by surprise.

'Sister Francis,' Andrews said. 'I'd like to ask you a question.'

The girl was still looking at him; the sad submission had been replaced by an expression of intentness. Max had the feeling that the controversy had excited her.

'I'll answer it, if I can,' she said.

'Do you intend to spend the rest of your life as a nun?'

The pause before she answered seemed interminable. The transformation that came over her was gradual; visibly, it went with a mental calculation. She seemed to straighten, the blue eyes roved over their faces; Max was again aware of their unusual colour and luminosity. One hand reached up to the veil that covered all but a line of dark hair at her forehead. Long, sensitive fingers touched it; he thought she was going to tear it off. But the gesture was enough; its significance was obvious.

'No,' she said. 'Not if I have any choice.'

She turned to face Holler when he spoke. His eyes were narrowed, and the look on his face shocked Max. He heard Minna draw her breath. She had come to stand behind him.

'You have no choice,' Holler said. 'Understand that. You'll stay in the custody of the nuns for the rest of your life. And be thankful for it!'

'Custody?' Sister Francis said. 'I've always felt I was a prisoner. Now I know it. And, of course, I know why.' She turned to the Reverend Mother; her voice fell to a soft, almost gentle tone. 'I don't blame you, Mother. You had to make me join the community. My aunt helped to persuade me, even though it was against my will.' She gave Curt Andrews another long, communicative stare. 'My aunt was very religious; she wanted to save my soul. She told me who my father was because she thought I'd spend my life as a nun in reparation for his sins.' She gave the Reverend Mother a slow smile. 'I thought it was silly at the time. But she was dying, and I wanted to make her happy. But I knew someone would come and rescue me.'

'Sister Francis,' the nun said, and anger had made her breathless, 'you are free to leave this House at any time. I, personally will be delighted!' She said furiously to them all, 'No one ever put pressure on her to enter religion. She has been perfectly free to go or stay.'

'Sister Francis,' Curt Andrews said, 'if you want to leave here, I am authorized to offer you the protection of the United States government.'

'I would be glad to accept it. From today.' The hand came up again and slowly drew off the white cap and the floating veil. Her hair was almost black and it formed a smooth helmet to a striking face. When you knew what to look for, the resemblance was incredible, even to Max who had only seen photographs. Not Eva Braun, with her round, dimpled face and fair hair, but the features, the colouring, and the eyes of Adolf Hitler. Holler had seen it when he looked at her; the magnetism had been passed to her too. She dominated the room. She was more effective and evocative precisely because she was a woman and not a carbon-copy male.

'No,' Holler said loudly. 'No, Andrews. You won't get away with this.' He spoke in English.

'She's too potentially valuable to our enemies,' Andrews said, 'and she can't be kept against her will. The story will get out. . . .' He paused to emphasize the point. 'And if anything happens to her, to a simple nun, dedicating her life to God – it could bring your government down, Holler. The best place for her is safe with us. The Russians aren't going to get their hands on this stick of dynamite.'

Sister Francis took a step towards him. 'Please take me with you. One day I shall have something to offer my country. I've always known it.'

Curt Andrews saw it first; Max heard a movement behind him, and then Andrews shouted and sprang forward. But he was too late; Minna Walther had fired twice before he reached her, and both bullets struck the smiling figure, bareheaded in her nun's dress. The third went wide, smashing the little red glass lamp that glowed in front of the Sacred Heart picture. There was a cry as Andrews struck, and the gun skidded across the floor. Max acted instinctively to protect her, but she had already crumpled to the ground, her right arm smashed from the savage open-handed blow. He held her against him, and she whispered to him, before she lost consciousness. 'I had to do it – forgive me, darling –' He saw Holler and the Reverend Mother kneeling beside the girl, Andrews bending over her. It was Holler who spoke first. 'She's dead,' he said to Andrews. 'You can take her with you now, if you like.'

Afterwards, when he was trying to remember what had happened, Max could isolate certain incidents with clarity; the rest merged into confusion. He knew that the Reverend Mother had come to help him lift Minna, and he remembered the whiteness of her face and the expression in her eyes as she looked up at him. 'Thank God for her courage. That brute has broken her arm. . . .' He kept seeing the dead girl, the triumphant smile frozen on her mouth, the nun's headdress still grasped in her right hand. The Reverend Mother had blood on her skirt. The American was coming over to Minna, and Max stood to bar his way. He had a clear recollection of the fury on the other man's face, and the way he clenched his hands into fists as if he wanted to hit her again and again. . . .

'She'll be put away for life!' The words were snarled at him. 'We'll make sure of that –' The door had slammed behind him so hard that the furniture shook.

Then Holler, very pale, but with a strange look of calm about him.

He had taken charge; the Reverend Mother was advised to change her clothes, gather her community into the chapel and stay there for the next hour. She had seemed to understand when he spoke to her in a low voice; Max heard only the words, 'Leave everything to me.' Then Holler began telephoning. Minna regained consciousness when they moved her. She cried out in pain. They wouldn't let him go with her in the ambulance. Holler's men had arrived, efficient and silent moving; they barred his way. The dead woman was removed, and someone was cleaning the bloodstains off the floor. Then Max too was taken; there was a gun in his side when he started to protest. He was pushed into a car outside and driven through the city. He was hurried up the steps into the police headquarters and shut up in one of the interview rooms. Somebody brought him a cup of coffee, but when he tried to ask about Minna they went out and locked the door. It was late at night when Holler came to see him.

He walked into the room and when Max tried to speak he held up his hand. His eyes were cold. 'Before you say anything, you'll listen to me. Sit down.'

'How is she? What have you done with her?'

'She's in hospital. I told you to sit down. I don't want to be unpleasant, Herr Steiner, but I shall ring this bell for my assistants, and you'll soon do as you're told. That's sensible of you. Cigarette?' He took one and lit it; Max shook his head. Holler set one of the chairs in front of Max, and sat down. He drew deeply on his cigarette.

'Did you know she was going to do this?'

'No,' Max said. 'For Christ's sake, if I'd had any idea, I'd have stopped her going near the place!'

'That's what I thought,' Holler said. 'She used us both very cleverly. You're her lover, aren't you – did you think Minna was capable of killing anyone? No, of course you didn't. Nor did I. But I should have seen through it. I should have known why she wanted to see the other half of Janus.'

'She said she had to do it,' Max mumbled. 'She said she was sorry. . . .' He raised his head; Holler saw the total weariness and despair in his face. 'What's going to happen to her?'

'We'll come to that in a moment,' Holler said. 'I'd like some coffee – have you had anything to eat?'

'I'm not hungry,' Max answered.

'You may change your mind, when you see food. I'll get some sent in.' Holler pressed the call bell. Max closed his eyes and waited for a moment. Minna. Minna. He could have cried her name out loud. He drank the coffee when it came, but he couldn't bring himself to eat. Holler smoked and ate sandwiches. The silence seemed interminable to Max.

'Tell me something,' the Chief of Intelligence said at last. 'Did you see the resemblance, or was it my imagination?'

'I saw it,' Max answered, 'the moment she took her head-dress off. I was looking for it, I suppose, but there was no mistake.'

'She had the same eyes,' Holler said. 'The same colour blue, the same power to draw you. . . . I used to watch him subduing other people, men of intelligence and education, generals, staff officers, people who should have seen through him at once. They couldn't withstand his power, whatever it was. She had it too. The nun recognized it.'

225

'She said it was evil,' Max said.

'She was right,' Holler said quietly. 'The Americans thought they could use her – Hindenburg and the army thought they could use her father. Who sups with the devil needs a long spoon.' There was a curious, twisted smile on his face. 'I'm having trouble with my American colleague. He's threatening to expose the whole story unless I take action against Minna. Not official action, of course. And I can't let the story come out.'

'What are you going to do?' Max asked him. 'You can't punish her –'

'I wouldn't have let that woman leave Germany alive,' Holler said. 'Minna forestalled me, that was all. She saw what could happen if Adolf Hitler's daughter came on to the political scene, masterminded by the politicians. If she'd been a fool, or even an ordinary woman, it would still have been dangerous for Germany. But his genes had passed to his child; his capacity to lie and to mesmerize. Andrews didn't even realize how she was working on him. Minna Walther did the best thing possible for us all. I hope you realize it. I hope you still love her, Herr Steiner, because she's going to need you. Now I've got work to do. You won't mind staying the night? They'll give you a bed.' He got up and stretched a little, nodded to Max and went out. The room was hazy with his cigarette smoke. A uniformed policeman came and escorted Max to a cell, where he was given pyjamas and asked if there was anything he wanted.

He shook his head. In his ears were still the words 'Minna Walther did the best thing possible for us all. I hope you realize it.' He dropped down on to the cot, and lay staring at the bare ceiling. Nobody had locked the door. She was in hospital somewhere in the city, under sedation. She had carried the gun in her bag, knowing that she was going to use it.

Holler said he hoped that he still loved her. . . . Her own whispered words to him before she fainted: 'I had to do it. I'm sorry, darling. . . .' He fell asleep, exhausted, without having answered his own question. The sleep was black and empty, like an abyss into which he had fallen.

'You put her up to it,' Curt Andrews said. 'You knew you couldn't hold the girl if she decided to come with me, so you fixed Walther's widow up with a gun and a guarantee if she had to use it. Very clever; no one can accuse you of acting against US interests, and you'll keep the whole mess under wraps. But you're not getting away with this, Holler. I'm going to string you up by the guts!' Andrews didn't shout; he had a powerful enough voice, even in a low key, to convey that he was capable of any threat he made. Prisoners in Vietnam Interrogation Centre 3 had learned to fear the anger in Curt Andrews's voice. It presaged dreadful pain. Holler hadn't spoken; he listened to Andrews with a lack of expression that was infuriating in itself. He didn't even light one of his interminable supply of cigarettes. Andrews was so angry that the muscles on his thick neck were standing out; he had taken up a fighting stance as he towered over the West German, balanced on the balls of his feet, ready to strike. He had always resorted to violence as the ultimate solution, and the habit had never died. The knowledge that all through he had been in contention with a brain even keener than his own increased his frustration. 'I've been watching you at work,' he said. 'You're no friend to the Western alliance: you're a Red, Holler, and you always have been – we had our suspicions about your friend Walther, right from the start – *détente* with East Germany, reunification – all the idealistic crap that you people have always fallen for.... It wasn't the Russians who killed him, your Department were just trying to mislead us! He was killed by the left wing, because they knew he was looking for Hitler's children, and exactly what would happen if he found them – only he was dead, so you got the widow to do it for you!'

'And is this your personal opinion, or is it the view of your State Department?' Holler asked; he sounded disinterested.

'You'll find that out,' Andrews snapped back at him. 'I'm going to put in a report about this whole business, and if there's anything left of you and your Communist-infiltrated service, it won't be my fault. We've had enough bullshit from people like you, Holler, trading on the goodwill of the United

227

States – this time, you've tried to give it to the wrong man. I smelt out Reds for two years in Vietnam, and I've had you and the Walther set-up in my nose ever since I got here!' He glared at Holler. 'I'm going to root you out,' he said. 'And none of you are going to like it.'

'I see,' Holler said. 'You wanted her very badly, didn't you, Andrews? What a coup for you and your service, eh? Adolf Hitler's daughter, carried off to the safety of the United States, where none of us wicked Europeans could try to make use of her. And she would have been useful, wouldn't she – the world is getting used to women in high places since the war. Golda Meir, Indira Gandhi, Mrs Bandaranaike. A son would have been the best, but that was quite an unusual woman, didn't you think so? She had a certain magnetism about her – I wonder how powerful she could have become in the future, with the right kind of backing –' He tossed aside his calm, and his eyes blazed hot with anger. His contempt was savage. 'You wouldn't give a damn what happened to us, to the German people, would you? If it brought some rotten political advantage to your service, you'd promote her and if we got ripped to pieces because of it that would be just too bad, wouldn't it? Well, I'll admit something to you, so you can put it in with the rest of your report. I wouldn't have let her go. If Minna Walther hadn't shot her, my people would have killed her, and you too, if they had to.'

'That's great,' Andrews said. 'I've got that on tape, Holler. Just go on talking.'

Holler shrugged. 'You can put it on the table as far as I'm concerned. Then you can edit out the bits you don't like, when you get home.'

'I won't be editing anything,' Andrews said grimly. 'I'm going to blow the whole stinking conspiracy up in your face. You tried to hide the existence of a daughter from me, but you didn't reckon on Mühlhauser – he told me the *whole* story. When you realized I couldn't be kept out, you primed Minna Walther to act as assassin. I guess when the pressure is on her she'll nail you, Holler, to save herself. You've got enemies in Bonn; they'll know what to do with this report when it comes back as an official United States note to the Bonn government. They'll dig you over like dogs in a boneyard – and you Krauts have a great way of cutting each other up. And it won't help to send Minna Walther on a nice convalescence where she can have an accident before anyone gets to question her. I'm putting that possibility in too; you won't be able to get rid of the chief witness without proving you were guilty with her.'

'It may surprise you,' Holler said, 'but murder isn't my favourite solution. If it wasn't necessary to bury this story forever, I would have Minna Walther tried for what she did. But I can't, because nobody must know that Hitler's daughter ever left the convent. As you said, if we discovered her existence then eventually so will the Russians; secrets as big as this always leave a trail behind them. Only it won't lead them anywhere. My friends in the Vatican will see to that. As for the accusations you've made against me, make them official by all means. I'm sure you think it will lead you a little nearer to your Director's chair. . . . But I doubt if this will.'

He reached into the drawer of the desk, and threw a blue folder on top of it.

'The originals are in safe keeping,' he said. 'You can take that away with you. You may want to use it as part of the famous report that you're compiling.' He walked to the door, opened it and went out, closing it quietly.

Curt Andrews was alone in the office. He picked up the blue file, and flipped open the first page. He lowered himself slowly on to the edge of the desk as he began to read.

'I want to make a deal,' Stanislaus Kesler said. He blew his nose; he had cried during the night, and his nasal passages were blocked. He was sitting opposite Paul in a cheap café on the outskirts of Geneva. They had a bottle of wine between them. Paul watched him carefully; Kesler looked haggard and heavy-eyed; he seemed to have aged suddenly.

'What are you talking about?' Paul said. 'You're lucky to be here in one piece. The best thing you can do is take what's owing to you, and disappear.'

'I'm not walking out on Maurice,' Kesler said.

Paul made a grimace of impatience. 'Don't be such a fool. If he keeps his mouth shut, they'll put him away for a few years. If he talks, or they connect him with the other murders, he'll be in jail till he drops dead. Forget him, there's nothing you can do.' He saw the expression on Kesler's face, and wished he'd been more tactful. 'I know how you feel,' he amended, 'but it's no use thinking you can help him. What happens if he trades you in to help himself?'

'Maurice won't shop me,' Kesler said. 'You don't understand us. We really care about each other.'

'All right.' Paul sighed. 'But what can you do?'

'I can put the West Germans on to you,' Kesler said. He poured himself a glass of wine. Paul had his glass in mid-air; the wine slopped out of it on to the table.

'Me! You'd set them on me –'

'Why not?' Kesler said. 'You know who pays the bills. And you'd soon tell them. You're not the courageous type. You would be a very useful bargaining point.' He finished his wine. 'I think that's what I'll do. If you run, you won't get very far.' He watched the other man lose colour, and the sweat begin to break out on his forehead and turn into little beads. Paul's mouth was slack with fright.

'I'll kill you,' he blustered feebly.

Kesler smiled. 'You couldn't swat a fly,' he said.

'You bastard,' Paul mumbled. 'You dirty pederast.'

Kesler kicked him under the table, catching him on the edge of the shin-bone. 'Be careful when you call names,' he said.

Paul couldn't speak; his face was twisted in pain. Kesler waited. He was very calm, as always in moments of crisis. He had spent his emotions in the last day and night, imagining Franconi being interrogated. He was going to save him if it was possible, and the frightened go-between was just the bait he needed. But if Paul was a coward, he wasn't a fool. He had a quick brain and a rat-like sense of survival. Kesler let him work out the problem for himself. It took him a few minutes. If Kesler betrayed him, he wouldn't have a chance. Raymond

230

would have him silenced before he had time to identify him as the paymaster. Raymond wouldn't be pleased about Franconi's arrest either. And he was sick of living with danger, of dealing with killers like the one sitting opposite him. He felt sick with fear and his leg was on fire from the kick. The thought of Raymond terrified him no less than Kesler. Only Kesler was here and Raymond was safe in his office in the luxury hotel. He decided that Fate had made the choice for him; the time had come to escape it all and enjoy himself in the distant paradise of the Seychelles.

'I'll tell you who pays,' he said to Kesler. 'I'll tell you enough to get Franconi out with a suspended sentence.'

Kesler nodded. 'I thought you'd see a way out for yourself,' he said. 'And it's all the same to me as long as it helps Maurice. I'll order some more wine. Or maybe you'd rather have a cognac. You look a bit pasty-faced.'

'How are you going to do it?' Paul asked. He had begun to calm down; he even felt relieved. Kesler could do the negotiating; if he was quick he could make his travel arrangements and be on a plane out of Switzerland by the evening. He could get the details settled later, when Raymond was out of the way. . . . The Seychelles, and the villa, waiting for so long to be occupied, and the big-breasted girl he'd picked out to take with him. He took a deep breath. 'Who are you going to contact?'

'You're going to advise me,' Kesler said. 'You know all the crooks in the police here; you'll get hold of one of them for me. I'll talk terms with him.'

'Me?' Paul's spirits fell as suddenly as they had risen a moment before.

'Yes, you,' Kesler said. 'You're going to ring one of your contacts and get him down here. I'll talk about money. And you'll tell me all I need to know before he gets here.'

'All right,' Paul said. He wouldn't get away before the morning.

'You'd better write everything down.'

They drove Max Steiner back to his hotel the next morning; the man who had taken him from the convent at gunpoint was very friendly. He suggested that he and Max have a drink at the bar, and he insisted on paying.

'How is Frau Walther?'

The detective had been expecting the question. 'She's well,' he said. 'They set her arm and she's under observation for a few days. Nothing to worry about.' He smiled encouragingly at Max. 'Herr Holler wants you to stay here for a bit; at our expense, of course. And enjoy yourself – Munich has a lot to offer. He'd rather you didn't telephone your magazine, or talk to anyone outside, just till everything's settled.' There was a glint in the brown eyes that was at odds with his smile.

'When can I see her?' Max said. 'I won't promise anything until I've seen her.'

'I'll ask Herr Holler, and let you know,' the detective said pleasantly. 'In the meantime, just do as he asks, won't you?' He paid the bill for their drinks, and stood up, waiting for an answer.

'I'll stay here till he contacts me,' Max said. 'I won't be talking to anyone.'

Holler's agent held out his hand. 'Good,' he said. 'Herr Holler will be in touch with you.'

Max watched him go. There were a number of people in the bar, drinking before lunchtime. He remembered sitting there himself, getting drunk enough to ring up his wife and say their marriage was finished. And Minna trying to tell him that they didn't have a future, only he wouldn't listen. She had known from the beginning what she was going to do when they found the other half of Janus. When they lay in each other's arms and he told her how much he loved her she had kept a part of herself intact, because of what she was going to do. But in the end she said she loved him. In the hotel lounge, at a corner table, now occupied by another couple. Two businessmen, deep in conversation. That had given him the courage to leave Ellie and his children. That and the brandy he drank after Minna had gone upstairs.

She had so nearly been killed that night. He thought of the

cyanide pen Holler showed them, and the young, good-looking man who had been betrayed at the identity parade by a little black and white terrier. He was the one who had watched Minna in the restaurant and in the lounge afterwards. Max had thought he was trying to make a pass at her. He had been jealous. . . . He thought of his anxiety for Minna after the experience, how he had tried to shield her, and how Holler had insisted that she was quite strong enough to look at the suspects. 'She's not quite as fragile as you think,' Holler had said. And he hadn't known that a few hours later she would take a gun out of her bag and shoot another human being.

Max signalled the waiter, and ordered a beer. He didn't want to drink too much; he wanted a clear head to try and answer the questions that were poised like daggers, aimed at his heart. Had she used him, as Holler said? Had she ever loved him, or only seen him as a means of completing what her husband had begun? If he hadn't known about Janus, would she have responded when he first made love to her, or was that part of the campaign she was conducting? There were no answers to the questions, and he knew there wouldn't be until he came face to face with her again.

Reverend Mother Katherine was in the chapel, praying. There were half a dozen nuns kneeling in private adoration; they were scattered, and the Reverend Mother knelt at a distance from them. She had made the announcement in the refectory the previous evening. Her bloodstained grey skirt was in the furnace; the shattered devotional lamp before the picture of the Sacred Heart had been replaced, and there was no trace on the newly polished floor of the grim stains that had been scrubbed away. She had made the announcement after grace was said, and before the meal began. Sister Francis had left the convent. That was all; the buzz of comment went on until the supper was finished and the community prepared for evening prayers. The Mistress of the Novices had come to her. 'May God forgive me,' she said. 'But I'm glad she's gone from us. I shall pray for her.'

'I'm glad too, Sister,' Reverend Mother Katherine said. 'We both knew she didn't belong here.'

'I never said it before, because I couldn't bring myself to pass such a judgement on any of our Sisters.' Sister Dominic hesitated. 'Sometimes I thought she was an evil influence. Pretending to be good. No doubt it was my imagination because I couldn't understand her.'

'No, Sister,' Mother Katherine answered. 'You imagined nothing. She was a lost child. But we will pray for her just the same.'

And she had tried to ask mercy and forgiveness for the dead girl, but there was no sincerity in the prayer. Her own hatred made a mockery of the *De Profundis* and her thoughts swung obstinately backwards, to the father who had been strangled to death without a trial, to her mother and herself, fleeing the vengeance of the tyrant they hadn't been able to kill. She couldn't pray for the soul of his daughter without knowing it was hypocrisy. That afternoon, in the quiet period reserved for meditation in the chapel, Mother Katherine tried again.

She thanked God first, for the deliverance from evil which she believed had threatened her own small community, and then posed a danger to her country and its people.

She thanked God for Minna Walther's courage, and prayed earnestly for her. And then she set her mind upon her duty, and began the *De Profundis* for the child of Adolf Hitler who had murdered the person she loved most in the world. And at last she was able to finish it, and mean it as she said the last line under her breath. 'Eternal Rest give unto her, O Lord, and let perpetual light shine upon her.'

'I've brought you your file back,' Curt Andrews said. He dropped it deliberately on Holler's desk. His face was set and expressionless; only the muscles under the jaw were tense.

Holler drew the blue folder towards him. 'Don't you want to use it? Sit down; I'll send for some coffee.'

'No, thanks,' Andrews said. 'I shan't be making a report. If you're offering hospitality I'd rather have a scotch and ice.'

Holler smiled. 'I'm sure we can manage that,' he said. Sunlight radiated through the big plate-glass window, shedding a nimbus of light around his small figure, with uncountable millions of dust motes floating gently downward through it. The office was high above the city, and there was a fine view from the window. Holler didn't like looking out; ever since his arrest by the Gestapo he had been afraid of heights. His own office in Bonn was on the first floor. He studied the American; he wore his well-cut suit and the blue shirt with buttoned-down collar; he looked like a man in transit. He gave no sign of hostility; he was as neutral as a machine-gun with the cap on its muzzle. Andrews nodded towards the file.

'Why did you hold this back?'

'I had to be sure it was right,' Holler answered. 'We didn't have time to investigate very deeply, but we found the first clues in the flat. Mühlhauser had an address book, and we checked out on the names. One of them didn't exist, nor did the address. But the phone number given was real enough. We traced it to a firm of contractors with business connections in Leipzig. That was his East German controller. My guess is, he was recruited soon after he was repatriated. And the fact that the Odessa helped get him settled in a good job here was just a bonus for them.' He waited while a tray of coffee, whisky and ice was brought into the office. He poured a strong drink for Andrews and filled it with ice. 'Odessa were told we were going to question him,' he said quietly. 'I knew it was an internal leak. We haven't traced it yet, but we will. So Kramer took a second look at the good Party member Mühlhauser, and decided to ask him a few questions. Your arrival was a godsend to him. He'd saved his life by telling Kramer what he hadn't told the Russians; and not just for that reason.'

'Why then?' Andrews asked.

Holler sipped his coffee. 'Because he was a Nazi deep down,' he said. 'He'd kept alive, but he consoled himself with the idea that he hadn't betrayed *everything*. And when he told about the twin, he hoped she'd be used by the right people. Either Kramer's friends or else a third party, like the CIA.... Someone who'd see a use for her in Germany's destiny, and he

235

probably believed that her heredity would do the rest. And of course he was going to feed his Russian masters everything he picked up while you were nursing him in Washington.... Anyway, now you know.'

'Sure,' Andrews said. 'Now I know I've personally recruited a Soviet agent and sent him to the bosom of the family. That makes me all set for promotion.'

'I thought the report you were submitting about the incident in the convent was going to do that,' Holler said gently. 'But if you were to forget about that, and unmask Mühlhauser yourself when you get back –'

'Or use him to pass disinformation,' Andrews said. 'That's the way I thought of playing it. On the understanding that you don't pass that file on to Washington before I have a chance –'

'My memory for sending in reports is no better than yours,' Holler said.

'I've forgotten mine,' Andrews said.

'That's good,' Holler nodded. 'When are you leaving for home?'

'I'm catching a flight this evening.'

For a moment they sat in silence; each looked at the other. Neither showed any emotion, each made a private vow not to present the other with a chance of balancing the score. Andrews had lost out, and it would always rankle. Holler would need to be very careful in the future. He got up and held out his hand. Andrews hesitated for a second and then took it; the handshake was brief.

'Safe journey,' Holler said. Andrews gave him a slow, hard look.

'Thanks,' he said. 'I won't forget this trip.'

Holler waited till he left the office. Then he picked up the telephone. His conversation was sparse; mostly he asked questions. 'You're sure this contact is genuine? No, no deal for Franconi. All right – it'll have to be a very big fish, if they want him let off the hook. No, I don't intend to, but play it along and see what you get. Right.' He set the receiver back, and took out a cigarette; he poured himself more coffee and drank it; it was no longer very hot. The ends were tying up; Andrews was disarmed, at least on this occasion. And the capture of Franconi had produced a very interesting offer from a source in Switzerland. The name of the top Soviet agent and head of the European assassination department of the KGB. It was very tempting; Franconi had given nothing away under interrogation. It was obvious to Holler that he was protecting an accomplice as well as himself. And it must be the accomplice who was bargaining for Franconi. He could be released through lack of evidence: intelligence was a game in which the scales of justice were adjusted according to what was most politically valuable. Holler had adjusted the scales many times before. He was going to do the same for Minna Walther. What happened to the multi-murderer Franconi was a different problem. He had silenced Curt Andrews and he could protect the widow of his old friend. It was time to let Max Steiner leave the hotel and go to see her.

'I've sent her home to Hamburg,' Holler said. 'Her arm is healing well; there's no reason to keep her in hospital any longer.'

'Then you're not going to take any action against her?' Max asked.

Holler shook his head. 'No. She did Germany a service. Fortunately I don't have to admit that anything happened, which makes life easier.' He gave Max a slight smile. 'It needed a little negotiating, but it worked out. So Minna is safe from prosecution. And you can see her now.'

'Why didn't you let me know before she left Munich? Why wait to tell me after she's gone home?'

'There was a reason for that,' Holler admitted. 'You don't act on impulse in my kind of work. There always has to be a reason. And this one was quite simple, really. Now she's gone home, you don't have to see her if you don't want to. You have been her lover; it would have been difficult to refuse to go to the hospital. Now you have an easy exit if you want one.'

'What kind of a bastard do you think I am?' Max demanded.

Holler pursed his lips and shook his head. 'I don't think you're a bastard at all,' he said. 'Minna wound you round her finger like a piece of ribbon. She has a way of making people love her. Sigmund worshipped her for nineteen years. I'm a little cynical about women, Herr Steiner, and it probably colours my view of the best of them. But Minna Walther is different. The women I've known have all been sensible, pragmatic; that's the new word, isn't it? They're supposed to be such impulsive creatures, ruled by the heart not the head –' Max saw the smile again, and this time it was a little sour and twisted. 'They're the most cold-blooded, the most calculating of the species. All they want is to survive, to protect their children and maintain the status quo. I speak from experience, but that's not important. Now and again history throws up the exception to the rule. Women prepared to die for an ideal. Or to kill for it. Do you still love her, Herr Steiner? That's why I sent her back home, because I owe her something. I wanted her to feel secure in her own house, among the people and the things she knows. If not –' He left the sentence unfinished. 'Her eldest son is with her.'

'Does he know?' Max asked.

'No,' Holler said. 'I told him she'd had an accident. He's very like Sigmund, but he has the strain of Prussian fanaticism dressed up as modern Liberalism. He's never understood his mother because he's got too much of her in him.' He paused. 'Do you want to go to Hamburg? Please understand; there's no obligation.'

'No,' Max Steiner said, 'there isn't. I can walk out of here and catch the plane back to Paris; I can write a long article about her husband and mention her in passing.... I can probably persuade my wife and children that I didn't mean it when I said I was finished with them and in love with someone else – no, there's no obligation on me to see Minna. I can file and forget, as the saying goes.'

'I haven't heard that before,' Holler said. 'There's a flight to Hamburg at eleven o'clock. I'll send a car if you want to catch it.'

'Thanks,' Max said. 'I'll be ready in half an hour.'

The memory of the first time he came to the house in Hamburg was so strong that for a moment he hesitated before going up the steps to the front door. Minna had met him at the airport, driving a fast car. He had remarked on the way she drove; there was an indication of the hidden side of her nature in the single-minded determination of her driving. It was an unusual trait in a woman. He remembered feeling uncomfortable as they cut through the traffic. So much had happened, and so quickly, since they entered her house together. He had been powerfully attracted to her even at that stage, going forward deliberately into a situation which was dangerous, because whatever Minna Walther was, she wasn't the type for a casual affair. He stopped at the front door and pressed the bell. Waiting there he felt as if he were going to see a stranger. The door opened and the housekeeper let him in, standing aside as he came into the hall.

'Good evening, Herr Steiner. Fräu Walther is in the sitting room. I'll go and tell her you're here.'

The house had a smell of lavender polish and Minna's distinctive scent; he glanced at the staircase. Her bedroom was on the landing facing the stairs. The big draped bed, and the chill of linen sheets. The changing tempo of making love to her. He would know in a few minutes whether it had meant as much to her.

'Come in, please, Herr Steiner.' The housekeeper held the door open for him and he went inside. There was a fire burning, in spite of the warm weather, and Minna was sitting close to it. Her right arm was in plaster and it was difficult for her to get up. He came quickly to her, and caught her outstretched hand. She looked very white and drawn, the grey eyes seemed larger, and the smile was uncertain. He couldn't put his arm round her because of the clumsy plaster; he saw tears swimming in her eyes, and felt the prick of them himself. He kissed her hand and held it. 'Oh, my darling,' he said. 'My darling.'

They didn't talk about anything for some time; he sat beside her, holding her hand. The fire flickered hypnotically and Max let himself drift, knowing only how much he loved

239

her and that nothing else mattered. She had recovered herself; she was very still, leaning against him, gazing into the fire. There was an idyllic quality about the time they sat there together, not breaking the silence. He didn't want to question her; he didn't want to spoil the harmony between them. He felt closer to her than ever before. But it was Minna who spoke of it first.

'Do you still love me, after what's happened?' She didn't turn to look at him.

'You know I do,' Max said. 'More than ever.'

'I wasn't sure,' she said. 'I saw the look on your face immediately afterwards. There were times when I was certain you'd never come back. That you couldn't accept what I'd done.'

'I've got to accept it,' he said. 'Because I love you. Perhaps I don't quite understand it. Why you, Minna? Why not leave it to Holler –'

'I couldn't take the chance,' she said slowly. 'I'll admit that at one moment I hesitated. Before she came into the room, I thought that perhaps if she was a nun it wouldn't be necessary. But as soon as I saw her I knew that Sigmund was right. He loved Germany, but he understood us all too well. We have a streak of self-destruction in us; it's in our culture, our ancient legends; part of us wants to triumph and then perish in a real Twilight of the Gods. That was the secret of Hitler, and why he overcame the reason and humanity of millions of decent, intelligent people. He had the dark side in himself, and he knew how to appeal to it in our nation. He didn't just offer us victory and world conquest – the alternative was always death and dissolution. I saw it in my own family and their friends; it's a kind of insane philosophy that insists on breaking ourselves before we bend. Duty, tradition, military honour – they're all fine words, Max, but they can be made to excuse the worst kind of crimes. You know that too. Nazism was the ultimate expression of the German sickness. That's what Sigmund called it, and that's why he started looking for this heir of Hitler's. Because he intended to kill it.

'He knew, and so did I, that what we had done once to the

240

world, we could not do again, and that the child of Adolf Hitler, man or woman, mustn't be left alive. Germany has had a wonderful rebirth; we've become a proud, respected people, and all we need is to be united as a nation. That will come in time. So there was no doubt in my mind at all. I decided to go on, after Sigmund was murdered, and to do what he would have done. I took his gun with me to the convent.' The grey eyes looked into his; their expression was steadfast, almost serene. 'She was truly evil, just as her father was. I shall never regret what I did.' She laid her hand tenderly against his cheek. 'I love you very much,' she murmered. 'Nothing can change that.'

'I want you to come away with me,' Max said.

She shook her head. 'I can't,' she said. 'My life is here, with my children.

'Ellie's getting a divorce,' Max Steiner said. 'The first time you met me, you asked how long I'd been away from home. Well, I'm home now. I want to marry you, Minna. I'll get a job in Germany, and we'll live in Hamburg if you like. Where's your son? I'd like to meet him.'

'He's upstairs,' Minna answered. 'But he won't accept you, Max. He won't have anyone take his father's place.' He helped her to her feet.

You'll be surprised,' he said, 'how people accept what they can't change. And nothing is going to change me. When does that plaster come off?'

'Six weeks,' she said.

He leaned forward and kissed her on the mouth. 'That gives me time to make friends with your son. Let's go and find him.'

Interrogation was an art as well as a science; Heinrich Holler was skilled in that art but the man known as Raymond to the clientele of a luxury hotel in Geneva was proving a difficult subject. He resented his kidnapping; his furious protest made Holler smile. It would take a long time to undermine him, patience and skill, no violence. Holler knew very well that that only hardened a certain type of man, and Raymond was a true professional. His defence would crumble when they proved him to be Russian, which Holler knew he was. He hadn't seen the Swiss, Maurice Franconi; he disliked that part of the negotiations too much to see him again before he was put on a plane for North Africa. All he had done was alert the Tangier police to the arrival of a dangerous international criminal. What they did about it was not his concern.

'I hate cocktail parties,' Helmut Walther said; Holler looked at him over the rim of his glass and smiled slightly. 'So do I. But this was a special occasion.' They both looked in the same direction: Max Steiner in the centre of a group of people, Minna beside him. They were smiling, Steiner was talking animatedly to a very important West German editor. There were rumours that the editor was making Max an offer to join him that could not be refused.

Holler turned back to the young man. 'They're saying that Steiner's articles on your father are the best political journalism published in the last decade. What do you think of them?'

Helmut hesitated. He liked and respected Holler, not just because he was such a friend of his father, but because the older man treated him as an equal. He did not patronize Helmut; he did not hesitate to disagree with him either. 'They're marvellous,' he said at last. 'I was very much against the idea at first; I didn't want my father to be fitted into any *Time*-type biography – you know the kind of thing – the journalist being clever at the expense of the subject. But Max was not at all what I expected. He spent a lot of time with me, asking my personal impressions. I got to like him very much.' He nodded again, emphasizing his point. 'I'm very pleased with the articles. Mother says they're going to be published as a book.'

'So she told me,' Holler said. He saw Minna, smiling and talking to someone close to Max. She looked very pretty, with colour in her cheeks. The broken arm had mended well; you had to look very closely to see that it was slightly crooked.

He turned again to Helmut. 'And how do you feel about the marriage?' he asked.

'I was against it to start with,' Helmut answered. There was an engaging innocence about his serious young face as he looked at Holler. 'But Max took me into his confidence; his wife was set on a divorce and determined to bring up the children in England. He told me how much he loved Mother and wanted to make her happy. He was working in the house here and we saw a lot of each other in the past year. He convinced me that I should go into politics after two years in Paris; he arranged for the introduction for me in France Soir. He was very helpful.' He shrugged slightly. 'I couldn't help liking him. That's when I began to accept the situation.'

'Yes,' Holler said gently. He forced back a yawn. He was very tired indeed.

Helmut Walther was still talking. 'He's changed Mother,' he was saying. 'She seems so much less inhibited now, more relaxed. When they do get married, it'll be very good for her. Father was so different – so warm and spontaneous. You knew him, Herr Holler, you knew what sort of person he was.'

'Yes,' Heinrich Holler said. 'He was a man you couldn't help loving, when you knew him. You remind me of him, in many ways, Helmut.'

'You couldn't say anything that meant more to me,' the young man said. 'I just hope I'll be worthy of him. I'll certainly try.'

'And don't underestimate your mother, 'Holler said gently.

'Oh, I don't,' Helmut protested. 'We get on so much better now. Thanks to Max; she never could show her feelings, you know. I found that difficult. I think marrying him will be very good for her.'

'Yes,' Holler said. 'I'm sure it will.' He nodded at the young man, and saw suddenly the same steadfast, immovable quality, bold and untrammelled by the shadows of the past. He was very much Minna's son, although he didn't know it.

'She deserves to be happy,' he said quietly. 'Your mother is a very remarkable woman.' He laid a hand on Helmut Walther's shoulder, and then he had slipped away among the crowd.